UNDER THE CANYON SKY

Canyon Crossroads

Books by Dick Brown

Under the Canyon Sky Series
Book One: Canyon Crossroads

Coming Soon!
Book Two: Heart of Gold
Book Three: Guarding the Treasure

UNDER THE CANYON SKY

Canyon Crossroads

Dick Brown

SPEAKING VOLUMES, LLC
NAPLES, FLORIDA
2023

Canyon Crossroads

ISBN 978-1-64540-945-8

This historical novel is dedicated to the pioneering men and women who had a hand in the Grand Canyon's transition from unbridled backcountry to one of America's greatest national parks.

Acknowledgments

My very special thanks to my wife Donna who accompanied me on many of the Grand Canyon's grueling backcountry trails, exploring abandoned copper mines, trudging along on endless field trips, and patiently enduring my time away while I plunged into periods of historical research. And then at home, conducting critical reviews of manuscript drafts, cautioning me not to stray into a monotonous history report, offering her thoughts and perspectives, and giving me emotional encouragement and inspiration every single day, all the while keeping the home fires burning. I also thank my publisher and editor for believing in this project and making this story come alive on the printed page.

Preface

The wonder, intrigue and stunning beauty of the Grand Canyon are beyond measure. This historical novel brings to life the struggle of nineteenth and twentieth century pioneers against monopolistic corporations while enduring rapacious government control. It is a human-interest story where the Canyon itself takes on a life of its own. The story underscores the obsession of the Santa Fe Railway and its captive enterprises to drive the independent entrepreneurs—the men and women who opened the Canyon for all to experience—out of business and off the land. Despite constant badgering and accusations of being squatters and trespassers, the canyon pioneers still managed to leave their indelible mark on this grand stage. What we see today at the Grand Canyon is not only the work of nature but the work of brazen pioneers who chiseled trails out of stubborn rock, erected primitive tourist lodges on the rim, discovered rich copper deposits below the rim, and guided daring mule riders to the river. This is their story—a story of passion, dreams and challenges.

Chapter One

BRINK OF DISCOVERY

Carving a life out of a Canyon carved before life began.

Angry clouds swept across northern Arizona's Kaibab Plateau. Jagged spears of lightning split the dark sky and thunder rolled across the Grand Canyon. Shivering on a slippery ledge, Levi Jackson, a burly six-footer, could not distinguish between the roar of rapids and the rumble of the storm. He had the look of a frontiersman, broad-shouldered and heavy set, with a clenched square jaw, snub nose, wispy eyebrows, and a grizzled mane grazing the collar of his tattered coat.

Rain splashed on the brim of Levi's hat as the storm reached the river's edge. Levi spotted a canvas knapsack in a snag of driftwood swirling in an eddy, compelling him to wade through the churning debris. With a firm grip on the knapsack, he turned toward the shoreline but the swift current sucked him under. Levi surfaced in the main channel. Where the river made a turn, he reached a sandbar and gained enough footing to drag himself out of the water. Windswept sheets of rain lashed Levi as he scrambled to higher ground.

The storm moved east across the Palisades and onto the plains of Navajo country. Levi asked himself, *Who belonged to this waterlogged knapsack? A fortune hunter? A lost trader? Perhaps a down-and-out prospector?* Among soggy socks, a mud-laden shirt, rotten beef jerky, and a disintegrating box of rifle cartridges, Levi found a sealed glass jar protecting a folded envelope. It rattled when he struggled to unscrew the metal lid. He smashed it against a boulder, releasing a letter addressed to Emma Lee in Kanab, Utah—and a handful of gold nuggets!

Levi read the letter. "February 6, 1877. Emma, as I am not long for this world, I am giving you the hiding place for that cache of gold you have been nagging me about all these years. There are five or six, can't remember now, cans of gold dust and nuggets, like these, stashed behind a small, shaded waterfall, about five hundred feet above the river, on the south side, on a line between Coyote Point on the Navajo Palisades and Apollo Temple. You were always my favorite wife, J."

Levi stuffed the letter and nuggets in a coat pocket. He stood and at once slid through slimy mud, caught a boot on a rock, and tumbled headfirst into the river. He wrapped an arm around a passing drift log and floated downstream for the next half hour, unable to fight the frigid current.

At first the rapids remained out of sight, but Levi could hear a steady, muffled rumble, then a loud roar as he drew closer. Frothy tail waves lashed him, and like a shot, he scooted between half-submerged boulders. His log leaped out of the river. His free arm slipped out of his coat sleeve as the log came crashing down and submerged. The under-current continued to tear at his clothing. He bobbed to the surface, coat-less. Tossed and buffeted again, he wrapped both arms around his log.

The current remained swift but the roar of the rapids faded with distance. The river held Levi in the center of the channel so any shore-line brush worth grabbing remained out of reach. Ten minutes later the sound of rapids again filled the air, and again the muffled rumble turned into a tumultuous roar. This time a yawning hole, a formidable whirl-pool, lay ahead. Levi and his log plunged into the hole, but after several dizzying spins, it released its deathly grip.

Between rapids, the river became placid, but the watery chaos that lurked around the next bend filled Levi with downright terror. The river roared like a wounded mountain lion. It plunged over boulders, taking him dangerously close to splintered driftwood wedged between rocks blocking the main channel. In fear of crashing—or worse—drowning, Levi, regretting not learning how to swim, hugged his log tighter. Then he sighed with relief as the river again set him adrift on quiet water.

* * *

Desperate to strike silver a second time, Monte Bridgestone plunged his pickaxe into the black granite, every blow exposing a glittering fortune. The tall, lanky prospector pried away a stubborn chunk of the hard, black rock and reached into the crevice with his left hand. It closed down on his fingers like a Gila monster clamping down on a fresh catch. Blood gushed from the hole. The mile-deep Grand Canyon had Monte trapped, and no one knew he was there.

With his Bowie knife in his right hand, Monte worked for hours removing sharp wedges of rock from around the hole that held him captive. Late in the day, he broke free of the granite jaws and tore off part of his shirt to wrap around his bloody fingers.

During his first twenty-five years, Monte had farmed the rich acres of Missouri, mined the silver fields of Colorado, and settled into family life in the bustling frontier town of Flagstaff in northern Arizona. Now, on a ledge about ten feet above the Colorado River, with the bleeding stopped, he threw down his knife and grabbed the chunk of sparkling granite at his feet. He fingered the prize rock. Bright yellow metallic flecks rubbed off and fluttered to the ground.

A man's shouting caused Monte to look up.

"Help! Help me, mister; throw me a line!" The man sounded desperate, having survived three sets of rapids while clinging to pieces of driftwood—and on the verge of entering a fourth.

Monte picked up a coil of rope, wrapped one end around his wrist and threw the line into the current. "Quick, grab this!"

The fellow reached for the rope, wrapped it around one hand, then released his log. Monte used both hands to pull the bedraggled stranger ashore, but then lost his balance and fell into the river himself. He felt a shooting pain when his right foot became wedged between two submerged logs.

"Quick! My turn to save you," said the stranger as he threw the rope and pulled Monte close enough to grab his arm, then yanked him clear of the raging torrent. The soaked frontiersmen sat on solid ground, panting like hound dogs.

"Well, we have just saved each other. My name is Monte Bridgestone and I believe I have a broken ankle."

"I am Levi Jackson, nothing broken but my pride. But dagnabbit, I've lost my dang coat!" He paused and looked around. "I've never ventured this far downriver. Where are we?"

"We're just downstream of the Redrock Canyon Trail. It's getting dark, but in the morning, if you can help me up to the plateau, I've got a horse and a pack mule waiting."

"Hey, your hand is bleeding! You must have hurt more than your ankle."

"No, I did that before you floated by. I got my hand stuck in a hole at my dig. I don't think I broke anything, but I have three mangled fingers."

Levi found a forked stick, stout and strong, and used Monte's dulled knife to fashion a crutch. The two rested on granite boulders, discussing their dilemma.

"I think I can get you up to that plateau and then we can ride up to the rim." Levi grinned. "I can't thank you enough for fishing me out of this dang river."

"Why were you in the river in the first place? You're lucky I heard you yelling." Monte, returning Levi's grin, rubbed his aching ankle.

"Well, I have several mines at the base of a trail that descends to the river from Navajo Point. When the storm came along, I scrambled for cover under a ledge. That's when I noticed a knapsack floating in the river. I fell in as you did, but this river stole my hat and tore off my coat. I had important stuff in a pocket!"

Lost coat? What could have been so valuable in his pocket? At first, Monte decided not to ask, but then changed his mind. "The way you're talking Levi, you'd think you had a pocket full of gold nuggets."

Levi appeared startled. How could this stranger possibly know about that? He scowled, then abruptly changed his tone and demeanor. "Sorry, Monte, I get upset with myself sometimes. What are you doing down here? Prospecting?"

Monte felt the need to be coy and not divulge too much information to this curious fellow. "I've got several promising copper claims but I'm always poking around in these side canyons, looking for more valuable minerals, say gold."

Levi perked up again with Monte's second mention of gold. "Yes, one of the great pleasures in life is to search after the heart—and gold would be a delightful find."

* * *

After a long restless night, the men began to stir. Monte yawned as Levi announced, "Well, we best get started; looks to me like you've got several hours of tough hobbling on that crutch."

As the men started up the trail, Levi mused, "I wonder if J stands for John. Ah, that's it! By golly, that letter belonged to John Lee. Last

5

time I visited Emma at the ferry crossing, she showed me some old newspapers reporting on his firing-squad execution."

The pathway was slippery and strewn with rocks and tangled debris from the storm. With one navigating on his crutch and the other dreaming of lost gold nuggets, the men dabbled in sparse conversation and made slow progress. Monte winced every time his swollen right foot touched the ground. And his mangled left hand throbbed.

Levi continued talking to himself, "I wonder who had possession of private correspondence between Lee and one of his wives?" He went over in his mind the key facts in the mysterious letter—Kanab eighteen-seventy-seven—five or six cans of gold—waterfall in the shadows.

Levi could not imagine why Lee hid the gold unless he felt it important to keep it safe from bandits or out of reach of Mormon tithing. Levi, himself a devout Mormon, concluded that Lee stashed the gold for safekeeping and future recovery.

Monte broke in, "How do you like my trail, Levi?"

Levi did not answer aloud but muttered to himself, "Not as good as my trail." His mind wondered back to Lee's mysterious note. He wondered how Lee came into possession of so much gold. Emma never mentioned Lee having a serious interest in prospecting. And why hide gold behind a waterfall? Down here, survival drives human interlopers to any source of water, whether a dripping spring, a trickling stream or a lively waterfall. The sound alone is a dead giveaway.

Monte, with a throbbing hand, a lame foot and piercing pains on every step, lagged further and further behind. "Levi, slow down, I can't keep this pace."

No answer came from the upper trail. Now on his own, Monte managed another switchback then paused at a long slab of red rock. He called out to Levi, but again no response. Exhausted and in pain, he rested. The slab tilted downward and threatened to grind its way toward the Canyon void. Monte dismounted as the rock slid over the edge, taking his crutch with it.

Far ahead, Levi stopped when he heard the crash. He looked back to make sure his disabled hiking partner managed the last series of switchbacks without too much difficulty.

"Monte, where are you? Can you hear me?" No answer.

"Monte Bridgestone, I'm calling you." Again, no answer.

Levi had far outpaced Monte and let his mind wander, likely dreaming about gold. Deciding to wait, he sat in the shade of an overhang, yawned and closed his eyes, savoring the canyon peace and quiet. In minutes, his snoring broke the silence.

* * *

"Monte, what in blazes are you doing? I waited for you but when you didn't show, I backtracked and here I find you sleeping on the trail! How's that broken ankle?" Monte cringed as he stood up to resume their climb. His hand started bleeding again.

"Hold up, Levi. I need to regain my senses." He smiled. "Do you see any driftwood hereabouts for a new crutch?"

With pains on every step, Monte resumed the climb, using Levi as a human crutch. After five grueling hours, the men reached what Monte called the Tonto Plateau, a sprawling mesa, still fragrant with the pungent scent of wet sage. Levi cut down a yucca stalk and fashioned a new crutch. He held the reins of Monte's horse in one hand and the yucca stalk in the other as Monte stood on his good foot and swung himself into the saddle.

"Here, you may need this crutch later. It's light and strong. Better take it with you." Levi climbed aboard the pack mule for the long trek up the next section of the Redrock Canyon Trail.

Monte asked, "Levi, what brought you to this part of the country?"

"Well, I'm told I entered this world in the Adirondacks of New York. I was the youngest of eight children. My family joined the Mormon Church and the westward migration, hoping to carve a new future out of an unknown frontier."

Levi looked down to see how far they had traveled, then up to the rim. He continued. "Encouraged by John Frémont's glowing reports of the Great Salt Lake country, our hard-charging leader, Brigham Young, continued moving his emigrant followers to land destined as Utah Territory. We blazed the Mormon Trail across Iowa to Winter Quarters on the Missouri River, and followed the Platte River to Fort Laramie, South Pass and Fort Bridger. Our route then veered southwest into the sprawling valley of Salt Lake, our promised land."

Monte looked back. "So, you've seen your share of rivers—the Mississippi, the Missouri, the Platte—and now the Colorado."

"Yes, and those were not my first dips in the Colorado, but that's another story. At twenty-two, I set out for California's goldfields near Sacramento, hoping to pan my fortune. With gold valued at several hundred dollars per pound, Brigham Young envisioned California as a source of tithing income from Mormon gold diggers. I found Sacramento to be a wild, lawless town where Forty-Niners fought ice-cold streams over their hidden treasures and fought each other over placer claims. Anarchy ruled as the town bulged with ruthless claim jumpers, bordellos with lethal ladies, and casinos with card game swindlers and watered-down, rot-gut whiskey." Levi watched Monte guide his horse around a sharp switchback.

"Having met with fair success, I figured it was time to leave the goldfields. I bought a ranch near San Bernardino and raised cattle and horses. My cattle business met the insatiable demand for beef in the northern goldfields."

"So, Levi, you are talking about Utah and California. What brought you to Arizona? I did not expect you to deliver your life story."

"I'm getting to that." Levi stopped talking. Something ahead caught his attention.

"Hey, Levi, what's wrong?"

"Quiet, Monte," whispered Levi, "I believe we're being stalked by a mountain lion. Let's keep moving but be on guard."

Monte, also whispering, challenged Levi. "I've never seen one this far down in the canyon. Mountain lions feed on deer and so hunt close to the rim."

Levi ignored Monte's offhanded assessment and continued, "In fifty-eight, I married Jenny Lewis, a home-spun woman, frail and shy, eight years younger than me and wary of moving away from family."

Monte interrupted. "Fifty-eight? That's the year I was born. I read that Teddy Roosevelt was born then too, Levi, in your home state!"

"Well Monte, you are a fountain of knowledge but since you asked for my story, would you allow me to continue?"

Monte saw Levi as a rather touchy fellow, not appreciating interruptions when expounding on his life story.

"I took my bride—wait, there he is! Looks to be a full-grown male and he's skirting our route," said Levi. "How much longer before we top out on the rim?"

"I'd say another hour or two. I spotted him scrambling up that talus slope. We need to keep a wary eye on this critter. Now, back to your bride." Monte wondered which would happen first, Levi reaching the end of his story or the two riders reaching the end of the trail.

"My bride and I settled in Utah, north of the Grand Canyon, where we raised horses and cattle and built a ranch. That's enough about me." After a short pause, Levi said, "I think the track of our mountain lion is running parallel to ours."

After another few minutes, Levi added, "So that's my story. That's why I'm here in Arizona, helping an injured fellow prospector up these sheer canyon walls. And now it's your turn Monte Bridgestone. What brought you here?"

"Ah, you would get around to countering with that question. My story is not nearly as exciting as yours, Levi, but here goes."

Monte took a deep breath and began. "I also came from a big family, the youngest of seven siblings. At age five, we moved to southwestern Missouri, nudging me closer to my Canyon destiny. Our farm, with its hundreds of acres, lay ten miles northwest of Carthage."

"My pappy died of old wounds from the Civil War. His will called for dividing the family farm among my brothers and sisters. I had one hundred and twenty acres of rich farmland in my name, but I grew restless and eager to try a new line of work. My brother John quit our Missouri farm life first and joined the Silver Rush in Gunnison County, Colorado. He influenced my life as a mining man by luring me first to Colorado and then to Arizona. To make a long story shorter, he was killed in a saloon scuffle and I married his widow."

They stopped to give their mounts a break. Just then, the mountain lion emerged from an overhang and let out a screech that startled the men and their horse and mule.

"Dang, wish I had a gun," said Levi, watching Monte draw his Winchester from its scabbard.

"Levi, he's just reminding us who's the boss. I'll fire a shot to scare him off."

"That's not good enough. You're wounded and this critter smells blood. We need to kill him before he kills one of us." Levi snatched the gun and took aim. The trigger jammed!

The mountain lion eyed Monte. As it sprang from a rock ledge, Levi took aim again. The gun fired. The lion fell at the feet of Monte's horse.

"Levi, I'm beholden to you. I reckon you have saved my life twice on this journey. We're getting close to the rim so I'll end my dreary spiel. Let's see, where was I? Oh, I gained prospecting and mining skills which I am now putting to good use here, when I'm not rescuing drowning Mormons from the Colorado." Monte cast a casual smirk back to Levi trailing close behind. "I was part owner of the Carthage Lode in the Quartz Creek Mining District and worked in mines named Flagstaff, believe it or not, plus the Shooting Star, Windsong and Black Diamond. And here I am, prospecting again."

"Yeah, prospecting, when you're not falling into the river or trying to reason with a killer cat!"

Monte changed the subject. "Levi, you are working claims below Navajo Point and I'm working claims around Redrock Canyon Creek. Have you considered how difficult it will be to get ore to the rim and shipped to a smelter?"

"Yeah, I have thought about it but since I don't have any ore worth shipping yet, I'm putting off how to solve that problem," said Levi.

"Well, it is really worse than that. Another problem may also need solving. At some point this Canyon may be invaded by government officials and business interests. Someday this place will draw tourists like a dead mountain lion draws flies. They may not take too kindly to mining and trail-building. There may be those who do not want to see the hand of man on this magnificent canyon. They may want to set aside Grand Canyon as a National Park like Yellowstone, and maybe outlaw mining altogether."

Levi had an answer. "So, Monte, we best get our prospecting and mining in now, before some maverick Federal agent rules that the Mining Laws don't apply here. I am not worried yet, but I share your prediction of government intervention and legal obstacles. Let's get back to work before it is too late. Oh, and one other thing; let's both try to stay out of the river."

On the rim, the two men thanked each other for their watery rescues and trail escapades, and parted ways, Levi heading east on foot and Monte heading south to Flagstaff on horseback, trailing his mule, both men wondering if they would cross paths again, and both wondering if they could carve a life out of a Canyon carved before life began.

* * *

After the town doctor tended to his broken ankle and bandaged his hand, Monte limped home to his wife. Townsfolk knew Marcy Bridgestone as the hot-tempered Irish lass, twenty-three years of age, who watched with alarm and growing resentment as her husband disappeared on long jaunts to the Grand Canyon. She refused to share his enthusiasm for prospecting and his optimistic hopes of soon striking a hidden bonanza.

Marcy also held little interest in saloon-keeping. After she married her late husband, John Bridgestone, she insisted on calling his establishment a tavern instead of a saloon. It sounded more upscale. But deep inside, she wished her new husband would abandon both saloons and prospecting.

"Monte Bridgestone, must I remind you a wife expects a husband to maintain a close relationship, to provide sustenance and security? Why can't you pursue a profession proven to be prosperous and productive in meeting such important ends?" Monte felt the income from his Ponderosa Tavern provided a good measure of sustenance and security, enough to afford some time away at the Canyon. Marcy would have continued her tirade but their baby son wailed for attention.

In no mood to discuss the matter, it bothered Monte that she did not notice his injuries. He did not dare mention he twice almost lost his life. He also withheld any news of discovering rocks containing gold flakes until he could empty his pockets at the assayer's office. He stood on the brink of discovery. "If I get a good report, Marcy's mood will surely improve."

Monte shrugged off signals of impending marital doom, willing to ignore them for the moment, secure in the belief fabulous wealth awaited him in the Canyon, enough to prove a powerful and healing medicine for their ailing marriage. He withdrew a small chunk of rock from his pocket and fingered its golden flecks. "Could this possibly be gold?"

For Marcy, incensed by Monte's frequent absences, this recent trip represented a turning point. Her affection for her new husband soured, and she cursed the Grand Canyon—which she had never seen—for subjecting her to long periods of loneliness. She longed for her former husband and missed the passion, societal standing and prosperity that John always provided.

Chapter Two

QUEST FOR GOLD

If prospectors can hug the trail's edge, trains can hug the river's edge.

The mysterious letter lost in the river spurred Levi to further explore below the rim. Endless tales of lost gold buried somewhere in the eastern reaches of Grand Canyon drove him to delve into the incised tributary canyons near the confluence of the Big Colorado and Little Colorado rivers. His second wife Molly tolerated his canyon treks and his searches for shiny metals, at least for a time.

Levi surmised that the river, laden with golden brown silt, had long been transporting native gold from Colorado's San Juan Mountains. "Could the sparkling flecks in the sand along the river's edge be gold? Could there be sizable nuggets, weathered by time and polished by abrasive transport, lodged in potholes, waiting for discovery? "Ah, most canyon rocks around here are sedimentary, not a chance," he muttered to himself, "but still, those gravel bars might hold a few colors when washed with a pan."

The Spanish explorers searched for gold and silver and ignored copper. With the Canyon's limited access and the cost of shipping copper ore, miners worried about the prospects of ever making a profit. But with the transcontinental railroad's steady westward push across Arizona, Levi envisioned a paying proposition for copper ore, once transported to the rim. Encouraged by recent copper showings, he developed several mining claims on the river. Levi and his young mining partner, Kirby O'Brien, improved a path used by the Hopi. The same route that led to Levi's claims also led to salt-encrusted walls, long regarded as sacred by the Hopi.

Coaxing their mules deeper into the Canyon, Levi started a conversation. "Kirby, my Navajo friends once used this same track to elude Kit Carson and government troops."

Kirby did not respond.

The trail began in the basin west of Cedar Mountain, contoured below Navajo Point, and crossed the western arm of a rugged side canyon. Levi and Kirby rebuilt the upper trail where it followed the ridges of the Spanish Buttes–Escalante and Cardenas. From there it dropped over the Redwall in a series of switchbacks, then sliced through talus slopes to the river.

"Kirby, ya still back there? For one who likes to jabber, ya sure are quiet this morning."

Levi viewed Kirby as a windbag, but a hard worker, less than half his age. Kirby's slender frame disguised his strength and endurance. His sweat-stained, broad-rim hat failed to keep him from squinting in the blazing sun. He wore a faded red shirt, frayed trousers held by suspenders, and cracked leather boots.

"Yeah, Levi, I heard what ya said about them Navajos. I'll tell ya what I think about this pathway ya want to call Jackson Trail. It should be the Jackson-O'Brien Trail."

"Kirby, what are ya mumblin' about?"

Levi and Kirby each trailed a pack mule. The train stepped around rocks and logs protruding from the sides of the trail bed. The four animals needed a wide berth to pivot around switchbacks.

"Levi, I heard this trail is part of a getaway route for horse thieves. Those scoundrels steal horses near Kanab, run them into the Canyon, and alter their brands. I don't know how they get them to swim across the river, but sure enough, they cross, somewhere above the mouth of the Little Colorado. Then they run along the shore to the foot of this trail—I mean our trail—and up to the South Rim and on to Flagstaff." After that spiel, Kirby needed to catch his breath.

"Yeah, I heard all that and here's the rest of the story. They sell the stolen horses in Flagstaff, then steal new horses, and trail them back across the Canyon to sell in Utah."

Levi and Kirby reached the river where Levi located several copper claims on the north side. Kirby, wondering how they planned to cross, asked, "Levi, do you have a plan for crossing?"

"Of course I do. Look up yonder at Mexican Rapids. Just above that spot, we'll unload our mules and stack our outfit on a log raft I have there."

"You have a raft? Is it safe?" Kirby seemed hesitant and nervous.

"Don't worry. A few years ago, I managed to snag a runaway raft from Lee's Ferry. I'm still amazed it drifted this far downriver. It's built strong and sturdy. All we need to do is climb aboard, push off and hitch a ride on a back-eddy."

Kirby felt several logs jostle underfoot as he put his weight on the raft. He crouched beside a wooden crate and closed his eyes. Before long he felt a bump as the raft rammed the north shore at the mouth of Mexican Canyon. Levi proudly announced, "Welcome to my Rattle-snake claim, a most promising outcropping of copper ore." After un-loading their supplies and setting up camp, they started work with pick and shovel.

Kirby struck the rock wall about a dozen times, loosening very little mineral. "Levi, how does this compare to mining in California?"

Levi hesitated, not wanting to get into a long discussion. When he noticed Kirby glaring at him, eager for a response, Levi said, "It doesn't." The two men worked well together, sharing an optimistic en-thusiasm that infected anyone who came in contact with them.

Anyone, that is, except Molly. She possessed a fountain of good cheer and maturity that belied her years. She understood that her man needed to get away and be alone for a spell, but Levi's canyon treks seemed to become more frequent. Not finding gold, she knew he had to settle for copper. She had yet to see any ore from the mines. The chances for prosperity dimmed. Molly paid a heavy price for Levi's long absences. She dreaded the lonely nights and the missing help needed to run their ranch.

* * *

The chief engineer for the Colorado & Pacific Railroad ended his first river expedition in disaster while directing a survey for a river-level railroad through the Grand Canyon to link Colorado and California. Three members of the survey party, including the railroad company president, drowned during the fateful run. They never found the bodies; the river rarely gave up its dead. When the engineer's second expedition came through the Canyon, it caught Levi and Kirby working at the foot of the Jackson Trail. The boatmen beached their craft and hopped ashore.

"Have you found any good copper deposits in that cross-bedded brown rock?" The engineer seemed knowledgeable about geological formations.

Not wanting to divulge too much information, Levi grumbled, "Yeah, some."

But then Kirby jumped in and with an excited tone in his screechy voice, said "Look at this!" He held out a blue-green rock with specks of native copper embedded in cracks. Levi cringed.

A boatman asked, "Is that gold?"

Before Kirby could answer, Levi narrowed his eyes and put a stop to the conversation. "Kirby, let's get back to work."

The intruders became so taken in by the look of Kirby's copper-bearing rock, which they believed surely must contain traces of gold, the engineer had to call his men back.

Levi did not speak until the expedition disappeared around a bend. "Kirby, one thing you must learn about mining; don't blab about your claim or you'll have a whole herd of greenhorn miners descending upon our mine. Now you've got those boatmen intrigued about the prospect of starting their own diggings."

Levi tried to educate his partner in the ways of prospecting, but Kirby resented being scolded.

"Don't lecture me Levi, I meant no harm." Kirby, eager to please, swung his pickaxe at the rock wall, chipping off pieces of copper ore, and building a new stockpile in record time.

"Hand me that banjo, Kirby." Chips stopped flying off the wall.

"What banjo? What are you talking about, Levi?"

Pointing, Levi said, "That short-handled shovel."

Kirby, perplexed, handed him the shovel. "Why did you call this a banjo?"

"Well, because that's what us mining men call a short-handled shovel—you need to learn what miners call things if you want to be a miner, Kirby."

Kirby played along. "So, what's the name for a long-handled shovel?"

Levi, with a snicker, said, "A long-handled shovel." And with that Kirby sunk his pickaxe deep into a crevice where it stuck.

"Kirby, you filed our Firewater claim with the County Recorder the last time you visited Flagstaff, right?"

"I did, but I had to wait in line for an hour. Ol' Emmett's assistant did not show for work that day. His foul mood told me to not ask questions about his delinquent helper."

His answer pleased Levi. Kirby always followed orders without question or pause.

The men on the survey must have imagined quartz seams filled with fine ore—enticing them to return and make their own mining claim. Later, rumors circulated that a deserter from the survey party found promising copper ore upstream of Levi Jackson's claims.

* * *

Around the campfire, after two cantankerous old-timers came in from their own diggings, Kirby asked if anyone had a good story. Prone to stretch the truth, Levi often boasted of dubious bear-hunting skills and outrageous feats. He raised a question sure to lead to a story. "Tell us Levi, how many grumpy ol' bears have ya killed?"

Levi heard a branch snap. "Hold it fellers; we may have company."

Chief Nez and his braves, having crept close to the fire-lit camp, prepared to attack the white invaders. In the next instant, Nez recognized his old friend Hosteen Shush, the name the Navajo gave Levi. The chief motioned his braves to back away. Spellbound, the old-timers did not know whether to go for their side-arms or run for their lives.

"Yah-ta-hey!" Nez entered camp. "You give me black water, then we go." Levi wrangled a blackened pot out of the flames and poured the old chief a cup of coffee. Nez guzzled the brew, threw the cup into the fire, and disappeared in the night.

"That was my ornery friend Jeremiah Nez. He must have followed you fellas into camp. Good thing I am with you boys tonight or your prospectin' days might have ended. Levi stuffed his pipe in his baggy trousers, filled his barrel-chest with canyon night air, and began his tale. "I remember out in the goldfields of California—a state that has a bear on its flag—killing lots of bears. I took an old large-bore gun, loaded it with nails and scrap metal, tied it to a tree where bears pass by, and set the trigger with a string so that the gun fired when the bear stepped in front of the muzzle. No one killed as many bears as I did." As it so happens Levi relished bear meat.

One of the old-timers joined the campfire chat. "Levi, I did not realize you were in California during the Gold Rush."

"Yeah, I met with fair success in wresting walnut-size nuggets from stream-beds. When the gold camps turned wild and dangerous, I decided to leave. Conditions deteriorated into discontent, injury and disease—and outright robbery to separate men from their newfound riches. Infectious diseases hit the goldfields. One of every three miners contracted cholera and one of twelve perished."

Kirby changed the subject. "Levi, how is it that you know that band of Navajos?"

"Well, I'll tell ya. My Navajo name is Hosteen Shush which means Strong Bear because my Navajo friends saw my strong arms as the branches of an oak. As you know, most Mormon men conceal their facial features behind a thatch of shaggy unkempt whiskers. Among my Navajo friends, I am known for one of the most prolific beards in the territory, descriptive of the bear. As the source of much amazement among the beardless Navajo, I became a trusted friend of the Navajo, Hopi and Paiute—they all hold the bear in great reverence."

"Hey, Levi, is that smoke comin' outta yer trousers?" shouted Kirby.

"Dagnabbit, I did it again." Levi jumped to his feet. "I keep fergettin' to make sure my pipe's out before puttin' it away."

Levi, wanting to quickly escape the embarrassment, embarked on a story of how he found his way into canyon country. "Perhaps you men have heard of the Mountain Meadows Massacre."

Kirby answered, "Sure, that's when a caravan of emigrants from the Midwest suffered a horrible ambush on their way to California."

"Yeah, they tried John Lee in court for the murder of one hundred and twenty men, women and children. I don't think he did the killin' but he became the scapegoat for those terrible deeds. After Lee's firing squad execution, Brigham Young ordered his California Mormons to dispose of their property and return to Utah."

Levi stopped to relight his pipe. "I came back, married my first wife, Jenny, and settled near the site of the infamous massacre, along the Virgin River, north of the Grand Canyon, where we raised a family. For over ten years, I traded with the Paiute, Hopi and Navajo. I provided for my family and assisted other Mormon families whenever the need arose. Then tragedy struck. Jenny died while giving birth to our fifth child, a daughter who followed Jenny to the graveyard two days later."

The men assumed mournful expressions but said nothing.

"Well, as you know, John Lee, a stout and devout Mormon pioneer, with a dark countenance, established a ferry crossing on the Colorado near the mouth of the Paria River. As one of the few places affording an easy crossing, it became key to the mission ordered by Brigham Young—to expand the Mormon frontier by colonizing the banks of the meandering Little Colorado River here in Arizona Territory. Because I earned the Navajo's trust and friendship, Brigham called upon me to handle issues involving these proud people."

"So, I imagine you will tell us that while Lee had established a crossing on the Big Colorado, you established one on the Little Colorado," said Kirby.

"Right, at Jackson Crossing. Molly, my second wife, and I established a home there and tried our hand at irrigation farming by planting corn, melons and beans, and raising livestock. As a member of the Joseph City Ward, I helped many Mormon families make agricultural claims along the Little Colorado. The settlers I guided through this rugged country viewed the Grand Canyon as little more than a gigantic inconvenience, a massive obstacle that one best avoid, a natural southern boundary for the Mormon empire. I did not see it that way. Restless and untamed as the creature for whom the Navajo had named me, I viewed the Canyon through the eyes of a seasoned prospector."

Levi purposely did not mention to Molly finding—and losing – Lee's mysterious letter as he still held out hope of finding the elusive stash of gold.

After swapping more tales, the men settled into a lively discussion on marksmanship. Levi, eager to interrupt, pretended to half-listen to Kirby's ramblings. He then cut into the campfire conversation.

"By golly, I used to beat everyone in shootin' matches. Once I bet a feller ten dollars that if he put his new hat behind a tree, I could put a bullet through it from one hundred paces." The men around the campfire scoffed at the outrageous bet as Levi continued. "I made the shot and when the owner retrieved his hat, it had a bullet hole through the crown. Do you want to know how I did it, boys?" No one answered. "Well, I'll tell ya anyway. I put a stone next to the tree to make the bullet ricochet against the hat!"

Courtesy toward the old man should have prevented any retort, but Kirby could not contain himself. "Now Levi, you'll recall our duck hunt at the lake on the Kaibab last year. Fellas, Levi blasted away with his old shotgun—with sorry results. The entire flock took flight without so much as losing a feather!"

Levi glared at Kirby as the men burst out laughing. "That's enough gibberish. I think it's time to end this jovial banter and for us to turn in. Kirby, we need to be deepening that new prospect hole after sunrise."

* * *

Discouraged, Levi needed tangible results. The back-breaking work on his canyon claims resulted in far less success than what he had known during his California Gold Rush days. He sent ore samples to the assayer and expected to receive good news soon.

"That sparkling red rock from the Firewater prospect hole is somethin' remarkable," he confided to Kirby, who detected a hint of desperation in the old prospector's raspy voice.

Levi reminisced. "I've mentioned this a dozen times, but I miss panning for gold in California. In the good ol' days, claims produced two hundred dollars a day." Kirby knew not to interrupt happy recollections.

Levi took refuge in a past of his own invention. Miners had their dreams but little else. Locked too long in hopeless thoughts, Levi despaired. He dreamed of striking it rich in a time when civilization reached his end of the Canyon—with river-level railroads running between canyon walls to transport fabulous treasure. If prospectors can hug the trail's edge, surely trains can hug the river's edge. Now in his dotage, he boasted of his many adventures, and all the money he earned, but never how he lost his money. His quest for gold ended in settling for copper in one of the most difficult places for mining.

It is no wonder then that Levi sold his copper claims to the two oldtimers for four hundred dollars. These two ragamuffins lived in a rock cabin at the base of a cliff where the Little Colorado River emptied into the main channel.

Crest-fallen when Levi quit canyon mining, Kirby protested, "Levi, maybe we didn't find enough copper worth mining, but there's always the chance of finding gold."

"Kirby," Levi said, bemoaning the chances of striking gold a second time, "The Canyon may very well be hiding gold—enough to starve on."

"Well, what about me, Levi? Where am I going to go? What should I do?"

"Kirby, you are a hard worker, skilled and dependable. It's been a pleasure having you as my partner. Do you know a fellow named Monte Bridgestone?"

"No sir, but his name came up when I last visited the County Recorder's office. Is he a quitter like you?" Kirby immediately regretted his question. Levi let it pass.

"Monte owns the Ponderosa Tavern in Flagstaff. But he is also a prospector and has several copper claims here in the Canyon, downstream of where we have been operating. I suggest you pay him a visit."

"Levi, I don't go in saloons. You know that."

"Dang it, Kirby, I don't either. All you need to do is hang outside the door until you meet. Tell him you've been working with me at the Canyon and are available as a miner, trail-builder, wrangler, whatever you want to pursue next. Monte hauled me out of the river a while back, then I returned the favor. We looked like drowned river rats on the trail and had quite a time climbing out of the Canyon. Since then, we have met occasionally when we both happened to be in town."

"Thank you for the suggestion, Levi. I'm sorry about my quitter comment. I have learned so much working with you and have enjoyed every minute we have spent together in the Canyon. Someday when I marry the girl of my dreams, I'm sure I will understand how one can trade the lonely life of a miner for the love of a woman."

When Levi left the Canyon, he journeyed to his ranch at Jackson Crossing and life with his beloved Molly. He took great pleasure in watching her long braid sway from side to side as she tended her garden. He found her gift of laughter contagious. As a caring companion, an industrious homemaker, and an excellent shot with a hunting rifle, Levi could not ask for more.

The day after his return, Levi and Molly strolled along the banks of the Little Colorado. They watched a small herd of deer grazing among their livestock. Molly broke the silence. "Levi, while your mining days have finally drawn to a close, what will happen to Kirby O'Brien?"

"I have recommended he visit with Monte Bridgestone. If their meeting goes well, I predict a rewarding mining career for Kirby."

Molly wrapped her arms around Levi. "I have waited so long for this day." She paused, then added, "Now if you ever get that urge to go prospecting again, just remember I am still a good shot with my trusty Winchester."

* * *

Although Flagstaff started as a rough one-street town, having got its chaotic start as one of Atlantic & Pacific's railroad camps, it emerged as the major outfitting center for Grand Canyon prospectors.

In the County Recorder's office on Leroux Street, a short distance north of the railroad yards, a divorced young woman worked as an assistant clerk. Sabrina Jaffa, a complex twenty-four-year-old, had a bewitching smile, alluring eyes so large and green a man could fall into them, and light brown hair, long by the looks of the large bun at the back of her head. Wearing a high-necked, long-sleeved, dark brown paisley dress, she made herself look dowdy and unavailable.

On the outside, Sabrina exhibited good nature and a cheerful disposition. But locked in a mundane job of processing documents—maps, surveys, property deeds, mining claims and other public records, she dreamed of an escape. She collected recording fees and annual mining assessment affidavits, all the while resenting her work as a file clerk. She detested her dingy corner of the office, the constant teasing by riff-raff patrons, and her supervisor's foul-smelling cigars. At times she did not want to report for work; other times she skipped a day or two. She ignored the threats and complaints by her boss and instead devised a plan to make her escape from her office drudgery.

In her clerical position she interacted with prospectors filing their claims, listening to them rave about their discoveries and their hopes of finding the elusive, precious metals hidden underneath the Grand Canyon's rocky exterior. Tales of hidden treasure somewhere in the mile-deep canyon intrigued her.

"Howdy, Miss Jaffa," said an old codger waiting to file a claim on the Jackson Trail. "You know, there are rumors circulating of lost gold somewhere near Levi Jackson's diggings. Some say it is a saddlebag with several pounds of gold nuggets dropped by horse thieves operating in the area. Others say it is the long-sought treasure the Spaniards were searching for and found, only to turn around and lose again. Still others think ol' Levi struck gold but then forgot where he stashed it. I'm filing this claim because I may have found a gold deposit, not the lost gold mind you, but a source I plan to develop, pending assay results."

After that long-winded dissertation, Sabrina felt she needed to add encouragement for the man. "Well mister, keep following those rumors and your dreams. You can't just chase your dreams, you need to also live your dreams. They'll give meaning to your wandering ways. And who knows, you may stub your toe on that old saddlebag." Sabrina half-believed her words to the babbling prospector also applied to herself.

When the old-timer left, two more arrived. "Miss Jaffa, take good care of these claim papers. We're finding rich ore deposits in the Canyon. Reckon we'll be back soon to file more papers," said one of the scruffy prospectors as they waddled out the door.

Sabrina responded under her breath, "I reckon I won't be here when you return."

Precious metals aside, reports of the awesome landscape inspired Sabrina—a vast wonderland of golden towers and red buttes, rippling mesas with broken edges, trickling springs, a cavernous stillness and countless side canyons draining into the mighty Colorado River. The time had come for Sabrina to get out of her drab office and venture into the wildest of Arizona landscapes.

Without so much as a courteous goodbye to her supervisor, Sabrina quit her boring clerical job in the County Recorder's office. She aspired to become a canyon prospector. Below the rim, she planned to stake her claim to freedom and adventure, to join the quest for gold, and perhaps prosperity.

Chapter Three

SETTLING FOR COPPER

Time runs out for a mule and a brother.

Monte endured his wife's fiery tantrums for another four weeks. By then his ankle had healed enough for a return to the Canyon. The time alone would offer emotional relief and quiet.

Marcy pretended to be sleeping when he left their house. As Monte hitched his team to his loaded wagon, he congratulated himself on avoiding another confrontation, but once on his way, wondered if he should have left a note about when he planned to return.

He spent the entire first day rounding the San Francisco Peaks on the primitive wagon road. He camped for the night a few miles north of a place called Little Springs where the forest gave way to the great expanse of the Coconino Plateau, promising a smoother ride the following day.

Monte thought the Klostermeyer Ranch at Little Springs seemed unusually quiet when he stopped to water his horses. As he swung back up into the wagon seat, he caught a fleeting glimpse of a woman peeping from the barn loft. He tipped his hat and moved along. In camp that night, he kept wondering why the woman seemed to be hiding. He put the thought aside; it was none of his business.

He just finished supper when he heard a rider coming up the road. Reaching for his Winchester, he watched for any sign of hostility.

"Hello in camp. May I come in? I mean no harm." The stranger brought his mule to a stop and waited for a response.

"Come on ahead. My coffee is hot and there's leftover stew on the fire," said Monte.

When the stranger emerged from the inky black of night, Monte saw a bedraggled frontiersman in tattered buckskins, small in stature, and showing signs of carrying many hard years on his drooping shoulders. Dismounting, he moved into the firelight; a jagged scar showed on his left cheek and stringy, sandy-brown hair grazed his shoulders.

"My name is Clancy Jennings. I'm on my way north for my first look at the Grand Canyon."

"Good evening, sir; I'm Monte Bridgestone and I'm headed that way too. You're welcome to stay here overnight unless you have a mind to ride in the dark." Monte felt he could use some friendly company.

"Don't mind if I do, Mr. Bridgestone. I've never traveled this road. I'd surely lose my way at night. Hot coffee you say?"

"Yes, fresh-brewed, and you can call me Monte." Jennings looked as though he had spent most of his life in the wilderness, bowlegged from years on the backs of mules. He stood about five-foot-six in boots. He accepted the steaming cup and crouched near the fire.

"Thank you kindly, mister, I mean Monte. You can call me Clancy and let me say I appreciate your hospitality. From the looks of your loaded wagon, I presume you are planning to stay at the Canyon for a spell—prospectin' are ya?"

Monte did not want to divulge too much without knowing more about this wayward fellow, lest he be a wanted outlaw. He did not answer but instead asked a question of his own.

"Clancy, where are you from?"

"It is rare for me to talk about my past but I'll tell ya. I hail from back East. My kinfolk say I came along in the late thirties. We lived on a farm in the foothills of the Smoky Mountains of Tennessee. At fourteen, my family moved to the Ozark Mountains and then we settled among the rolling hills of Missouri." Clancy helped himself to a bowl of stew.

"Missouri? I lived there once," said Monte, then divulging his own past, "I came long after you, on the Cedar River, just upstream of Waterloo, Iowa. I remember living on a Missouri farm, nothing about Iowa, but I'm told a twenty-year-old boatman on the Cedar River named Jack Sumner became a member of Major Powell's expedition through the Canyon. He actually planted the idea of running boats down the Colorado in Powell's mind. More coffee?"

Clancy declined but said, "Go on, I'm listening."

"Well, I dreamed of moving further west and trying something other than farming. I bought a new horse, saddle and bridle and joined my brother in the Colorado Rockies in seventy-nine. From that rude introduction to prospecting and mining, I still feel the vibrations of the pick handle striking that silver-laced quartzite."

"Ah, so Monte, you are a prospector. I might have guessed," said Clancy. "Having any luck at the Canyon?"

"Yes, although not silver. I've staked three copper claims. I reckon you might have prospecting on your mind too. Ever done it?"

"I'll tell ya Monte, you mentioned Colorado; I joined the Pike's Peak Gold Rush in fifty-nine. I recall Horace Greeley, the eccentric editor of that "penny daily" *New York Tribune*, reporting that if the gold estimates were not exaggerated, the fortunes of silver were beyond estimating. With rampant reports of millions of dollars of gold in the Rocky Mountains, the Gold Rush drew hordes of prospectors, miners and investors from California where the placer claims had played out. And from the east came settlers with picks, shovels and the slogan 'Pike's Peak or Bust' painted on their wagons."

"So how did you do?" Monte, enjoying the campfire discussion, drew two more logs from his wagon and laid them on the embers. Sparks flew into the night air.

"While many Fifty-Niners found good diggings and made fortunes, I had no such luck in finding gold. I traded the mountains for the plains, despite having lived in mountains most of my life," said Clancy, "but one good thing came out of it! I encountered William Cody, better known as Buffalo Bill, also leaving the goldfields."

"I shouted 'Howdy Bill! Clancy Jennings here. Any luck finding gold?' He answered, 'None, but there's a rumor that a fellow named Lee had great success. I'm headed back to the flatlands.' As we rode along together for a spell, I suggested, "Someone should post a one-hundred-dollar reward for the person who nabs the damn fool who started that dad-blamed gold rush." Cody nodded his agreement. 'I'm a buffalo hunter Clancy, not a gold-seeker.' "I figured Cody had buffalo on his mind as he seemed to be only half-listening to my ramblings. That gold rush marked the limit of my pitiful prospecting experience."

"As for my Colorado mining experience, the isolation and loneliness of the tiny mining community, the lack of knowledge of silver market prices, and the bone-chilling high-country winters combined to take their toll on my brother and me. As the first prospectors to scour the carbonate fields along Quartz Creek in the San Juan Mountains, we settled in the mountain community of Quartzville, Colorado's first mining camp west of the Continental Divide, on the wagon road to Ohio City and Missouri Flats. We worked many silver claims northeast of Gunnison and west of where John Frémont ended his ill-fated fourth expedition. It was hard work. Too hard. We moved to Flagstaff and became the proprietors of the Ponderosa Tavern. Now I reckon we should turn in. I want to get an early start in the morning. You tagged along with Buffalo Bill once; you're welcome to tag along with me."

"Sorry for boring you and your horses with my long-winded story. Hey, something is spooking my mule!"

"Clancy, it's just a lone coyote; we all should rest."

"Coyotes have never bothered him. It could be something else."

Monte yawned, then mumbled, "See you in the morning."

* * *

The men, exhausted from the long journey and late-night discussions, fell into a deep sleep, even with Clancy's obtrusive snoring. As the eastern sky glowed brighter, a mountain lion circled the camp. Monte's horses shuffled their feet and strained their tether lines.

Loud screeching and wild braying woke the men. The cat clawed the air, then the throat of Clancy's mule. Monte jumped to his feet, grabbed his Winchester carbine and fired a shot at the commotion.

Clancy shouted! "You killed my mule!"

"No, that big cat killed your mule." Monte pointed to the animal slinking away from camp. Clancy knelt in a pool of blood as his mule exhaled a final time.

"Sorry there, Mule, I guess your luck ran out. You would have liked seeing the Grand Canyon."

"You named him, Mule?" Monte was sorry for the incident.

"Monte, I need to borrow a shovel. I don't want the buzzards to get him."

"You want to bury him? That will take hours, even with both of us digging." Monte realized he had a dilemma on his hands. He wanted an early start on the wagon road but he could not abandon Clancy in mountain lion country.

"Monte, if you had died, I would not leave you out here for the buzzards."

"That's comforting, Clancy, but we're talking about an animal, not a human. I need to get moving and I can't leave you here."

"Well, I'm staying. How much do you want for a shovel? Throw in a pickaxe too. From the looks of this rocky ground, I'll need both."

Monte walked over to his wagon, wincing every time his right foot touched the ground, and returned with two shovels and two pickaxes.

"We need to set aside any rocks we pry loose. We'll need them to keep coyotes from digging up the grave," said Monte, as he handed Clancy a pickaxe.

After an hour of scratching the surface, Clancy threw down his pickaxe.

"Monte, I reckon we have chosen a bad place for grave-diggin'. We're hitting hard black rocks. Shall we try another spot?"

Monte sighed and waved his arm in a circle. "There's not enough dirt for weeds and sagebrush to grow! We're standing on a giant lava field! Clancy, we can't bury Mule here and we can't move him. We need to be on our way. I suggest you throw his saddle and your gear in my wagon."

Monte, while happy to be moving again, kept reliving the mountain lion attack in his mind. The cat may have turned on Clancy or himself next. He concluded that he may have saved their lives. As the wagon team plodded northward, Clancy gazed at the trail of dust until he lost sight of ol' Mule.

* * *

"Hello gentlemen! Welcome to Cedar Ranch; I trust your journey around the Friscos went well," said the sheep rancher.

"Are you the owner?" Monte scanned the facilities as he waited for confirmation.

"Yes, I homesteaded here three years ago." The rancher spoke with distinct pride.

Monte found the place to be rather primitive. The outbuildings were livestock sheds with deer antlers hung on weathered sideboards. Overnight accommodations comprised a small one-room log cabin with a stone fireplace, a floor constructed of split logs and simple beds made by heaping sheepskins on the floor. The owner stuffed the largest cracks with coyote skins.

"My name is Monte, this fella is Clancy. He could use a horse or mule. I reckon we'll stay the night."

The sheepherder agreed to sell a mule to Clancy, then pointed to a stack of firewood and left the travelers to themselves. Clancy soon had a fire blazing to heat a pan of beans for supper. Monte added thick-sliced bread to the meal.

Clancy started a conversation. "Monte, I hesitate to press a man for details of his personal life as I hold a man's privacy as sacred as his freedom, but seein' as we are traveling together and sharin' stories, do you mind if I ask you if you are a married man?"

"The answer is yes; I have a wife in Flagstaff, no doubt still stewing about my prospecting trips. We are opposites. Marcy has a red-hot Irish temperament and does not take kindly to my absences. What about you?"

"Never married, never even came close," said Clancy. He then changed the subject. "Last night you mentioned you and your brother owning the Ponderosa Tavern in Flagstaff."

"Well, it's just me now. An accidental gunshot killed John while he tried to quell a disturbance in our saloon. Like ol' Mule, my brother's time ran out."

"Sorry to stir up unpleasant memories," said Clancy. "I was just trying to make conversation."

Under Monte's management, the Ponderosa continued to flourish as Flagstaff's most popular gathering place. Positioned at the crossroads of early canyon travelers, Monte could not miss hearing stories of intrigue and mystery, of lost gold and exposed ledges of sparkling minerals. Tales of wondrous beauty and fabulous potential wealth glowed brighter with every shot of redeye whiskey. As one experienced in prospecting and mining, he found himself instinctively drawn to the Canyon.

* * *

When Monte and Clancy reached the South Rim, they parted ways. Clancy's reaction to the stunning vista must have been profound. He set about exploring along the rim to the west of Monte's trail. He tied his new mule to a scraggly juniper, then tripped on an old whiskey bottle and watched it tumble down a rocky draw—and followed it.

Rough life had given this slight and wiry frontiersman a courage that would not fail before the gaping chasm he entered. He would come to know Grand Canyon in his own way, on his own terms. Grand Canyon, with its immense collection of castles, towers, temples and pyramids, in return would come to know—and to claim—a soft-hearted but tough man, devious but straight-shooting. Clancy, known as congenial and good-natured—a sentimental man, would not hesitate to help a friend or a stranger in need. His closest friends would pay him perhaps the highest tribute of all, recognizing a trait important to canyon ecology. He lived at peace with nature, never killed an animal except for meat, and never cut down a tree except for shelter.

Sometimes Clancy Jennings seemed to live the life of a recluse; other times he sought attention by describing the outcome of his latest venture to anyone who would listen.

On his first encounter with the Canyon, he not only stood on the rim, but he followed an old Havasupai pathway and descended part way into the Canyon's awesome depths. On a second descent, Clancy reached the river, touched the sinister red flood, heard the dull roar of this growling monster, and vowed to return. He would later expound on how he lived on jerked antelope, dried apple slices and stale biscuits for three days.

Like Levi Jackson and Monte Bridgestone, Clancy had no idea what lay hidden in the rock strata but hoped perennial erosion exposed valuable minerals, waiting for discovery.

With that trip to the river, Clancy gave prospecting another shot. He used to say, "In my way of thinkin', I reckon the river has already done the diggin' so's good ore should be exposed and there for the takin'."

For most self-respecting prospectors, not finding imagined glory holes did not do enough to destroy their drive to keep looking. For them it became an obsession, but not for Clancy. If success eluded him, he would move on to something else.

* * *

Monte made a habit of asking Ponderosa Tavern patrons known to have been poking around in the Canyon, "What have you found so far in your canyon wanderings?" Answers ranged from "sorry-looking rocks" to "black and pink banded walls that sparkled in the sun." Once an old timer reported, "I've been finding limestone formations with blue and green layers; can't figger what they are." Monte knew the blue-green telltale sign of copper compounds and asked the old-timer to bring in a sample the next time he visited. On another occasion, a prospector confided, "I found a surface deposit of gravel with pale yellow crystals that glittered in the sun."

"Tell no one", he whispered. "I don't want to start a gold rush until I can stake my claim, but I believe I've hit it big."

Monte played along. "Did the crystals crumble in your hand?"

"Yeah, I think so."

Monte hesitated, trying to break the news gently. "I'm sorry to tell you, mister; that was mica, which is brittle, not real gold." The prospector groaned.

"So that saying is true; all that glitters is not gold," recalled the prospector.

"Mister, gold shines; it does not glitter at all." Monte felt sorry for the poor fellow. "Here, let me buy you a drink." He explained how he fell into the same trap. "I too should have known better. I left black rocks with gold flecks at the assayer's office a while back. Turns out the report on the flecks, or crystals as you call them, came back as mica, not even fool's gold, just an iron-sulfur compound." Based on his initial prospecting ventures in the Canyon, Monte doubted that gold would be found in paying quantities. He already resigned to the fact that he would have to settle for copper.

To strangers, Monte seemed quiet, short on words until he knew folks better. Then he made friends and associated himself with a group of prospectors who could not resist the gnawing urge to explore below the Canyon's rugged rim. Monte often wondered why his late brother had not caught the urge to search for minerals worth mining at the Canyon.

It was not the Canyon that attracted John Bridgestone to Arizona but the progressive town of Flagstaff, with its transcontinental rail service and burgeoning lumber industry. John married Marcy Parker of Albuquerque and settled in Flagstaff. He became one of the town's leading businessmen, investing in brokerage and banking enterprises, and took great pride in seeing Flagstaff grow into a viable community. That ended with a deadly bullet.

Monte tended to the needs of his brother's widow. He worked with a Flagstaff attorney and the probate judge, William O'Neill, in Prescott on the sale of John's estate. His role changed from that of a caring brother-in-law to a substitute husband. Marcy had a well-built, petite frame, a fair complexion and reddish-brown hair. Monte found her to be defiant and outspoken, and at times downright difficult. In contrast, he had a calm demeanor and quiet disposition—dignified of bearing, soft-spoken and always sensitive—qualities that appealed to his brother's grieving widow. His sense of honor and his abiding affection for his late brother must have guided his decision to marry. Monte built a new house for Marcy. When she gave birth to a son, they named him Benjamin after the newly elected President Benjamin Harrison.

* * *

While studying natural history at Harvard, Teddy Roosevelt lost his father who taught him honesty, bravery and resourcefulness. Teddy's mother died on the same day his wife died after giving birth to a daughter. In the span of four years, he lost both parents and his wife. The grief-stricken twenty-five-year-old New Yorker resigned his state house position and journeyed west in search of a new life. He hunkered down on his Elkhorn Ranch on the banks of the Little Missouri River in the Badlands of Dakota Territory.

Inspired by the late Senator Thomas Hart Benton of Missouri, proponent of America's western expansion, Teddy learned to ride western-style, rope cattle and hunt buffalo. He mused about protecting America's wildlife and natural resources. In seeking peace and quiet while in direct contact with nature, he became concerned about devastating damage to the West. He imagined himself as a conservationist—someday firing up citizens to protect America's great treasures, including the forest lands of the Northwest and the canyon lands of the Southwest.

Teddy worried about environmental damage to the western frontier. After a few years, he returned to the East where he could influence national leaders to address such national concerns. He learned he had a gift—swaying crowds—while campaigning for Harrison.

* * *

While serving as a Senator from Indiana, Harrison had seen photographs of the Grand Canyon. They inspired him to introduce legislative bills on three separate occasions to create Grand Canyon National Park, but they all failed. Now back from the frontier, Roosevelt no doubt influenced Harrison about preserving America's natural resources, including the Canyon and the wildlands of Dakota Territory.

When Harrison won the presidency, he rewarded Roosevelt by appointing him Civil Service Commissioner.

"Theodore, I want you to work on civil service reform." It is a wonder why Roosevelt accepted a desk job in Washington City. He detested political machines and yet he aspired to a career in national politics.

During his first year in office, Harrison admitted North and South Dakota into the Union.

"Mr. President, thank you for signing the statehood bills for the two Dakotas, even though I would have preferred seeing the territory become one state, not two," said Roosevelt while visiting the President in the executive mansion.

"Theodore, I wish I could have spent time in the West as you did, but right now America is entering an age of conflicting ideas and interests, increasing control and regulation, and economic instability. Perhaps you have noticed our American way of life drifting away from an agricultural base toward an industrial base, with factories and urban centers, and attendant big business."

"Yes sir, and inventions and railroads are changing the face of our nation." Roosevelt glanced at a mural of the Grand Canyon on the office wall. "What bothers me the most, Mr. President, is that our western frontier may fade into the past, gone forever."

* * *

It is a saloon's clientele that determines its ambience. Rowdy cowboys and rough railroad men patronize certain establishments, while quieter townsmen and weary travelers prefer gentler surroundings such as the Ponderosa Tavern on Railroad Avenue, near the train depot. It became a first-class operation, despite the strained interplay of a plinking piano and a scratchy fiddle, alleged to be fine music.

On a slow night, with only two or three patrons in the saloon, Monte sat down in front of his chief bartender, Silas Taylor.

"Silas, do you recall my brother's killing? I was on a canyon prospecting trip at the time."

"Reckon I do, Monte; I had the duty that fateful night and saw it happen." Silas continued wiping the bar as he launched into his dissertation. "As you know, by tacit agreement, the boisterous elements and the more genteel folks kept to their own parts of town, neither likely to cross the boundaries of the other, as both preferred the comfort and security of kindred associations."

Monte listened intently as Silas continued.

"It was mid-January, back in eighty-seven and the blast of night air in Flagstaff carried a bitter chill. When a whiskey-filled cowboy staggered in here, his ruckus and loud insults shattered the evening calm. Simon Nelson, one of several regular patrons gathered around a Faro table, asked him to simmer down. When the cowboy turned his attention to other patrons, Nelson repeated his icy command. His cold, blue eyes remained focused on the cowboy. 'Simmer down or get out!'

Frustrated and somewhat confused by the cool disdain, the troublemaker swaggered back out into the frigid night. He returned after midnight, more annoying than ever."

"Sounds like trouble," said Monte as he shifted position on the bar stool.

"You're right," added Silas. "Max Nelson handed his brother a pistol. Both went after the drunken cowboy. Simon struck him on the back of the head several times. General confusion ensued when another stranger came through the door as Simon and the dazed cowboy stumbled into his path. The stranger tried to subdue Simon from behind but only had him around the neck, not knowing the cowboy as the real cause of the ruckus. Your brother, at the far end of the bar when the scuffle started, then yelled. 'Watch out! He's holding a gun!' Simon gripped his gun with both hands in front."

"John ran around the bar to wrest the gun away from Simon. In the ensuing scuffle, the pistol discharged and John cried out. The Nelson brothers, tripping over the dazed cowboy crumpled in a heap at the doorway, ran out into the street. Then the ornery cowboy staggered to his feet and also ran outside, followed by the stranger—all four men disappearing into the night. John slumped to the floor. The bullet had entered his stomach and exited near his spine." Silas paused for a minute and drew two beers from the tap.

"Your brother lingered a day before he died. As you know, the entire town mourned the tragic loss of the good-natured thirty-three-year-old tavern proprietor." Silas handed Monte a beer and held up his mug. "Here's to John Bridgestone—a dear friend and an upstanding citizen of Flagstaff."

"Much obliged, Silas. Either Marcy did not know these details, or she chose not to tell me." Monte emptied his mug and said goodnight.

Chapter Four

UNDER THE CANYON'S SPELL

Time has a way of stealing away fact and replacing it with legend.

"It's about time you got home. Now your supper is cold." Marcy's tone telegraphed her foul mood. Monte hung his hat and coat on the hook near the door and reached out to her. Marcy stepped back, avoiding any contact.

"Well, if you must know, I got talking to Silas down at the Ponderosa. I finally got the straight story about John's accidental killing."

"Accidental? He was murdered by those no-good Nelson brothers. And no one has been held accountable for what happened that dreadful night." Marcy stomped into the kitchen.

Monte raised his voice. "Silas saw everything and swears it was an accident. Sorry I brought it up. I did not mean to upset you. Now I know why you never want to talk about it."

He waited a few minutes for Marcy to settle down. "By the way, I'm going up to the Canyon tomorrow. Just a two-week trip this time."

The backdoor slammed shut.

* * *

Flagstaff's fledgling lumber industry harvested the vast timber resources on the broad flanks of the snow-tipped San Francisco Peaks and delivered ties and lumber to the Atlantic & Pacific transcontinental railroad. One prominent lumberman insisted that someone named the peaks after San Francisco, California but the local padre corrected the timber tycoon. "Sir, pardon me but sixteenth century Franciscan friars, while conducting missionary work with Native Americans in this region, named the San Francisco Peaks in honor of their Patron Saint, Francis of Assisi, who taught that man should cherish and admire the natural world."

"Thank you, padre, I appreciate your enlightening me on the proper origin of the name. I do indeed believe we must cherish nature around us, but I also share the notion that, with great care, we can take advantage of nature."

For emigrants traveling west across the vast Arizona plains, the Peaks stood out as a beacon of hope and inspiration. On the Fourth of July in seventy-six, a party of emigrants stopped at a spring south of the Peaks. Cyrus Taylor, the older brother of Silas, loved to tell the story: "To celebrate the nation's centennial, they stripped an eighty-foot ponderosa of its branches and hoisted a thirty-six-star American flag. For travelers who continued west, that 'flag staff' became a landmark, and for those who stayed, it served as the namesake for a new town."

One man who stayed, Clancy Jennings, who Monte encountered on the Coconino, became a well-known settler in the area. That pipe-smoking pioneer spoke in a whining voice. He loved to tell outlandish stories, delivered with a faint grin and a glint of mischief in his blue-gray eyes.

Flagstaff's first citizens platted the townsite seven miles south of Frémont Peak, one of six San Francisco summits that encircle the caldera of the dormant volcano, and named after John Frémont, who then served as Governor of Arizona Territory. Despite all of Frémont's transcontinental travels, the "Pathfinder of the West" skirted Arizona's most impressive piece of topology—the Grand Canyon of the Colorado.

Clancy knew everyone in town. One day he commented to Cyrus, "The railroad gave sawmill owners ninety sections of government timberland south and west of Flagstaff. Progress on the railroad had bogged down between Flagstaff and Winslow where construction of the two-hundred-foot-high trestle across Canyon Diablo awaited special prefabricated bridge spans and supports."

"I remember that, Clancy. The sawmill machinery orders sat on flatcars stranded in Winslow. It bothered the lumbermen to no end. Without the bridge, hired hands moved wagons with ox-teams, and skirted the deepest part of Canyon Diablo by using the old bedrock crossing, hauled the machinery to Flagstaff and built the largest sawmills in the territory."

Cyrus continued, "Those mills began ripping ponderosa well before the first locomotive whistled into Flagstaff. They supplied millions of ties, bridge timbers, telegraph poles and fence posts to the Atlantic & Pacific, Union Pacific and Mexican Central."

While lumber became the mainstay of business in early Flagstaff, ranchers raised large herds of cattle and sheep on the grasslands east and south of the Peaks. The bustling town became the major supply center for northern Arizona.

Clancy concluded, "I reckon the lumber industry and the railroad get the credit for building this fine town." Cyrus nodded his agreement.

* * *

Clancy liked to talk about the ugly wounds he received in a skirmish with marauding Apache. He conjured up a different story every time someone asked about the dent on his left forehead or the gash on his cheek.

Known as a drinking man, late one Saturday night, Clancy took another swallow of his second beer. He noticed a fellow with a hangdog face at the end of the bar. Clancy nodded and went on about his drinking. The stranger broke his bloodshot stare and asked, "Hey mister, how d'ya get that nasty hole on yer forehead?"

Clancy sported more scars, including a bullet hole in his chest, than any man he knew—and he had a supply of yarns to go with each badly-healed wound.

"Aw, it ain't so bad," drawled Clancy, sensing a chance to spin one of his yarns. "'Twas back in the year of sixty-nine when I escorted settlers through Apache country."

Clancy watched several others gather around, providing inspiration for his prolific imagination. He stalled, waiting for a few more men to sidle up to the bar.

"Like I say, I was guiding a party of settlers when suddenly forty or fifty Apaches ambushed us. A flying hatchet struck me!"

"Well, that shoulda killed ya," said the drinker. Clancy put down his beer mug and raised his right hand. "See this?" pointing to what remained of his index finger. "I put my hand up to fend off the hatchet, but it sliced off the end of this here finger. I figger it slowed the hatchet and saved my life!"

The men, even Silas Taylor, the barkeep, stood spellbound, gasping with disbelief. Clancy allowed time for the fire of their imagination to melt away the absurdity.

"I've got this notch on my left ear from a stray bullet; wanna hear about that?" Clancy offered. Without pause, "No," shouted the man at the end of the bar, "We've heard enough fer one night. Sorry I asked."

"So, you are the miserable town drunk, sitting at the same spot every night," Clancy speculated.

The fellow answered, his voice rather slurred, "Naw, we do not have a designated town drunk here in Flagstaff; it's not an easy job so we all take turns!"

That seemed to put Clancy Jennings in his spot. Throughout his life, by mingling fact with fiction, Clancy could always conjure up a good story, far better than any town drunk.

"Now mister, don't be too hard on Clancy here," Silas interjected. "Fact, folklore, legend, history—however told, most Old West stories are intertwined, albeit, often so tangled one never completely unravels the real truths, right Clancy?"

The storyteller, suppressing an impulse to retaliate, guzzled the rest of his beer and departed the premises, but not before looking back over his shoulder and stating, "Silas, I never let the truth get in the way of a good story. However, I often bend the truth a mite." He stopped and turned toward Silas again. "I've always believed the truth would understand."

Clancy worked for a season as a stage driver for the run between Flagstaff and Canyon Diablo—the lawless railroad town—named after the nearby Devil's Canyon. For a year it marked the end of the line for the westbound railroad. Construction crews and their frustrated foremen sat idle, stopped dead in their tracks, waiting for materials to construct a long wooden trestle over the deep canyon. Compounding the delay, mounting Atlantic & Pacific's financial problems led to the line being taken over by the Atchison, Topeka & Santa Fe Railway.

Clancy often talked about his time at Canyon Diablo. "That hell hole became a stronghold for outlaws and gunslingers. Footloose drifters down on their luck risked permanent residency in the town cemetery south of the tracks. It was a deplorable town, with drab shanty saloons, bawdy brothels and gambling halls lining Hell Street, and deadly broken-bottle confrontations in back alleys. Until completion of the bridge, these houses of ill-repute along Whiskey Row roared night and day with the drunken laughter of painted dance hall girls, card sharks, disbarred lawyers, raucous cowboys, idle railroad workers, disillusioned prospectors and dusty drifters—the dregs of western civilization. The town cemetery filled up before anyone died of natural causes."

Clancy paused and assumed a more mournful tone. "I'm ashamed to report that newcomers were gunned down on the mere suspicion that their pockets might hold something of value. And before the unfortunate soul was dragged off and thrown into Diablo Canyon, the scoundrels stripped the dusty saddle off his horse and the scuffed boots off his feet."

Until the tracks could resume their westward progression, freight wagons with trailers hauled dry goods, mining equipment and sawmill machinery from the railhead to Flagstaff. When the first train crossed the completed trestle, the rip-roaring town seemed to die overnight, the riffraff drifted away, and the need for a stage line, including Clancy's services as driver, faded into oblivion.

* * *

As the first permanent resident on the South Rim, Clancy claimed a one-hundred and sixty-acre homestead on public land—forested land. He lived in a rustic log cabin among the ponderosa, near a spring, one of the few reliable water sources on the rim. His homestead offered a stunning view of the Colorado River where it breaks through eroded plateaus, carrying its golden sand, grit and silt through Granite Gorge.

With Stuart Casey and Cole Campbell, two Flagstaff ranchers, Clancy located about forty mining claims—no gold, some copper, but plenty of asbestos—on the north side of the river. The men found asbestos wedged in cracks of the brown mudstone which lay atop the pink and black-veined Granite Gorge. Here, ancient forces pressed elementary constituents together and fused them into long fibers the prospectors called "mineral silk."

To access their claims, Clancy converted the rugged Havasupai pathway he had used a few years earlier into a trail that started near the front door of a second cabin perched on the rim. He called it the Whiskey Trail after stumbling over a Twin Oaks whiskey bottle. The trail penetrated deep into the east arm of a tributary canyon that Clancy named Whiskey Canyon. Along the way, the trail passed a spring below the Redwall, then followed the trickling stream in the Tonto sandstone, a prominent ledge capping the colorful up-thrusting bands of Granite Gorge. He needed ropes to get past several small waterfalls. Before sighting the river, he heard the deafening roar of a tortured torrent. Sockdolager Rapids, named by the Colorado River explorer John Wesley Powell for a slang term meaning a heavy knockdown blow, as in a boxing match, featured mid-stream boulders that whipped the flow into ferocious tail waves. The Whiskey Trail served as an important access into the Canyon for most of the early prospectors and visitors.

Clancy set his mind to spend the rest of his life on the South Rim, prospecting, building trails, mining, guiding early tourists and regaling them with outlandish tales. He established one of the first tourist camps at the Grand Canyon by erecting a log building to serve as kitchen and dining hall. He advertised himself as a canyon guide, charging tourists for his trail guide services, a group rate of twelve dollars plus one dollar per head for meals and another dollar for tent lodging. Sleeping quarters for his canyon visitors comprised white canvas tents erected on wood platforms, furnished with table, chairs, Navajo blankets for rugs, iron bedsteads and squishy mattresses. A tent city blossomed among the ponderosas—single units for ladies and dormitory units for men. There were several small wooden edifices erected suitable distances from Clancy's lodging, each containing thick mail-order catalogs serving in dual capacities, one being reading. On his trail, he guided some of the first canyon tourists to the river and back.

Summering on the rim and entertaining tourists, Clancy prospered enough to carry himself through the winter months. He wintered at his second home—a rock cabin built in the mesquite, a vertical mile below the snowbound rim. Here, at the foot of his trail, Clancy set up a base camp for exploring and prospecting. By switching between his rim and river camps, he adjusted the climate to suit his liking. He spent weeks prospecting alone in the Canyon's hidden reaches, splitting rocks, hoping to expose a glittering fortune. He memorized dripping springs, explored broken walls of ancient dwellings, pondered stone murals with the curious marks of those who lived there long ago, and collected pottery shards or what he called "prehistoric puzzle pieces."

Living with the Canyon, Clancy discovered and shared its thousand moods. Though he had little money, he never refused to help a friend or stranger in need. Old-timers remembered him as a sturdy, weathered man, skilled in hunting and woodcraft. The congenial, good-natured fellow, with a twinkle in his eye and a sly sense of humor, called himself Captain—but those close to him called him Cap. His friends treated the title as honorary, there being considerable doubt about a military phase in Clancy's mysterious past. Some close friends regarded him as a captain of tale-spinning. Among the knickknacks on his cabin's fireplace mantle, there sat a picture frame displaying embroidered letters that spelled out Clancy's simple outlook on life: "Old wood to burn, Old wine to drink, Old books to read, Old friends to trust."

As self-appointed guardian of the Grand Canyon, Clancy entertained audiences with fantastic accounts of personal escapades. He enjoyed the tourist season, with its opportunity to bluff greenhorns with sensational stories, and achieving the apex of virtuosity. Ol' Cap laughed with the giddy, talked sense to the serious, and spun yarns to the gullible. He told so many whoppers he disguised the truth about himself and his times at the Canyon. His stories arose spontaneously, often triggered by a visitor's innocent question or by a situation at hand. Clancy seized such opportunities and designed a tale to fit the occasion, often twisting and embellishing the truth to bolster his self-importance. Some viewed his ramblings as protective colorings to hide a checkered past.

Sitting around a canyon campfire at river's edge, greenhorn visitors felt inclined to coax a story out of their guide. "Captain, tell us about one of your early experiences down here."

"Wal, when yer travelin' alone in this deep canyon, ya need some sorta alarm clock to wake up the next mornin'. I would just draw in a gallon of fresh canyon air until my lungs are ready to explode and then yell 'Wake Up!' as loud as I could before goin' to sleep. The echo would return in the morning and stir me into action." Clancy looked around; no one said a word until a young lady, with a mischievous smirk on her face, broke the silence. "Why Captain Jennings, that's preposterous; an echo would return much quicker than that. You'd only get a couple of hours of sleep!" Clancy felt bushwhacked and outwitted. He found himself caught, by a lady no less, without a sprightly comeback.

Early visitors stopped at Clancy's Whiskey Spring well below the rim for a lunch of canned tomatoes, stale crackers and coffee brewed over a small campfire. Leaving part of their supplies, but not the coveted coffee pot, they ventured further down the deep canyon and camped for the night. The next morning, the explorers woke up naturally, without the need of a booming wake-up call ricocheting off the canyon walls. After lowering themselves down on ropes several times, they reached the river and passed several restful hours watching the reddish-brown flood slide past their feet.

Clancy Jennings guided a churning mix of tourists—folks he likely would not see a second time—from Flagstaff to the Canyon, following the wagon tracks from Cedar Ranch to his primitive tourist enterprise. The wagon road put Cedar Ranch on the map as an important campsite for early prospectors, as a halfway house for early tourists to the South Rim, and as a relay station for the Grand Canyon Stage Line.

* * *

During Flagstaff's frontier times, many strong-willed, hard-working men and women settled within sight of the San Francisco Peaks. In town, the lure of the silent canyon walls grew stronger, often when Captain Jennings and other wayward prospectors burst through swinging saloon doors, bubbling about their adventures below the rim. Their stories circulated about town and grew more enticing with each telling.

Stuart Casey and Cole Campbell, both homesteaders on Anderson Mesa southeast of Flagstaff, surrendered to the call of the Peaks and the Grand Canyon. Casey, an early sheep rancher, a public-spirited townsman, and an adventurer with a passion for prospecting, drove himself hard. Skinny as a rail, erect as a lance, and wiry as a steel spring, his face appeared drawn and melancholy. On one hand, with high cheekbones and pencil-thin mustache, he exhibited a laconic homeliness, but on the other, undaunted confidence.

Cole Campbell, a respected stockman and a skilled lumberjack and blacksmith, always saw himself on a path to good fortune. He befriended others with a cheerful grin. Despite the difference in age, Casey being fifteen years older, the two men became lifelong friends and trusted partners in their ranching and mining enterprises.

On one early summer day, Cole accompanied Casey on a week-long cattle drive on the Coconino. "Casey, we've both been so busy rounding up cattle, driving them to good pastures and tending our herds, we've hardly taken time to get to know each other better. It seems as soon as I settled near you on Anderson Mesa, I plunged my-self as deep into the ranching business as you. I understand you have some experience in mining."

"Cole, do you know Levi Jackson?"

"Can't say I do. But I've heard him mentioned a few times about town." Cole wondered why Casey asked about that old-timer.

"Well, like Levi Jackson, my mining expertise stems from Califor-nia. I was born in the mid-forties in northeastern Missouri. My family journeyed by wagon train across the Great Plains and the Rocky Moun-tains and settled in the Sacramento Valley in the mid-fifties. As a young man, I found work in the goldfields, although the intensity of placer mining had long subsided. I married Sarah Robinson near Oroville, in the northern extremity of the Valley. Two years later, with most mining claims played out and diminishing prospects for other work, we set out for Arizona, spending two years in transit, herding sheep along the way."

"Sheep?" exclaimed Cole. "So, you were a sheep rancher before a cattle rancher."

"Hang on youngster, I'll get to that. In our covered wagon on the outskirts of a nameless town, Sarah gave birth to our first child. I found the stubble-studded plains of Nevada to be rather unsightly and unsuit-able for grazing livestock, even sheep. And the baron brown mountains were not much to look at either. So, I vowed to move on as soon as Sarah regained her strength. We made our way to Arizona and wintered near the base of Bill Williams Mountain. No doubt you've heard about the town of Williams there."

"Sure, I visited there once but I know nothing about this fellow Bill Williams," said Cole.

"Ol' Bill served as the guide for an ill-advised winter crossing of the San Juan Mountains when the Frémont expedition met disaster in deep snow. Now back to my story."

"As you know, my family homesteaded a quarter-section of land on Anderson Mesa. I understand why you favor the area, with those large grassy meadows interspersed among the tall ponderosa."

Stockmen like Stuart Casey always searched for better range land. He continued.

"By the late eighties, we had about two thousand head of cattle and a large number of horses. In winter months, our cattle grazed on the tall bunch grass and leafy weeds on the high plains near Canyon Diablo. In summer months, like now, our Black Angus cows ranged over the high country. And here's the best part; sometimes our cows drifted all the way to the South Rim, luring me to within sight of the Canyon. From my first encounter, as happened to Clancy Jennings, whom I'm sure you know, I had a lifelong obsession for further exploration." Casey paused, then continued, "Sarah gave birth to eight more children, three girls and five boys. As our sons reached their early teens, I drafted them into ranch work. Sometimes we drove our livestock to the brink of the Canyon and that's when I carved out time to prospect with Clancy, and work on various mining claims."

Cole interjected. "So, you are a rancher and a miner. I came to Arizona in quite a different and round-about way. I was not part of the great westward migration via horse and wagon on the Mormon, Oregon and Santa Fe overland trails. I was born in Stonington, a farming community in central Nova Scotia. While growing up in Canada, I heard stories about my uncle who had traveled across the American West to California. Hungering for adventure, my uncle found himself in the

Bear Flag Rebellion serving under John Frémont as the Mexican-American War spread into California. Then, early in forty-eight, my uncle, a millwright in partnership with John Sutter, made a discovery that would trigger the greatest mass migration in American history. At Sutter's water-powered sawmill at the confluence of the American and Sacramento rivers, he noticed yellow flecks in the mill's sluiceway. He became the first to pluck gold nuggets from the ice-cold waters of the South Fork of the American River. Sutter's Mill became the epicenter for the California Gold Rush."

"Aha, so your uncle is the one who started the mad chase for gold! Interesting. I wish I had an earlier start on the Gold Rush." Casey sighed. Thoughts of a lost opportunity raced through his mind.

"I was too late also, Casey," said Cole. "Now here's my story. At age sixteen, I left my family, including two brothers and a sister, on our farm, and set out on my own. Inspired by my uncle's letters about his adventures in California, I boarded a steamship to Panama. Upon anchoring in a natural harbor on the Caribbean side of the isthmus, a scow ferried me and my fellow passengers to shore. A row of dilapidated fishing huts separated civilization from the mosquito-infested inland jungle where the risk of contracting yellow fever deterred many travelers. I crossed the isthmus on the American-built trans-Panama railroad and booked passage on a California-bound steamship. I entered the United States at San Francisco. Knowing California forests would long outlast California gold, with most of the gold placers already played out, I found work as a lumberman at logging camps and sawmills on the slopes of the Sierra Nevada. The planks I sliced from ponderosa logs helped meet the Far West's insatiable demand for lumber."

Cole continued. "I worked with several veterans of the Mormon Battalion who stayed in California to help develop the new territory. In fact, some veterans worked at Sutter's Mill and other mechanized sawmills around Sacramento. Whether felling trees or working at sawmills, lumbermen earned a dollar-fifty a day plus room and board. I became an expert at pushing logs through screaming gangsaws where, in one pass, multiple blades ripped ponderosa and fir logs into planks and boards."

"I had no idea you had milling experience. You've come to the right place. If you tire of herding cows, Flagstaff's lumber industry could use a skilled sawmill operator," said Casey. "But how did you find your way to Flagstaff?"

"Well, still restless like my famous uncle, I journeyed eastward across Nevada, southwestern Utah and northern Arizona, crossing the river at Lee's Ferry. Still on the move, I passed through Navajo Country and down New Mexico's Rio Grande valley. I settled in Silver City, New Mexico, a silver mining town, where I met my future bride. I then traveled to Arizona with Mormon emigrants and tended their cattle at Mormon Lake, about twenty-five miles southeast of where you and I homesteaded. Amanda and I married in Prescott and started our ranch near yours. And as you know, we're raising two children, quite enough for us; can't imagine how you and Sarah can raise so many more."

"Well, Cole, we're managing but Sarah dreads being left alone when I come up here with the herd. She raises even more of a fuss when I venture below the rim."

* * *

The bawling cattle ranged over the high country, drifting northward during the summer months. Stuart Casey followed, keeping an eye on his herd, trading tall tales with his ranch hands, and his foreman Slim Broadway, and helping them round up strays.

"You know Slim, I first tried my hand at sheepherding and had done well. Our enterprise took care of Sarah and fed the children—all nine of them. When I sold out and switched to cattle ranching, Sarah raised a ruckus! It hadn't done a lot of good to explain—women just couldn't fathom how a man could give up a good thing just because he wanted to try something new."

Slim grunted his approval about women but his eyes rolled when Casey resumed.

"Well, I'd done all right. Selling my herd of sheep at a good price allowed me to buy four hundred head of cattle. And as for our family fortunes, this herd of cattle here has grown five-fold and enabled us to afford a second family home in Flagstaff so our children can attend school." Slim seemed to be only half listening, thinking about his own lot in life. But he let his boss ramble on, nodding occasionally as if interested.

The herd halted its northward drift. Casey motioned to Slim to stay back as he dismounted and picked his way through the cows, staring straight ahead, anticipating the shock. But once again the gaping abyss dropped away, never failing to fill him with that cold dread, at first terrifying, then awe-inspiring, that peripheral horror that lasted less than the time to move a step closer to the rim. Upon the heels of primal terror rushed an overwhelming beauty that weakened the knees and stunned the heart. His senses seemed crushed by the majesty of the age-less mesas and towers spread out like an unraveled, worn-out doormat. Casey let his breath escape, savoring the slow recovery of his senses.

Something more profound than prospecting fever drew Casey to the Canyon. He knew he had to venture there whether or not he found anything of value. He mused that this monstrous gash in the planet could yield great wealth. Casey couldn't imagine Sarah putting up with another—as she expressed it—chase after the rainbow's end. To get started, he planned to give the boys more and more responsibility around the ranch. He climbed back on his horse and allowed himself a dry chuckle: "Good thing Sarah hasn't seen these dangerous cliffs."

Casey twisted in his saddle, then settled back and gazed out over the great chasm. As it had so many times before, the continuum of horizontal striations of multicolored stone fascinated him, exciting him anew. He imagined that each layer may hold its own special treasure. Great wealth must lay hidden somewhere in that vast depth, waiting for a prospector possessing the courage and determination to go after it.

Cole Campbell, he thought, stands out as young, hardy and ambitious. Though he lacked mining experience, the logging camps and sawmills of the West had hardened him. As a cattleman, the independent Canadian lad impressed Casey. He had the strength and endurance needed to prospect in the Canyon.

Looking back at his foreman, he thought Slim might also be up to the task. He'd broach the subject of a prospecting venture at the appropriate time. Casey convinced himself that the threesome could not fail to amass a fortune and that, since the majority of the digging had already taken place eons ago, they would not have to work too hard.

He chuckled again. He sounded just like Clancy Jennings. The ranchers enjoyed the Captain's tangled tales last time he had made a foray into Flagstaff, but his talk of Lee's lost gold captured most of their attention. Dreams of lost gold and hidden treasure have always been an integral part of the mystique and lure of the American West. Gold fever flared once again deep within Casey's being—once a prospector, always a prospector. He then jerked to his senses, remembering what someone once said about lost gold, that time has a way of stealing away fact and replacing it with legend.

Sarah invaded his thoughts again. He squirmed a little in the saddle, as though he could hear her scolding. He could almost hear her inevitable outburst, "That Canyon will be the death of you!" She never yelled at him but instead pleaded with him, saying he had duties and responsibilities to his community and to his family.

Casey thought for a long minute, the measure of a man is by his work and his family, by his friends and his community. Well, he had served his community well in the Territorial Assembly as a representative from Yavapai County—had worked hard pushing for a new county by carving out a piece of Yavapai to create Coconino County. Yavapai officials cheered as they had tried many times to drive Clancy Jennings out of their county. By giving up nearly twelve million acres of their regional administration for a new county, they rid themselves of the tale-spinner. Casey also sponsored a piece of legislation supporting a plan to build a railroad from Flagstaff to the Grand Canyon. Despite a completed line survey and an approved legislative bill making the Flagstaff and Grand Canyon Railroad tax exempt for six years after completion, construction never started.

The Flagstaff community looked at Stuart Casey as a well-known and respected citizen, and—as for his responsibility to his family—he provided comfortable homes, both on the ranch and in town, and both having excellent standing among his neighbors—a good life. His older boys volunteered to take on more of the ranch workload, allowing Casey time for his own pursuits that could further the family's fortune beyond Sarah's wildest dreams.

Sarah, however, could not abide prospecting and prospectors. She needed him at home, not out in a distant canyon where she had to worry about him sliding down a rocky ravine or drowning in a river.

From somewhere deep inside, a cold wind blew and an icy hand closed around his heart, causing Casey to shudder. She had warned him. In her quiet way, Sarah let him know her patience had run out. He didn't want to lose her; he knew all the gold on earth would not buy her back.

As fate would have it, Stuart Casey, Cole Campbell and Slim Broadway fell under the Canyon's spell and spent countless weeks together picking at canyon walls, searching for its hidden bonanza. Campbell and Broadway, as understudies, learned the ways of prospecting. They admired Casey's knack for reading the rocky pages of an ancient book, deciphering the veins and outcroppings that teased prospectors with traces of mineral. The men had many mining camps and claims on both sides of the river, and often prospected with Clancy. They staked copper, galena and asbestos claims, some spanning the river itself, and all of their claims spanned the time when men challenged the Canyon to reveal her mineral resources.

Cole Campbell also found time to work in Chet Kennedy's sawmill in Flagstaff, occasionally filling in for the company foreman. Chet and Cole had both gained valuable experience in the lumber industry while working in northern California so it pleased him to no end to again apply his skills at the Kennedy sawmill.

* * *

Cowboys, lumbermen, railroad workers and miners all congregated in Flagstaff saloons to trade fantastic yarns, gamble away hard-earned pay, wash dust-dried throats with redeye whiskey, and celebrate the good life by raising a ruckus. As the redeye flowed, tales grew wilder, stakes became more fabulous, egos assumed greater proportions, and tempers grew short. The bark of a Colt revolver often punctuated an evening's revelry.

One evening in the crowded Name-Your-Poison Saloon, Clancy mentioned to two scruffy lumbermen at the bar, "You know, for a while we had no cemetery here in town."

One man scowled, "So what's yer point?"

"Well, we decided to hang a man to get one started," answered Clancy, startling the entire establishment. The piano player stopped on a high note, the barkeep overflowed a beer mug, and the rip-roaring Faro game came to an abrupt halt.

"Yeah, on a cold windy night last year we tried to hang an unscrupulous bad guy, to give the town's new cemetery a start."

Clancy had their attention. "I can picture that night as clear as last night. A rowdy lynch mob gathered around a tall ponderosa. Someone yelled, 'get a horse, let's hang 'em!' The culprit whined, 'I hate horses. A fellow holding a rope said, 'You won't be on that horse long.' Out of desperation, the man made a final plea, 'I'm a loving husband and devoted father. Anyways, I ain't done nothin' wrong.' The ringleader placed the noose over his head."

"I reckon that noose signaled the low point of this poor soul's reckless life," explained Clancy. "Then wouldn't you know it but a pinecone dropped out of the tree, hit the horse's rear end, and set it rearing, front legs flailing in the air. I could see this would not be a proper hangin' so I went for my knife and cut the rope. The lynch mob protested when they saw their night's revelry coming to an abrupt end. The fella slumped to the ground, gasping for air as two sympathizers spirited him out of sight." Clancy paused and looked around the room, just to make sure he still had everyone's attention.

"Here's the worst part—the cemetery would have to wait another month for its first entry."

With that, Clancy guzzled the rest of his beer and left the premises. The piano player resumed his plunky tune, and the barkeep resumed filling beer mugs. The Faro game resumed with several players grumbling the interruption brought them bad luck. And a fellow with a squeezebox, singing off-key, took up a position next to the piano.

Before long, a scuffle started up at the gaming table. One player pushed another who crashed into the wall. A lighted lantern dropped to the floor and flames ignited cotton window curtains. Soon fire consumed both the floor and the wall. The barkeep ran over and swatted the flames with his apron. Instead, he caused the flames to leap higher.

Everyone ran out into the street as the fire spread to the ceiling and tables and chairs, and the piano. With the entire saloon engulfed in fire, one fellow ran back in to scoop the money off the table, but came back out empty-handed. He ran in again and never returned.

As a young frontier town, contractors constructed most of Flagstaff's buildings with lumber from Kennedy's sawmill. Constructed as wood-frame fire traps, with posts, beams, ceiling rafters and cedar shingle roofs, like the saloon, they stood little chance of surviving a fire.

After an hour, the raging fire destroyed the Name-Your-Poison Saloon. Empty lots on either side of the building prevented the fire from spreading to other buildings. But one poor soul perished, cremated in place, leaving no body to bury in the empty town cemetery.

Chapter Five

BOXCAR JOURNEY

Old age takes hold when regrets take the place of dreams.

Dan McLain propped his loaded shotgun against the sideboard of his wagon, standing it upright against the seat. He treasured this long, rusty, wire-wrapped, double-barreled blunderbuss. Having it nearby could mean the difference between life and death.

On primitive wagon roads in 'Canyon Country', as Dan called it, one knew a man lived longer if he kept himself ready, alert to the possibility of sudden danger, ready to meet it with less than a second's notice. A seasoned frontiersman who had herded wild mustangs, hunted bear and trapped wolves, he took great pride in his endurance, agility and basic good horse-sense. One had to start out early to get the drop on Dan McLain.

The picture of frontier confidence and savvy, Dan swung himself up into the driver's seat. He acted like a mulish, cantankerous teamster but he knew when to compromise and never hesitated sharing with his fellow man. Snapping the reins, he shouted "Yah!" to his team of wiry Arizona horses. The sudden lurch of the wagon jarred the shotgun which sprayed buckshot into the wagon-master's right shoulder. Dan, tougher than hardtack, recovered from his wounds—and his embarrassment.

Dan wanted one more shot at seeking his fortune before old age set in. He hired young Kirby O'Brien, to assist in a mining operation where he found copper showings in the limestone caprock, about fifteen miles southwest of Clancy's place.

"Dan McLain, you are the most obstinate man in the territory," cried his wife, Sadie. "You couldn't settle for shooting yourself in the foot. Instead, you shoot yourself in the back! I declare, you are in no shape for back-breaking work on a skimpy surface deposit." Ignoring Sadie's protests, Dan planned to poke around the area for a month or two.

When Sadie went back in the house, Dan whispered, "Kirby, we need supplies and we need to get this mining claim recorded." He handed Kirby several folded papers. "My back is killing me. I'd like you to ride into Flagstaff and take care of these chores."

A thought flashed across Kirby's mind. He had heard about a pretty assistant clerk working in the County Recorder's office. His heart raced when he realized this would be an opportunity to get a look at her.

"Kirby, did you hear what I said?"

His mind flashed back to the present. "But these papers describe a spring, not a mine."

"If you want to work for me, do as I ask and get yourself to the Recorder's office. Tell ol' Emmett there you are filing the Never Mine on my behalf." Dan appeared agitated.

"Dan, I heard about prospectors making claims under the Mining Laws to protect a spring or road that has nothing to do with mining. It seems you are trying to claim a spring as a mine."

Kirby could see the anger building under Dan's derby hat. "Dang it, I'll go to the Recorder's office myself. You stay here." He tried to hide the sharp pain when he grabbed his papers from Kirby.

Kirby regretted questioning his new boss and the lost opportunity to meet the assistant clerk. In time, his snide comments faded from Dan's memory. Trust settled in and grew, and the two made good progress exposing copper deposits on the South Rim.

* * *

One summer day, while Clancy fetched a bottle of Tennessee whiskey from his home state, Stuart Casey and Cole Campbell sat in rockers on Clancy's cabin porch. The fellows had not known each other long, but long enough to have endured several of Clancy's wild tales. Cole, glancing over to Casey, blurted out, "I don't know about you, Casey, but it amazes me how visitors are so easily drawn to Clancy's quaint stories."

"Yeah Cole, and there's that drawling voice of his, reaching a crescendo as his story approaches a climax. By the way, thanks for calling me Casey. I never liked my first name."

"No doubt about it," Cole added, "Clancy has a knack for leading listeners along a trail of plausibility, intertwining fact and fiction, then turning them down sharp switchbacks that stretch his tale far beyond reason, and then letting it snap into absurdity, confounding his listeners with doubts—including doubts of whether to laugh or scoff."

"Well, that's putting it eloquently. Where did you go to school, Cole?" He didn't wait for an answer. "Anyway, in the end, those listeners laughed, mostly at themselves for being led so far astray."

Clancy appeared in the cabin doorway with a bottle and three glasses. He poured two fingers of whiskey for his friends, three for himself—his hand shaking. "What are you boys talkin' about?"

"Ah, nothing much. Careful, you're spilling! Make mine three fingers too, will ya? Casey here just asked where I went to school. The answer is eastern Canada. What about you Casey?"

"The Midwest," Casey answered.

Clancy followed, "I used to live in the Midwest. Didn't like it much, too flat, not like the Smokies or the Ozarks. Let's drink to where we are now, not where we're from."

"I'll drink to that," said Casey and Cole at the same time.

Clancy added, "Here's to the Grand Canyon—surely the most majestic, sun-splashed place on the planet."

"Now who is spouting eloquent words? Between you and Cole, you make me feel like an uneducated bumpkin. Quit yer speechifying and talk normal," urged Casey.

"Clancy, you sure picked a good spot here. You have a spring, firewood, shelter—but you are missing one important element," observed Cole.

"Yeah? What's that?"

"A view of the Canyon. You are down in a cove here and you cannot see the 'majestic, sun-splashed canyon' as you call it."

"Ah, that's why I built another cabin right on the edge, about a hundred yards northeast of where we are sitting," explained Clancy. "That's where I sit and conjure up ideas for new stories to entertain my visitors."

Casey added, "And you are quite the tale-spinner . . . and whiskey drinker too."

"Well, my best stories come to mind with a nip of this fine Twin Oaks whiskey," said Clancy, taking a healthy swig, then adding, "But a few of my best stories come with too much whiskey. The problem with that is I forget 'em before I can tell 'em."

After another swig, "Casey, you think I'm a heavy drinker. I'm touched by your concern. Sure glad I'm still drinkin' . . . saves me the humiliation of falling off the wagon."

Tales told on the trail often served as gentle but effective admonishments to exercise caution, to follow instructions or to keep a safe distance from the edge. Tales told in safe comfortable surroundings, like on Clancy's cabin porch or around a campfire, became long drawn-out ramblings told for the mere joy of a corking good time.

New arrivals would gather around Ol' Cap as he opened with some unusual remark and those who understood him knew he seemed primed and ready to spin a dandy. His blue-gray eyes would sparkle as he fingered his long moustache. He had an uncanny way of pulling a leading question from those around him.

* * *

Having read newspaper accounts of John Wesley Powell's river expeditions through the Grand Canyon, Clint McCarty left the State of Maine and headed West. As a man of implacable drive and youthful enthusiasm, he radiated authority, self-confidence and a keen sense of judgment. Behind mystic dark eyes, there burned the will of a glory hound. His striking good looks disguised his air of superiority; his firmness came like claps of thunder. Despite his forceful personality, he possessed impish humor and an infectious, disarming smile.

In a quiet fishing village in southern Maine, Clint McCarty came into this world eight months after Arizona had been carved out of New Mexico and made into a separate U.S. territory. Although educated in public schools, he augmented his knowledge through extended private study. He worked as a fisherman on schooners trawling the Grand Banks, all the while harboring his desire to go west. As a store clerk in Gloucester, where he received a monthly paycheck of forty dollars, Clint weighed his options and promptly quit his job. The twenty-year-old adventurer rode the rails to Arizona, arriving in Flagstaff a year after the first tracks had reached the frontier town.

Stuart Casey saw McCarty hop off the smoke-belching train. "Welcome stranger; where you coming from?" inquired Casey.

"Back East, name's Clint McCarty," replied the newcomer, as he craned his neck to get a better look at the town.

"McCarty? You ain't related to Billy the Kid, are ya? I'm joshing. We all know the McCarty name as an alias used by the Kid and other notorious outlaws."

"None of my kinfolk performed such dastardly deeds. Eastern newspapers were full of stories about the Kid, his gang of cattle rustlers, and his death about two years ago at the hands of Sheriff Pat Garrett of Lincoln County, New Mexico Territory," volunteered McCarty, apparently well-versed in western lore for an easterner.

"My name's Stuart Casey. I usually go by Casey. Come on—I'll buy ya' a drink at the Ponderosa Tavern, best place in town," smiled Casey. "I was jest foolin' about, ya know. It ain't every day we see a newcomer arrive by freight car."

"Oh, I can explain that. Two outlaws forced me off a Santa Fe passenger car at a water stop called Canyon Diablo and robbed me at gunpoint. Then they ordered the train to roll out, leaving me and some others stranded. I hopped a westbound freight and continued my journey. I'd appreciate that drink," sighed McCarty, "as those outlaws relieved me of all my pocket money." The two men grumbled about the lack of law and order as they walked along Railroad Avenue.

"Casey, it looks like one of your town's buildings burned down recently."

"Yeah, that pile of scorched lumber used to be the Name-Your-Poison Saloon. The fire took the life of one poor soul, burned beyond recognition. We need to build with stone instead of wood." After pausing outside the stone-faced Ponderosa to watch the train pull out, they stepped inside and ordered drinks.

"Monte, two beers, please," ordered Casey as the two sidled up to the bar. "Clint, I'd like to introduce you to Monte Bridgestone, proprietor of the Ponderosa Tavern and Monte, Clint McCarty here just arrived in a boxcar."

"Boxcar?" Bridgestone's hand slipped off the beer tap. "You don't look like a hobo, Mr. McCarty; what happened?"

"It's a long story, but it's a pleasure meeting you fellas," replied Clint, in a classic slow New England accent as he hoisted his beer. Casey and Clint moved to a corner table and the two launched into a deep discussion about railroad transportation and westward migration.

While Europeans built railroads to connect cities, Americans built railroads across barren prairies and inhospitable mountains to induce settlers to establish cities. It would not be long before five transcontinental railroads steamed to completion. Several of the railroad company names had "Pacific" embedded in them, thus emphasizing the great feat of westward expansion. Transcontinental rail lines offered inexpensive travel at forty miles per hour, and safe transport at that—Canyon Diablo being one exception.

As track-laying crews worked their way westward, they created a series of frontier towns like Flagstaff. The government awarded Atlantic & Pacific Railroad three million acres to build a line following the "Albuquerque Trail" along the thirty-fifth parallel. The Atlantic & Pacific line faltered several times over the years but its army of graders, tie-cutters, tracklayers and spikers continued its surge across northern Arizona to California.

Investors and businessmen saw railroads as instruments of expansion and prosperity. They did not hesitate to nuzzle up to railroad officials to learn the location of the next railhead. By the turn of the century, bound by steel rails, the Atlantic married the Pacific, allowing the commingling of Americans under one nation.

One historic union occurred at a place called Promontory Point, just north of Great Salt Lake in Utah Territory. Kirby O'Brien, the young partner of Levi Jackson and Dan McLain, then only six years old, witnessed the Central Pacific shaking hands with the Union Pacific, not understanding the significance of two engines meeting face-to-face. He had accompanied his father who worked as an accountant for the westbound Union Pacific line. During the celebration, Kirby had the honor of shaking hands with Leland Stanford, President of the east-bound Central Pacific line.

Clint McCarty, who associated with a banker named Jesse Parks, remained vigilant for business opportunities, always charting a course forward, whether plunging through Atlantic waves or clerking in a Gloucester business venture. When the Bank of Flagstaff receded into hard times, followed by foreclosure, its new stone building became available. Clint bought it, and added two wood-framed buildings and seven vacant lots to his real estate holdings. Now a substantial property owner, he partnered with an Ohio man named Walter Hatfield to purchase a dry goods business. Exercising his business savvy earned during his employment in Maine, Clint established the McCarty-Hatfield general mercantile store.

After Monte introduced Clint to the Canyon, they outfitted occasional prospecting parties, befriended other prospectors, and soon fell under the spell of the Canyon.

Townsfolk saw Clint as an ambitious man, brimming with energy and imagination—a leader, a fighter and a hard-driving businessman. His youthful clear gaze, ingratiating smile and outgoing personality drew townsfolk to this trim, handsome young man. Tireless, optimistic and persuasive, Clint exhibited great potential for public life—the ideal politician perhaps.

Journalists described Clint as having "the spiritual endowment of a sunny temper and the supreme physical gift of a winning smile that turned his eyes into points of light". Old-timers would say, "He's the first to rise in the morning, and has the campfire made before you're out of your blankets. And he's already smiling when he hands you your first cup of coffee." His pluck and perseverance showed in his fight to overcome the obstacles of nature at the Grand Canyon and transcended into his success in public life.

Townsfolk admired Clint's ready smiles and lauded his commercial success. Appreciating his vision for Arizona statehood, they elected him to the Territorial Legislature. There, he helped move the territorial capital from Prescott to Phoenix.

Clint continued to divide his time between canyon ventures and his blossoming political career. He served two terms as sheriff. The criminal element avoided the jurisdiction of the intrepid lawman known for tracking down desperadoes and bringing them to justice. Later he would reflect, "I saw my capture of law-breaking scoundrels as revenge for the unknown assailants that greeted me in Canyon Diablo a decade earlier."

Politics, sheriff duties and prospecting left little time to mind the McCarty-Hatfield general store. Clint had prospered in its operation and his success as a local businessman helped in politics. He considered capitalizing on his success by selling his business interests.

* * *

On a raw April morning, two German immigrant brothers from Ohio, Ernst and Otto Bergner, arrived in Flagstaff, by then a town bustling with eighteen saloons, each attracting its fair share of railroaders, loggers, cowboys, ranchers and prospectors. The town population swelled to one thousand. It had battled back from a series of devastating fires when the Bergners' train stopped at Flagstaff's boxcar depot. What the latest fire had left of the town seemed lifeless in the early morning gloom. The outlook worsened when a late-season snowstorm dumped two feet of snow on top of burned-out buildings. To Ernst, the town seemed nothing more than a charred husk of a frontier whistle-stop. "Look at this town, Otto. It would do well if the town fathers promoted building with brick-and-mortar rather than rough-cut lumber." Otto shook his head in agreement and the two stepped off the train. "Let's find a hotel, Ernst, assuming there is one still standing."

The town's aspect must have improved as the sun ascended and townsfolk moved about, many of them busying themselves with shoveling heavy wet snow and resuming repairs of the dismal aftermath of Flagstaff's latest conflagration. Chet Kennedy's sawmill operated day and night churning out new lumber for rebuilding. And from the stone quarry south of town came a steady stream of wagons loaded with building materials that will not burn.

Ernst, kind and respected, became the guiding force in their business ventures. While strict in his dealings, he always had a soft spot for the underdog. Otto seemed easy-going, unassuming, more of a follower than a leader, but always smiling. The men took pleasure in seeing the town constructing more buildings of stone rather than wood.

The Bergner brothers' dreams of building a new life turned into new business opportunities. They knew of no comparison in Ohio to the grandeur and beauty of the towering San Francisco Peaks or the surrounding pine-studded foothills and sweeping grasslands. The transcontinental railroad had opened the area to settlement and commerce, and western fever already had a grip on the brothers. They built a commercial empire, starting with the purchase of the general store, where fellow Ohioan Walter Hatfield became their most trusted and valued employee. They then bought several cattle outfits and soon diversified into real estate, mining and Navajo trading posts—enterprises destined to make an indelible impression in the economic development of northern Arizona. The trading company that grew out of the McCarty & Hatfield general store would grubstake many a canyon prospector.

* * *

Monte Bridgestone befriended Clint McCarty and together they made excursions to the South Rim. Flagstaff had become a major crossroad on the American frontier and Monte had reached a major crossroad in his life. As happened to Levi Jackson and Stuart Casey, his canyon escapades spelled difficult times for his marriage. In fact, Marcy saw little value in Monte's prospecting trips. She shared none of his adventure and enthusiasm, and cursed the Canyon for the weeks and months when her husband left her alone in town. To Marcy, it seemed his unbridled passion for mining replaced his passion for family life.

Like his late brother, Monte had considerable mining experience. He associated himself with a group of prospectors who could not resist the gnawing urge to explore below the Canyon's rugged rim. With Clint McCarty and Slim Broadway, he often trekked across the Coconino to the rim, and dropped into Redrock Canyon on week-long prospecting trips. These men built a rustic camp on a majestic promontory that Monte named Summit Point, west of Clancy Jennings' tourist camp. For Monte, in the bewildering vastness of the Canyon, that special place on the South Rim surpassed all others.

"Clint, have you ever built a log cabin?" Monte asked. Clint signaled no.

"Slim, what about you?" Also no.

"When you look around at the trees on this rocky point, what you see is scrawny pinyon and stunted juniper with gnarled trunks and exposed roots. What we need is ponderosa and they are further back from the rim. I don't mean the stately trees with cinnamon-colored bark but the jack pine, the younger trees with black bark, what I call blackjack."

Slim understood. "So we need lots of blackjack logs, maybe six to eight inches in diameter. Let's get to work, boys."

The three men set about felling trees, trimming the branches and dragging them out by mule to Summit Point. Monte directed cutting them to length and notching the ends. The men spent several days erecting the building. They cut no openings for windows but placed a doorway facing the Canyon. They set a long ridge pole in place and cut smaller logs for roof rafters. Monte explained, "Think of the ridge pole as the spine and the rafters as ribs." Once they completed the skeleton or framework, Clint announced that he had business in Flagstaff and started back.

Monte commented to Slim about the sudden departure, "Well, Slim, I guess that leaves you and me to finish the job."

"It's not that he doesn't like hard work but Clint is always thinking ahead to the next project. It is not unusual for him to leave the details to others. I've not known him long but I've heard others regard him as the planner in his business enterprises."

About this time, another enterprising planner, William O'Neill—the young probate judge from Prescott—took a pragmatic interest in the Grand Canyon. As a dashing, flamboyant adventurer with a penchant for melodrama, O'Neill bluffed often and seldom yielded. His friends saw him as a man of controlled discipline and cool restraint, but with an uncanny knack of striking at the right time and in just the right place—he should have prospected for gold. His actions came across as swift but often reckless.

O'Neill hailed from St. Louis, Missouri, the Gateway to the Wild West. While his father had been a leader of men in the Civil War, the son became a leader of boys—always in the lead of a mock attack upon the National Capitol, or in miniature cavalry sweeps across the rolling meadows around Lee Mansion in Arlington to take the battle into the teeth of his father's erstwhile enemy. Reared and schooled in Washington City, O'Neill seemed destined for western adventures. He worked as a journalist in Phoenix and Tombstone where the first signs of his rambunctious nature surfaced as bets in poker and faro games.

From his first encounter with the abyss, O'Neill sought ways to exploit the region. He scampered down a pathway used by the Havasupai to a place he called Canyon Gardens. There he staked claims in various side canyons, betting, with the same misguided confidence of Arizona's wildest gambling houses, that his holdings contained minerals of value. To O'Neill, prospecting was gambling. This forward-thinking canyon pioneer wasted little time developing copper showings in the limestone outcropping below the rim and a few miles back from the rim where Dan McLain and Kirby O'Brien had been scratching the surface.

O'Neill also built a log cabin, with help from Kirby, on the rim overlooking Canyon Gardens and there he entertained visions of mines, hotels and a railroad depot at the brink of the Canyon. He often said, "I see things with a clear eye; and quite frankly, I like the view." Although his time at the South Rim turned out to be short, his influences on its development would be everlasting.

In his cabin, O'Neill spun dreams grander than the grandest Jennings' tales. This young visionary foresaw the potential of both the mining business and the tourist trade—and the railroad that would come to the Canyon to serve both industries.

As in every other undertaking in his short life, O'Neill distinguished himself in his term as a lawman. As the youngest ever to wear a badge, he built a reputation as being one of the best—remembered for his courage and iron resolve. Like others who became legendary in the annals of frontier justice, he trailed outlaws and desperados alone, laid his life on the line and single-handedly captured his unsavory prey. He received endless congratulations when he captured the four men who kept robbing trains at Canyon Diablo.

Bandits targeted stagecoaches and freight trains whenever they stopped at Canyon Diablo. Flagstaff merchants counted themselves lucky when they received complete and undamaged shipments from the East. While the town decayed into ruin with completion of the trestle bridge, the location continued as a railroad water stop and became notorious for train robberies. When four masked men relieved an express agent of fifteen hundred dollars and passengers of their timepieces and jewelry, Sheriff O'Neill and his posse captured the desperados but failed to recover the loot.

Like many a hero, however, William O'Neill had his fatal flaw. In all things, he seemed impulsive yet smug and confident, impatient yet cunning and aggressive. In his business dealings, on the trail of a vicious outlaw, or at the gaming table, he took a direct approach—his goal, immediate results—win or lose. He accepted a loss or a win with the same cheerful grace.

In the Tombstone gambling houses, O'Neill would plunge into a reckless faro card game, laying down his last double-eagle chip with the same carefree grin as the first. The heyday for faro occurred during the California Gold Rush but men played it in mining town saloons throughout the Old West.

With the backs of early faro cards featuring the image of an African tiger, players called the game "Bucking the Tiger". A smart player could make a fortune bucking the tiger as the house had a low percentage. Such an edge often caused sleight-of-hand faro dealers to cheat the players, increasing the profits for the house, and expanding their own cut.

At the faro table, many gamblers could play at one time and the hands played fast. Betting against the dealer, players bet on the card rank of their choice. The dealer then exposed cards in pairs, regretted paying off winners but reveled in collecting from losers.

O'Neill found himself "bucking the tiger" in every phase of his life, gaining him the nickname Buckey. Once, in declining an offer to join several Tucson businessmen in a mining venture, he said, "The only difference between mining and gambling is the element of time. In gambling, well, you win or lose, and don't have to wait long to find out which it is." One businessman reminded Buckey of what Mark Twain used to say, "There are two times in a man's life when he should not speculate—when he can't afford it and when he can."

Bristling with ideas thirty years ahead of their time, Buckey O'Neill ignored the position he advocated to the men in Tucson. He would promote the Canyon's copper deposits to eastern investors, plan a railroad to serve those investments, and work several mines himself.

* * *

Ben Saxton, a heavy-set fellow, had a dark, sallow face with a pock-marked complexion. With a high forehead undercut by two furrows and the nervy look of a thoroughbred, he stood six-foot-six. Born in the East, he never knew his father but understood he sailed around Cape Horn at the tip of South America—where howling winds, gigantic waves and frigid temperatures challenged even the most experienced sea captains—and joined the California Gold Rush. Ben later learned that his father made it to San Francisco and the goldfields around Sutter's Mill, only to die of cholera in a mining camp on the Sacramento River. In grammar school, he attained the fifth grade and bounced around from one odd job to another. The concept of hard work always eluded Ben but he found work on an eastern railroad as a dispatcher. With deteriorating health due to a burgeoning aneurysm, doctors urged him to live out his remaining months in the arid Southwest. Ben settled in Williams from where the new transcontinental railroad still pushed westward. As a frontier town, Williams comprised livery stables, storage sheds, fourteen saloons, and a long row of tents next to the tracks.

"What do you know about railroad work?" scowled the construction foreman.

"Well," Ben responded in his gruff manner, "back East I worked as a dispatcher."

The foreman sneered, "That's not construction!"

It was Ben's turn to lash back. "I know a rail weighs five hundred pounds, it takes two dozen spikes and three or four blows per spike to pin a rail to ties and, under the whip of a good supervisor like yourself, a crew can lay two pairs of rails per minute and four hundred rails per mile."

Ben made up those numbers, hoping the foreman didn't know such details. The foreman hired him on the spot and for the next few months Ben labored in Williams' railroad yards—as assistant foreman.

At the time, Emma Lee lived in Ash Fork, eighteen track-miles west of Williams. Ben learned that her late husband, a major in the Mormon Battalion, had been executed for his alleged participation in the Mountain Meadows Massacre. He befriended Emma and visited her whenever his work took him to Ash Fork.

One day Emma confided in Ben about her husband's stash of gold. Rumors floated about claiming Lee hid several tin coffee cans filled with gold nuggets in the Canyon. She showed him a keepsake nugget Lee had given her one time when he ventured out of hiding. She also showed Ben a crude map she had drawn from memory, based on subtle clues that Lee had shared with her over the years. It marked the gold's location in the eastern reaches of the Canyon, the same area explored by Levi Jackson, but it contained so little detail that Ben wondered if the map could be of any use at all.

Such calamities kept rumors of lost gold alive. Of all the stories that persist through time, those involving hidden treasure, whether heists gone bad or treasure buried but location lost, or abandoned gold mines, they always captured the imagination of men like Ben Saxton.

Emma complained that her old age clouded her memory and warned Ben that searching for rumored lost gold is a waste of time. Ben countered, "Emma, old age takes hold when regrets take the place of dreams. I still have dreams and I believe when gold's about, it always reveals itself. There will be time enough for regrets later."

Gold fever spread like the wind. One fortune-hunter bent on finding the alleged lost gold learned that Ben had a map showing the gold's location. He hired Ben to guide him down the Jackson Trail, a trail Ben had never traveled. In fact, Ben had never seen the Canyon. Despite Emma's constant reminder that memories dim with passing years, his party snaked its way down the trail.

That expedition turned into disaster with the loss of a string of five heavily-laden burros. A fallen tree on the upper trail blocked their way, and as they turned their saddle horses, one of them bucked, knocking all of the burros down a steep talus slope. One burro had a loaded rifle strapped to its pack, and as the hapless animal rolled over and over, the weapon discharged. The frantic burro had landed pack down with legs flailing in the air. The stray bullet struck the man who hired Ben. He survived as perhaps the only person ever shot by a burro. This misadventure is the kind that could inspire Clancy Jennings to spin a yarn about an armed burro.

Chapter Six

COPPER STRIKE

The river is a living testament to the power of nature and the passage of time.

One late-March morning, three men left Flagstaff, their wagon bulging with picks, shovels, blankets, and provisions for two weeks at the Canyon. Trailing three pack burros, they followed a muddy wagon road which skirted the Peaks, snaked through the ponderosa forest, and then stretched across the northern plains of the Coconino Plateau. By six in the evening, the threesome reached Red Rock Hill and set up camp for the night. The brutal spring winds that gusted all day showed signs of dying down. The temperature also started on its way down. Huddling around the coffee pot that night sat Monte Bridgestone, Clint McCarty and Ben Saxton.

Ben Saxton, thirty-eight years old, now a sullen drifter hanging around Flagstaff, occasionally found construction work, but often found himself unemployed. He had finished clearing land south of town for the Citizens Cemetery—Clancy's story about getting a cemetery started became a reality. As a canyon prospector, he helped locate several mining claims and build the early trails, but Monte often regretted including Ben on excursions below the rim. He found him to be moody, impulsive and quarrelsome, often creating an issue where none existed. Ben seemed awkward in movement. Monte often viewed him as being prone to violence, more dangerous than productive, but he needed a strong worker, and so settled for the burly vagabond.

In the flickering light of the campfire, Monte recorded the journey in his pocket diary, with penciled phrases capturing the day's highlights. When he closed his book, Ben started bragging about his first canyon visit.

"You fellas may not know I poked around the Canyon before you two. I led a search party for lost gold near the point where the Little Colorado flows into the Big Colorado. We matched up every detail on our map with the buttes, mesas and ravines."

That got Clint's attention. "So, what happened? If you struck it rich, you wouldn't be regaling us with a wild tale tonight."

"Our burros got away from us. We had no supplies for an extended stay so we turned back. Once I find my map, I'll put together a new outfit and resume the hunt. But I do wonder what happened to that string of burros." Before Ben finished his short spiel, Monte had fallen asleep.

The men spent the second night at Cedar Ranch. On the third night, the prospectors camped below a forested ridge one and a half miles from Red Horse. They spread their bedrolls on a springy mat of dry pine needles. A sinister hush came stealing along the ridge like a slinking coyote as the men breathed in the pungent smell of pine pitch.

Early in the afternoon of the fourth day, they arrived at Clancy Jennings' cabin and got their supply wagon stuck in the mud. Ben gravitated to Clancy while Monte and Clint unhitched their horses and started unloading the wagon.

"Ben, quit your jawboning and get over here and help," complained Monte.

"I'm comin', hold your horses," chimed the free-loader in a harsh, grating voice.

They camped there for the night and invited Clancy to supper. In return, their story-telling host waived his standard camping fees.

81

"Monte, yer my best friend—aw—I'll admit it, my only friend, since you killed ol' Mule. After all, if it were not for you, I may never have found my way to this magnificent canyon. The least I can do is accommodate a few weary travelers."

"Best friend, huh," returned Monte, "well then, I question your judgment but be that as it may. And by the way, I did not kill Mule; that big cat killed him."

Ben had to jump into the conversation. "Clancy, how long have you been here at the Canyon?"

"See that ravine over there? When I arrived, the whole canyon was that size."

The men chuckled and helped themselves to the coffee pot. Clint put another log on the campfire and then raised his own question for Clancy.

"I've heard you tell folks we are seventy-five hundred feet above sea level here on the South Rim. I know all about sea level but how do ya know how high we are?"

Clancy stroked his stubbled chin for a minute, then with a twinkle in his eye, explained, "Wal, I jest drilled down until I hit saltwater, then I took a measurement." The men delivered a blank stare.

Clancy then continued. "I think I need to tell ya more about this ol' river we call the Colorado. It is rather special, ya know. It works night and day, much harder than most rivers, going about its business, doing its darnedest to cut deeper and wider, carrying mud, sand and bits of weathered rock downstream."

Clancy, looking at his visitors and with all seriousness, added, "It's a simple matter of gravity, moving eroded material from high places and transporting it to low places. The river is a living testament to the power of nature and the passage of time."

Ben interjected, "What has that got to do with elevation or saltwater?"

Clancy stopped and pondered how he would explain the river's real intentions. Clint offered some coaching. "You know, Clancy, an odyssey can take one below the rim but imagination can take one anywhere."

Clancy had no idea what Clint tried to say but it did not matter. He thought of a way to personify the Colorado River. "Like you and me—well maybe just me—the river has a goal. My goal has been to attain the poverty level. Having recently achieved my goal—"

Clint interrupted, "Clancy, get on with it."

"This ol' river lives for the day when it finally reaches sea level. Now mind you, it still has another half a mile of scraping and scouring before it equalizes level with the Gulf of California. When you think about it, you wonder why it's in such a hurry to reach the sea, but when it does, that's when seawater will flood into the Grand Canyon."

Clancy added, "I won't be here when that happens. Sorry, but you fellas won't either. At its current rate of excavation, it will take millions of years to get the job done."

With that wild explanation, the men retired for the evening. The following morning, they realized Clancy had already departed for parts unknown. Riding horseback and leading their string of pack burros, the men dropped below the rim between Spanish Butte and Sinking Battleship.

Monte expressed concern about their progress and his frustration with Jennings' Whiskey Trail. "Clint, we've had a hard time of it ever since we started down."

"Yeah, a very hard time, almost as hard as following Clancy's exasperating yarn last night. We've had to unpack and repack three times," responded Clint.

Ben glowered, then grunted in agreement. At last, they arrived at camp about a mile below Whiskey Spring.

The next day, they left camp for the river. They had to cross a small stream many times and at one point had to leave their horses and pack burros behind and dropped forty feet by rope ladder to the creek-bed. They reached another place with a thirty-foot rope ladder. All along the way, they prospected and staked a claim they called the Texas Ranger. Monte found their return to where they tied their horses and burros to be most strenuous. He wondered how Jennings, being more advanced in age, managed the climb.

Further west, Stuart Casey and Cole Campbell laid claim to a mining location that included Grand Canyon Springs, as they began their own prospecting venture.

Monte and his partners spent several days digging prospect holes. They put in a shot of giant powder and retrieved pieces of rock from the blast hole.

Ben remarked, "I see ya like giant powder better than standard black powder that railroaders use."

Monte looked at him and saw a tenderfoot. "Yeah, everyone knows it ignites quicker and has a better shattering effect on these layered canyon rocks. Very little black powder has been used since the seventies because it has a habit of delaying its explosion and sometimes failing to explode at all. Anyone these days who has worked on railroad construction knows that, Ben."

By mid-afternoon, sheets of rain pelted the men. Tired and wet, they started back to camp, a distance of about four miles. Monte grabbed his daybook and noted that it rained so hard they stayed in camp and finished scratching their names under a rock overhang.

When the weather cleared, the three prospectors struck a trail down river by climbing out of Whiskey Canyon and trekking west across the

Tonto Plateau, blazing a new route with pack burros. They passed a prominent red mesa; hugging the western edge of its base, they made camp where the east and west forks of Cottonwood Creek converged in a stand of spindly Frémont cottonwoods. The prospectors had skirted Windsong Mesa, not realizing that it held copper minerals and native copper that would later prove to be their richest strike. The next morning, they left Cottonwood Camp and traveled westward across the Tonto, making their way to a nameless creek. These men would soon know the terrain over which they now picked their way as well as they knew the names of all of Flagstaff's saloons.

One late afternoon, the men came across Casey and Campbell camping in a rocky ravine and there spent the evening. After supper, they sat around their campfire, smoking their pipes. Casey broke the silence, "I'm sure you fellas know about the law that President Grant signed to promote development of our nation's mineral resources."

The men nodded and Monte added, "Sure, we know—it passed with pick-and-shovel prospectors like us in mind." It seemed Casey had something on his mind.

After another round of silence, Casey spoke again, "While Congress was eager to encourage recovery of our young nation's hidden mineral assets, some lawmakers found the Mining Act to be so generous they considered it to be not in the best interest of the people. With that in mind, I'm worried fellas; I think there's something in the wind that may later prevent prospectors and miners from making claims on public land like here in the Canyon."

"Aw, Casey, you—" Monte interrupted Ben.

"That's certainly true. A prospector simply placed stakes or rock monuments at the corners of his strike, posted a discovery notice, usually weather-protected in a tin can or glass jar, and recorded the location of his claim with county officials."

"Casey, you worry too much," countered Ben.

That ended the evening discussion but Monte shared the same sentiments. Mining men depended on their ability to make claims by right of discovery and to operate their mines without interference—an important tenet for canyon prospectors. Monte, having read about the establishment of the United Mine Workers of America two months earlier, thought Casey might be right; maybe the founders of that labor union had the same concerns.

* * *

One day while prospecting below the rim, Monte and his partners made a startling discovery—not gold or copper but a rider on a gray swayback mule approaching from the West. As the stranger reined in, the men stood aghast, seeing a woman in their midst. She wore a blue-striped shirt, patched knee trousers, woolen stockings protruding from her boots, and a bandana around her neck. Ben stiffened as she dismounted.

"Howdy fellas, bet yer surprised to see a female prospector down here!"

"Prospector?" exclaimed Monte, as the men also dismounted. "Who are you? How'd ya' get down here? Who ever heard of a woman prospector?"

Monte knew the emancipation movement for women had been underway for some time but he never dreamed it would include prospecting and mining.

"My name is Sabrina Jaffa; pleased to meet you fellas. I've been pokin' around these rocky ravines for three days but I ain't findin' anything of interest."

"I'm Monte Bridgestone and these two *male* prospectors are Clint McCarty and Ben Saxton," said Monte, motioning to his partners and emphasizing the word male.

Sabrina, while well-educated, used prospector jargon, hoping to be accepted in the male's general pursuit of valuable metals. She had a small trim body, large green eyes and a bewitching smile. Seeing the men still aghast, she took off her slouch hat and, unable to resist practicing her female wiles on three male strangers, she uncoiled her long brown hair and let it cascade down her back. "See? I'm a woman; surely, you've seen women before?"

"Not down here, we ain't," griped Ben, sensing violation of their canyon sanctum.

Monte still couldn't believe this rare sight—an attractive woman below the rim, riding across the Tonto, alone! Sabrina explained that she had been working as a clerk in the County Recorder's office where she learned about mining prospects in the Canyon. Planning her first visit, she thought of herself as a free-spirited woman miner before her time, inspired by Calamity Jane's foray into a man's world, even wearing a man's shirt and trousers.

"Fellas, I'm in my mid-twenties, recently divorced, and in dire need of a change. I want more out of life so I quit my clerking job." The men stood spellbound, trying to adjust to this breathtaking discovery. Sabrina added, "I'm searching for more excitement and pretty metals, and I figure the Canyon is a good place to start. Wish me luck."

With that, she put her hat back on, mounted her mule and continued her eastward journey along the Tonto.

Clint, who had been speechless during the whole encounter, had to say something. "Fellas, this is not a good omen. To my way of thinkin', a woman's place is in the home, not in a clerk's office, not out here on the Tonto. I hope she doesn't jinx our prospecting."

Ben, aroused by the mere proximity of a beautiful woman in their midst, replied, "Maybe so, but she sure is a good-looker." He longed for a woman to take care of his physical needs.

The prospectors watched Sabrina's long hair sway across her slender waist, matching her mule's swishing tail. Before disappearing around a red butte she looked back over her shoulder and in a final tease, waved farewell to the startled men.

"Well, I never knew her name, in fact, I paid her little notice during my visits to the Recorder's office," said Monte. "She sure looks a lot different in the saddle."

Ben resisted the urge to follow as Monte urged them to go on about their work. They located two adjacent mining claims and spent the next three days working them. Around the evening campfires, they sat perplexed about their encounter with the mysterious woman prospector.

With ore samples tagged and packed in canvas bags, the prospectors started the long trek back to Flagstaff. They camped at Cliff Gulch where it empties into Bighorn Creek. After crossing the Tonto they climbed a steep pathway to the rim that Buckey O'Neill used to access Canyon Gardens, the same path whose footprints are now more of the white man—and now white woman—and less of the Havasupai. The caravan of tired men and burros reached the snow-covered rim near sundown. After a short break, they resumed their overland journey to Flagstaff, at least until dark. It took four days, with overnight stops at Red Horse, Cedar Ranch and another camp eighteen miles northwest of town. By mid-afternoon, they rode into Flagstaff.

* * *

When Monte filed their mining claims with the county recorder, he could not resist inquiring about Sabrina Jaffa.

"Hey Emmett, I understand you lost your office clerk recently."

"Yeah, she suddenly quit about two weeks ago and I've been short-handed ever since."

Monte enlightened the fellow, "Well, you won't believe this but we ran into her in the Canyon, prospecting no less!"

Emmett fumbled Monte's claim papers. "In the Canyon? So that's where she went, crazy woman, she don't know nothin' about prospecting."

Monte tended to agree but he did not know. Perhaps their paths would cross again someday. After delivering canyon ore samples to the assay office on Railroad Avenue, he went home to his family.

Meanwhile, below the rim, Cole Campbell prepared to lay claim to the trail the men had just traversed. He located and recorded it as the Tonto Trail.

Monte's homecoming, neither pleasant nor restful, gave Marcy another chance to raise a ruckus. She watched with alarm and growing resentment as her husband abandoned her more frequently, apparently favoring long jaunts to the Canyon over her company.

Marcy Bridgestone, like Sarah Casey and Molly Jackson, took a dim view of prospecting. All three women felt their men had obligations to earn sufficient income to support their wives and children. Marcy shouted, "Surely there were other professions—even ranching or storekeeping—that offered steady work!" She charged that Monte neglected his job as proprietor of the Ponderosa Tavern, not knowing he put Silas Taylor in charge of daily operations. Marcy also charged that he had been neglecting their son.

"Before long, Ben will ask about you," she scolded. "He will need your attention and praise as he learns how to do things."

Monte, not focused on her rant, mumbled, "Ben tagged along with Clint McCarty and me to the Canyon, not that he did much work." Marcy seemed perplexed.

"What?" she declared in alarm. "I'm talking about our one-year-old son!"

Monte replied, "Oh, I'm talking about Ben Saxton, the worthless helper with me at the Canyon!"

Marcy shook her reddish locks in exasperation. Prolonged separation bred loneliness, anger and mistrust. As two opposites, their marriage seemed destined to fail.

* * *

Within two weeks, Monte and his associates, grubstaked by Jesse Parks, organized another prospecting trip to the Canyon. By most accounts, Parks had the honor of being Flagstaff's first settler, arriving a few months before the Fourth of July wagon train. He homesteaded northwest of town and later built the Bank Hotel building at the corner of Railroad and Leroux Avenues. The men, being joined by Slim Broadway, pushed hard, encouraged by assay returns on samples from their previous trip. Anxious, indeed desperate, to develop their mines, they hoped to generate revenue and pay off their debt to Parks. After three days, they reached the rim as the setting sun thrust its final light shafts into red buttes which cast serrated shadows upon their eastern neighbors.

On an April Tuesday, Monte's party started into the Canyon. The descent went well until one of their pack horses fell about five hundred feet. Despite this loss, they arrived at Clancy's rock cabin around mid-afternoon. From there they continued their journey, arriving at Cottonwood Creek four hours later, just in time for an early evening rainstorm.

The men had clambered down the Whiskey Trail, but forfeited a rest and water stop at Clancy's primitive camp. Near where Whiskey Spring seeped from the impervious shale, Clancy had built a crude rock cabin and corral. With its shade and water, this camp became a popular rest stop for early prospectors and tourists, many of whom scratched their name on a wall protected by an overhanging ledge. The men then circled around Windsong Mesa and made camp for the night. Just before drifting off, Monte glanced at the star-studded Milky Way, just as a fireball streaked across the sky, leaving a sparkling trail of stardust in its wake.

The next morning, they ascended the west wall of the mesa, located an outcropping of blue and green-tinged limestone, and staked the Shooting Star mining claim. It would be the Grand Canyon's greatest strike, but at the time of discovery the men named as locators—Ben Saxton, Monte Bridgestone, Slim Broadway, Clint McCarty and Jesse Parks—did not know what they had.

From Cottonwood, the men caravanned across the Tonto to Willow Creek and prospected in the gulch. It rained all day so they busied themselves by again scratching their names into a wall of sandstone. Despite the wet weather, Clint carved some dry humor into the rock—"Hotel de Willow Creek" with an arrow pointing to the creek-bed, and added his mark: "Clint McCarty 1890".

The prospectors left their Willow Creek camp the next day and journeyed through the Tonto sagebrush, shuffling along the base of massive buttes, and skirting deep side canyons. By late afternoon, they rounded the north tip of O'Neill Butte—named by Buckey himself when he had staked a claim at its base—and arrived at Six-Gun Creek.

Operating from their base camp, the men prospected in the deep side canyons where mica glittered in the black granite. There, Monte and Ben located the Black Diamond while Clint and Slim claimed the

Black Knight. Altogether, they located and surveyed sixteen lode claims.

On the first day of May, the men sent Ben Saxton home with ore samples, including greenish-blue rocks from the Shooting Star claim. They spent another week deepening the Black Diamond claim where the rude clatter of picks, shovels, rock drills and ore samples landing in a pile shattered the canyon silence.

The men spent considerable time working the Black Diamond Mine and similar sites but for naught. Monte glanced at his left hand, scarred and mangled from the time he reached into a crevice in the granite wall several years earlier. Black Diamonds—worthless mica deposits—had drawn prospectors into the Canyon from the beginning. Again, and again they returned to the black rocks, only to have their hopes shattered in dismal empty holes.

For another week the men worked on prospects in Six-Gun Creek and Bighorn Creek, but by then their food supplies had been exhausted. They determined to leave but rather than trudge the rugged trail through Canyon Gardens to the rim, they backtracked to Willow Creek, killing a pink rattlesnake at Hotel de Willow Creek before making camp there.

Starting out from Willow Creek, Monte, Slim and Clint journeyed to Whiskey Canyon where they set up camp along the creek. The next day they ascended Whiskey Trail and retrieved their wagon, cemented to the rim by hardened mud from an earlier excursion. Their return journey along the rutted wagon road took them to Red Horse, Cedar Ranch, and Jesse Parks' ranch northwest of town. They arrived in Flagstaff, only to find that Ben Saxton had already broken the news of their mining claims.

In the nineties, reporters found slim pickings for local newspaper stories. They often had to fill a page with lodge meeting notices, comings and goings of townsfolk and strangers, but assay findings caught the attention of readers, more so than shootings which gave towns bad reputations.

The Saturday edition of the *Frontier Times* carried the following report: "Mr. Ben Saxton, who is interested with Monte Bridgestone and Clint McCarty in some mining properties in the Grand Canyon, came in last Monday from camp with fine-looking ore samples. As soon as he gets confirmation of good results from the assayers, these parties plan to develop their canyon mines."

Another short sentence at the end of Monte's mining claim report raised considerable interest: "Mr. Saxton also reported encountering a female prospector below the rim." That's the only information he disclosed. Perhaps intending to track her down on his own and not wanting any competition in his pursuit, he declined to give her name or where the sighting occurred. Such a story would have produced a sudden increase in the *Frontier Times'* readership.

Monte Bridgestone received the assay results in a report in late May. Most of the rocks had little evidence of precious metal. Ore from the Black Diamond in Six-Gun Creek had mere traces of silver and gold. Shooting Star ore from Windsong Mesa had traces neither of silver nor gold, but assayed at a remarkable forty-five percent copper. The partners recorded the Shooting Star Mining Claim in June, and made plans for further exploration and development of this promising copper discovery. In time, they paid Jesse Parks for his share.

One warm day in mid-July, news reached Flagstaff that John C. Frémont, former territorial governor—but better known as the Great American Pathfinder—had passed away at his home in New York City. Retired from politics and destitute, he and wife Jessie survived on her writings. In an executive order, President Benjamin Harrison called for expressions of sorrow in the death of Frémont and gratitude for his military and public service.

The Shooting Star Mine heralded an era of rambling hopes, unyielding hardships, and wavering prosperity in hard-rock mining ventures at the Grand Canyon—the same traits which typified the life and times of John Frémont.

Chapter Seven

BLACK DIAMONDS

Man awakens interest in the potential mineral wealth that sleeps in the Canyon.

The glitter of black diamonds in Granite Gorge continued to draw prospectors below the rim. Even after locating copper deposits on Windsong Mesa, these canyon pioneers returned to the hard, black, rock walls, hoping to find mineral more valuable than copper. Their discoveries led to a blizzard of mining claims filed with the County Recorder in Flagstaff.

With forests on both rims of the Canyon, prospectors worried that President Harrison's Forest Reserve Act might threaten their right to file and work their claims. The men stockpiled only a few tons of ore, and of that, hauled only a fraction out of the Canyon. Forest reserve or not, the men faced a serious dilemma. The laborious tasks of hauling ore by burro to the rim, then by wagon to Flagstaff, and shipping it by rail to distant smelters, raised considerable doubt about ever making a profit in canyon mining.

One gray November day, Flagstaff's *Frontier Times* reported: "Several of our people plan to spend this winter at the Grand Canyon prospecting and developing their mining properties. Monte Bridgestone, Clint McCarty and Ben Saxton will leave this week. Stuart Casey, Cole Campbell and Slim Broadway are there now."

These men applied themselves to the monumental task of improving Casey and Campbell's crude trail, an old Havasupai pathway by which the mysterious Sabrina Jaffa found her way into the Canyon.

Casey and Cole wanted a shorter route to their Six-Gun Creek claims. They agreed to surrender their right to the trail if Bridgestone and McCarty made improvements and allowed them free use. The men spent most of December and January widening the trail, easing the way for pack animals to transport supplies and ore between the rim and canyon diggings. Monte, Clint and Slim labored long and hard on the trail. Ben helped, but not nearly as much as the others. Monte included a strong fellow like Ben in the work party, despite Ben's poisoning presence.

Monte grinned as he approached Slim. "We appreciate your help in improving access into the canyon depths so we can haul out good ore."

"I've been helping Casey and Cole locate claims on a pyrites ledge on the north side. Since this trail will help get our ore out of the Canyon, I'll pitch in and help build the trail. So's I'm willin' to post eighty dollars for blasting powder and provisions."

Monte responded, "Slim, that's exactly the kind of help we need. Thank you."

"Since I'm investing time and money in this enterprise, I'd like to give it a name."

"What do you have in mind, Slim?" Monte agreed that a trail destined to become a major thoroughfare for footmen, mule riders and pack burros needed a proper name.

Slim responded, "Let's call it the Pioneer Trail!"

"Okay boys, you heard it," Monte proclaimed, "We're building the Pioneer Trail." The men looked up, nodded their agreement, and resumed work.

Monte suspected Clint hired Slim to work in his place at times, freeing him for sheriff duties and other political pursuits.

One day Ben did not return from town with supplies, leaving the others stranded. The partners offered little sympathy. Ben, in his grumpy and combative manner, argued that deep snow hampered his wagon team and delayed his overland travel. He often made excuses for not completing an assignment. Monte used the incident to rid himself of this stubborn, unreliable worker.

"Ben, you're fired! We cannot depend on you and you've never done your fair share of the work." Monte's patience had run out. Ben cursed the work party, claiming trail-building to be too difficult for him and too dangerous at that. Later he found the partners had banished him from trail ownership.

Those who later used the Pioneer Trail to explore the wonders of Grand Canyon could not imagine the dangers and hardships faced by the men who built the trail. Injury lurked at every bend, and death awaited any relaxation of caution. Clint delighted in telling the story of Slim's flirt with death.

"We had been making good progress on the trail until we came to a giant boulder. When we tried blasting the rock out of the way, it split in half with one piece tumbling down the talus slope in spectacular fashion, the other landing right where we wanted the trail. Before going ahead with the work, it became necessary to remove this massive obstruction."

Clint, who harbored a knack for telling amusing stories, continued. "We drilled holes in two sides of the rock and set off the blasts. Slim assumed both charges went off at the same time, and after the explosion, approached the rock. The rest of us, convinced there had been only one explosion, warned him to get away, but he laughed at our warning. He sat on the rock and rolled a cigarette. I yelled for Slim to jump and he did, and not an instant too soon. As he left the rock, the powder exploded and pieces of the stone shot in every direction. The blast knocked him to the ground and covered him with rubble. Except for a few scrapes and cuts, and a bruised ego, he was not hurt."

The men extended the trail where Six-Gun Creek meets the river. Over the years, the route and grade of various sections changed with increasing use by prospectors, miners and stockmen. Canyon Gardens served as the miners' base camp for treks across the Tonto or descents into the inner reaches of Granite Gorge.

* * *

"Slim, I filed our papers; now it's time to get back to mining," said Monte.

"What exactly do the papers do for us?" Monte decided to take a few minutes to explain.

"By filing a notarized certificate and plat with the County, we create a franchise to operate the Pioneer Toll Road from rim to river. Arizona territorial laws provide that a person desiring to construct and maintain a toll road must file in the Office of the County Recorder a certificate and plat showing the location and route. We can then collect tolls in hopes of recovering our development expenses, like your eighty-dollar investment, and maybe even reap a small profit by assessing tolls on folks using our toll road."

Monte's paperwork described the trail as starting on the Colorado River west of Skeleton Creek, continuing through Canyon Gardens, and ending at a stake on the rim and marked "Pioneer Toll Road".

As crafty individuals, prospectors located many mining claims along the Pioneer Trail. They knew mining claims could give them the exclusive right of possession. They could not own the land until the claimant proved it contained valuable mineral, at which time they could receive a patent and valid title or deed certifying ownership of the land and its mineral resources. In the meantime, their property right enabled them to interfere with, and even prevent, public access. To some prospectors, the mining laws amounted to just a passel of vague legal talk, so they staked locations where no mineral existed. While considered suspect, and sometimes fraudulent, the practice continued for years.

Clint McCarty knew well how the scheme worked. When Slim pressed him for details, Clint explained, "When we stake our claims, the General Land Office—that's the agency that doles out public lands to citizens—has no incentive to investigate the validity of our mining locations. As valid claimants, we can maintain our rights for an indefinite period by performing at least one hundred dollars of development or assessment work each year until we bring the claim up for a patent."

"One hundred dollars!" exclaimed Slim, "I just invested eighty dollars in the trail. Another hundred is a lot of money!"

Clint clarified, "It's not real money, Slim; it is just the estimated value of labor spent on the claim, say a ten-foot tunnel, shaft or trench. During the patent process, the Land Office surveys and examines the claim. If minerals are present in paying quantities and the claimant is actively engaged in mining, it issues a patent."

"So, what's the catch, Clint?"

"Well, by performing modest amounts of annual assessment work on claims, and certifying completion of such work by filing an affidavit of annual assessment, a claimant can hold the land as if it were under long-term government lease. Failure to comply assumes an abandoned claim, in which case it reverts to the public domain."

Slim, suspecting Clint pushes the law to the limit, felt obliged to clarify his position. "I'm an honest man and want no involvement in shady operations. Clint, are you sure this is the way the system works?"

Clint did not answer, but under his breath he warned himself that he best keep a close eye on Slim, at least try not to imply there is anything illegal in staking claims for toll roads or mines.

Unlike placer claims for surface minerals, lode claim rules restricted claims to fifteen hundred feet along the apex of the vein and three hundred feet on either side, so that a full-sized lode claim was six hundred by fifteen hundred feet—or about twenty-one acres. Also, with each claim, the locator could stake a five-acre mill-site in the vicinity to set up machinery for ore reduction and smelting.

Some prospectors, including Clint, conniving and confident, took advantage of a loop-hole in the law. With no time limit between claim and patent, the law permitted the locator to maintain control of land by complying with annual assessment requirements. This led to a long agonizing conflict at the Grand Canyon. While prospectors made mining claims ostensibly for mineral, some claims encompassed viewpoints on the canyon rim, trails routed to include precious springs, and river crossings in such a way as to give the claimants control of land to which the public should have free access. The law also gave claimants the opportunity to levy tribute on the tourist. While most canyon prospectors did not engage in such skullduggery, the government charged Clint with fraudulent claims along the Pioneer Trail and around the trailhead. His mining properties became so entangled in bitter conflict, legal challenges and controversy, years, perhaps decades, would be needed to settle the matter.

* * *

One day in early February, Monte, Clint and several other men descended the newly constructed Pioneer Trail and followed the Tonto Trail across the plateau. The men navigated their string of burros below an unnamed point on the South Rim, around the head of Six-Gun Creek basin and past the northern tip of O'Neill Butte. Rocks clattered beneath their burros' feet. Their awkwardness sent small boulders tumbling over the brown-varnished ledges of Tonto sandstone and crashing into jagged walls of black granite.

While tempted to descend one of the side canyons and prospect in the same black and pink-banded rock that showed in the gorge, the miners continued eastward to a camp they called Ribbon Creek. The next day the party resumed their trek across the Tonto, passing Boulder Creek, rounding a lone butte, then skirting the deep ravines of Bridgestone Canyon, named in honor of Monte's departed brother. Upon arrival at their base camp at the fork in Cottonwood, Monte scribbled a brief entry in his pocket notebook: "Reported for work on the Shooting Star."

Monte had a question. "Clint, what do you know about copper?"

"Not much," said Clint, "I think it is used to make cartridge shells and cookware."

"Well, I've been reading a geology book and here's what I learned."

Clint rolled his eyes as Monte launched into his dissertation.

"For untold millennia, the Redwall limestone formation in the Grand Canyon held its copper treasure captive beneath a rust-red cloak stained by the iron compounds of higher rock strata. This massive six-hundred-foot wall of pure limestone is replete with resonant amphitheaters, shaded alcoves and hidden caves. Inside the blue-gray limestone, we call it 'blue lime', is a matrix of interlocking passageways and chambers formed as trickling water dissolved the carbonates and sulfates. Some of these solution cavities and channels collapsed, then refilled with debris, leaving only jagged pipelines to convey mineral-laden water, cementing the shattered rock and choking the flow. Are you listening Clint?"

"Of course, this is very interesting." He found Monte's ramblings rather boring but faked his interest.

Monte continued. "In time, sulfates precipitated in the breccia pipes to form mineralized zones. Still later, water percolated down through brecciated limestone chimneys, leaching copper and depositing it as rich veins of ore. The folding and faulting of mesas, like Windsong Mesa here in the Canyon, facilitated the percolation of rainwater and snowmelt, forming copper traps deep within the Redwall. When exposed at the surface, these ledges become oxidized outcroppings of sage green and azure blue ores."

"Ah, I understand," said Clint, still pretending to be interested in Monte's long spiel on canyon geology, "These colorful ores are just waiting to be discovered by prospectors like us. Monte, you could be a geologist!"

* * *

By spring, two prospecting outfits roamed the Grand Canyon between Whiskey Rapids and Bighorn Creek. Clint McCarty, Monte Bridgestone, Ben Saxton and Slim Broadway concentrated their work on the south side of the river and operated as the Shooting Star Mining Company. The other contingent—Stuart Casey, Cole Campbell and Clancy Jennings, and sometimes Slim Broadway—centered their activity on the north side, although some of their claims spanned the river. The Casey group operated as the Jennings Asbestos & Copper Mining Company.

These prospectors often crossed each other's territory so that the side canyons and mesas became a maze of lode claims. Development work on the canyon mines varied from a shallow prospect hole to penetrating tunnels and deep shafts. The men borrowed tools and equipment from each other and moved from one site to the next. They often left picks, shovels, rock drills, miner's spoons, explosives, and even burros, at one of their diggings, returning later to either resume work or to pull up stakes.

Casey spent less time in Flagstaff and more at the Canyon, performing manual labor on over sixty copper lode claims below the rim, often retrieving tools and equipment from one claim and moving to another. While Clint served in one political office after another, Monte and Slim managed their properties. Both served as the front line of defense in protecting their canyon holdings.

With mining claims on both sides of the Colorado, the river itself presented a tremendous obstacle. The miners used makeshift canvas boats to navigate the four-hundred-foot-wide river, ever fearful of being drawn downstream into formidable rapids before they could cut an angle on the current. Casey and Campbell used two river crossings, one called Jennings Crossing just below Bedrock Rapids, and the other Casey Crossing, where Cottonwood Creek dribbles into the river. This outfit staked asbestos claims on the north side in washes that drained Angel's Gate and neighboring buttes.

In June, Clint, Slim and Ben, grubstaked by Flagstaff businessmen, followed the old Jackson Trail to the river and located several copper claims above a ledge of Tonto sandstone, a mile south of where the Little Colorado emptied into the Big Colorado. After venturing out of their customary territory for the first time, the men risked overlaying new claims upon old claims in the Little Colorado Mining District that Levi Jackson established a decade earlier. The intriguing tale of Lee's lost gold weighed heavy on Ben's mind. For years, many versions of the story circulated around northern Arizona.

One story described a leather ore sack stuffed with gold nuggets hidden behind a waterfall west of the Jackson Trail. As the story goes, an old prospector, following a dead man's water-stained map, found the cache and crammed a few precious stones into his pants pocket.

When the old prospector tried to return for the remaining nuggets, he could not find the waterfall. For years, the old-timer wandered in search of his former discovery. With each shift in canyon scenery, each bend of the rocky ravine, he thought he heard the sounds of splashing water. Moseying along canyon walls, he poked at rocky clefts by day, dreamed beside his campfire by night, and started again the next day. If the gold existed, perhaps a rockslide buried it or a thundering flood swept it away, or perhaps it is still there behind those elusive falls.

* * *

In the early nineties, canyon prospectors hurried to file their claims with the County Recorder. When Congress and the Harrison Administration passed the Forest Reserve Act, the prospectors felt threatened. They worried about how restrictions would affect their mining activities at the Canyon.

"I told ya. Yep, I told ya," said Casey. "Harrison's act is only the first step where the President can withdraw forest lands from the public domain," pointing his finger at Monte and Clint sitting on a rock ledge.

Monte added, "Setting those lands aside as national forest reserves, not mining reserves, is a big problem. With forests on both rims, I suspect this new act may eventually limit our right to file and operate mining claims."

"Don't worry too much, fellas," cautioned Clint, "when you think about it, we have lots of claims but little actual mine development."

Monte could not help counter Clint's flippant statement, so he chimed in, "Yeah, well I hope that will change, or we're just wasting our time stockpiling tons of ore. I reckon we not only need to increase production but we need to haul thousands of tons out of the Canyon."

Casey scowled, "Just how are we going to do that?! We need a rail-road from the Santa Fe mainline to the South Rim. When I was in the Territorial Assembly, I sponsored a bill to build such a railroad—the Flagstaff and Grand Canyon Railroad. The bill passed and authorized the survey of a route to the Canyon. Although the line would have been exempt from taxes for five or six years, no one stepped up to finance the project. So, construction never started. Clint, you like dabbling in politics. Why don't you see if you can get that project resurrected?"

"Fellas, I propose the South Rim terminal be near Summit Point which hovers over our claims on Windsong Mesa," suggested Monte.

Before Clint could respond, Casey interjected, "I might suggest the head of Pioneer Trail. It has the best access into the inner canyon."

Clint cautioned, "Hold up fellas, we're getting ahead of ourselves. I am involved in some local politics, but I have no clout with the Territorial Assembly. I'll talk to the Bergner brothers to see if they have any ideas about financing a railroad project."

The men continued to sit on the rock ledge, gazing at the Canyon, with all its sublime grandeur, and wondering if the Administration that succeeds Harrison would allow building a railroad through a forest reserve. No one spoke but each man realized a railroad could finally make canyon mining a profitable enterprise. Each man also worried about the impact of belching black smoke and grinding wheels on the brink of this magical place.

* * *

That fall, Casey, Campbell and Broadway started for the Canyon with a winter supply of provisions and a few head of cattle as a winter meat supply. They camped one night at Cedar Ranch. Driving cattle made progress very slow. It would be another three days before they reached the South Rim.

Clancy joined the party as the caravan of miners rode over to the Pioneer Trail and down to Grand Canyon Springs where they left the cattle and some horses to winter. With burros packed with provisions and mining supplies, the party then continued to the river. Casey pointed to his old canvas boat still anchored with rocks. "There she is; SS Plunger, right where I left her this past summer."

The men stood stone-still on the muddy shore, staring at the swirling current, wondering who dared to be first. Also, on their minds, the boat seemed well-weathered with canvas torn in places along the gunwales. The men stalled, wondering if they should attempt a crossing in the rickety craft.

Clancy, who never let a difficult situation impede a good story, fingered his beard and conjured up a tale to raise the men's spirits.

"I had a similar situation last year. 'Twas when I guided two young women down to this very spot. One of them asked, 'Mr. Jennings, how do you know if the river current is too strong to cross?' Wal, I told them someone jests stick their head in the water and listens. 'Listen?' the other woman asked, 'what do you mean, listen?' Just what I said, listen." Clancy let the question sink into the minds of his fellow miners.

Casey interjected, "Clancy get on with it. We've got work to do." The others remained glued to Clancy's every word.

Clancy waited another minute or two, then continued, "As I was saying, before Casey here so rudely interrupted, I asked one of the women to dunk her head in the river and listen to boulders rumbling and tumbling along the bedrock bottom."

Cole played along. "And what does that tell you, Clancy?" Slim stood spellbound. Casey, paying little attention, fingered the frayed canvas along Plunger's gunwales.

At last, Clancy delivered the punch line. "If ya hear boulders rumbling along the bottom, then the current is too strong to cross. If it's quiet like a gurgle or murmur, then ya know it's safe to cross!"

Casey could not hold back any longer. "Clancy, I have a mind to throw you in right now! Men, help me steady this ol' scow. Sea Captain Jennings will be the first to venture across!"

The men ferried across the river and swam their burros behind the boat. Then they trudged up a side canyon for a distance of three miles to some of Casey's claims. He had sent a sample of the copper ore to Denver; it assayed at one hundred and sixty dollars to the ton. When the men had accumulated a good pile of ore on the dump, Cole declared, "We need more ore sacks, at least fifty or sixty." Casey agreed and sent Clancy back to Flagstaff for a hundred sacks.

While promising ore lay tantalizingly close at hand, the cost of extraction and transportation seemed to nullify any profit. The men found it maddening; profits seemed to be ever elusive.

When Clancy reached town, he went straight to businessman Ernst Bergner. Clancy burst through the office door and announced, "Hey, Ernst, we have a tremendous opportunity to make a lot of money from mining in the Grand Canyon."

After studying some promising copper ore from the north side mines, Ernst replied, "I'll put up two hundred and fifty dollars for ore sacks and mining supplies." He also staked Clancy to a new Studebaker wagon, four Navajo mules, and new harnesses. Loaded up with provisions, Clancy set the team in motion. Just then, Ernst flagged him down.

"Clancy, wait a minute, tell the boys I'm thinking about building a cableway across the river to help transfer ore and supplies." He held on to the lead mule as the team settled down. "I'm not sure I can fund such a project but I'll talk to Otto and others about town. We may need to form a group of investors but a cableway sure would make life easier."

Ernst bid Clancy farewell, and with a slap of the reins Clancy again started the team on its way back to the Canyon.

Clancy camped at the head of the Pioneer Trail where he found Monte and Clint camping. "Where ya headed, Clancy?" asked Monte.

"Back to our north side mines."

"Are you men finding high grade ore over there?" Monte had his doubts but let the old man respond.

"We think so but assay results will tell the story."

The next day, Monte and Clint helped load burros with ore sacks and other mining provisions. Clancy packed the gear down to Canyon Gardens, across the Tonto, down to the river, then across and up to their copper claims—a gruesome trip taking several days.

"Casey, I'm back. Good meetin' with Ernst Bergner," reported Clancy. "He grubstaked us with everything we need and wait till you see the new wagon parked at the head of the Pioneer Trail! Oh, and one more thing, he's thinking about financing construction of a cableway across the river."

"I knew we could count on the Bergner brothers. Now men, let's get back to work," said Casey.

Everyone dreaded the next task—filling ore sacks, loading them on burros and packing ore from the northside mines down to the river, transferring sacks to the boat, ferrying across, reloading on pack saddles, and driving ore-laden burros up to Canyon Gardens. After this long torturous trek, Casey and Cole arrived on the South Rim with their pack train.

Casey spent the next three days with Buckey O'Neill arranging an option on some asbestos claims in which an eastern investment company expressed interest. He then planned to travel to Flagstaff to talk to the Bergner brothers about their cableway idea before returning to the Canyon. Meantime, Ben Saxton, who needed a ride back to town, helped Cole load the ore in the Studebaker wagon. After hitching the four Navajo mules, they started off on the long haul to Flagstaff.

In town, it dawned on Cole to run an assay sample before shipping. "Ben, maybe we should get an assay done."

"Aw, them rocks look good," countered Ben, always looking for an easy way out. But they sent a batch of samples to Denver anyway. After three weeks, the report came back. It showed a value of only twenty dollars to the ton—not worth shipping! The hard-headed north rim miners spent four months in the Canyon that winter, stockpiling blue and green copper ore in hopes of better assay results.

Casey and his partners returned from their extended mining trip, undaunted by the low grade showing of ore that Cole hauled to Flagstaff. They contended that the richest ores lay hidden in ledges on the north side. They sported specimens of heavy, silver-gray ore, known as lead glance ore or galena. And as a bonus, the ore carried a small percentage of silver. The prospectors also located a three-foot ledge of copper glance ore. When it assayed at thirty percent copper, they made plans to work that claim during the next several months, even though their recent labors resulted in ore not worth shipping. Regardless of logistical and financial issues, the men had awakened interest in the potential mineral wealth that slept in the Canyon. More mining enterprises would surely follow.

* * *

Casey and Jennings disagreed on how to construct a cableway across the river. Casey stated his vision. "I contend we need a hand-operated aerial cableway with a traveling block system. I envision a wheeled structure with a suspended cable-car that rolls along on two stationary

109

steel support cables and a third moving cable or rope for hand-over-hand propulsion.

Clancy, being his contrary self, interrupted, "Why two support cables? One should do it just fine."

"Two for stability when squirrely winds drop to river level," snapped Casey. "I contend the cableway needs to be at my crossing because it's closer to our mines."

"Your location would require rock excavation on both sides of the river to form a landing platform where we can load burros, ore and an operator in the cable car. My crossing already has natural landings," Clancy argued.

Casey gave an additional rebuke, "But your landings are just above the waterline; the cable would sag and the car would submerge in the river. I can picture the poor passenger hanging on for dear life, or worse, drowning as the ore is swept away."

"Well, my location has softer rock for drilling anchor bolts into the granite wall," Clancy responded, knowing the cables needed firm anchors. "And another thing—"

Casey cut him off. "We cannot settle this right now. Maybe the Bergners can hire an engineer to design a system that best fits our mining needs at a location that is best for crossing the river."

"Or maybe we need a bigger, stronger boat," Clancy mumbled to himself.

"What was that?" asked Casey.

"Oh nothing," answered Clancy, as he rolled over some boat ideas in his head.

"Well, you said something; if you have a better idea, let's have it."

Clancy presented his boat idea. "Back in Missouri, when folks needed to cross deep rivers, a flimsy canvas scow would be the last thing on their mind. They would build rigid wooden boats from strong planks, with wood seats and a center section with oar locks. So, they rowed across rivers rather than swim or pull themselves along on a cable system." Clancy thought he'd stop there for the moment before expanding on boat landings, docks and moorings.

"In the part of Missouri I lived in," argued Casey, "we did not have rivers squeezing between canyon walls which means your riverboat idea would work well. But here we have rock walls, swift current and limited shoreline for beaching boats. A cable high enough to avoid sagging into the water makes better sense. A bridge would be better yet but that's a more expensive proposition for future consideration."

Casey, trying to ease out of a conversation going nowhere, added, "Let's see what Cole and Slim think about wood boats and cableways."

Chapter Eight

WHEELS NORTH

In Granite Gorge, one takes full measure of the river slicing through canyon rock walls and the continuum of time.

As the westbound Overland Express pulled away from its boxcar depot, a small, inferior-looking fellow, having just stepped off the train, walked over to the office of the Grand Canyon Stage Line in the Bank Hotel. The two-storied red sandstone building stood at the corner of Railroad and Leroux streets. Besides the stage office, the first floor of the hotel building included an opera hall, Jesse Parks' Arizona Central Bank, and a Wells Fargo express office; the second floor contained lodgings.

The hotel became a hub for rail travelers—stiff passengers who could step off the train at the depot a block away and spend the night at the Bank Hotel, then the next day take the Grand Canyon stage to the South Rim. Alternatively, they could be on their way the same morning of their arrival in town. The stranger wanted to continue his journey right away. With a somewhat meek countenance and an outward gentle manner, he introduced himself to Jeff Fox, part-owner of the stage line.

"Sir, I'm Ryan Perkins and I'm looking for passage on your next stage to the Grand Canyon." Ryan hooked his thumbs into his vest in a gesture of self-importance.

"Well sir, we have a stage leaving within the hour; can I take your carrying bag?" responded Jeff, sensing an important visit by a distinguished gentleman.

"Certainly, here you go." Ryan extended a handshake. Jeff noted his weak grip, but with his slate-gray eyes trained straight and level, he seemed serious about getting to the Canyon quickly. The sandy-haired, bespectacled Ryan was a jittery fellow, meticulously dressed, more for a business meeting than a sight-seeing trip.

Early canyon visitors suffered three or four arduous days astride a horse or grasping a bone-jarring wagon seat on their ride from Flagstaff to the Canyon. By eighteen ninety-two, stagecoaches bounded over the Coconino in one long day, following the deep wagon-wheel ruts to Clancy Jennings' canyon ranch.

With business slow, Jeff engaged in light conversation while the genial stranger waited. "Not that long ago," volunteered the stage owner, "canyon visitors and prospectors had several routes between Flagstaff and the South Rim. They often traveled by the wagon road that weaved its way through the forested flanks of the 'Friscos, across cedar-studded flatlands, and then through pine forests of the Coconino Plateau to the brink of the Canyon."

"Friscos?" asked Ryan, noticing the proprietor's words had a descriptive flare.

"Yeah, that's what we call the mountains behind us." Jeff continued, "They made their first night camp near a ranch at Little Springs, their second camp at Cedar Ranch, and their third camp at Red Horse. They often stayed with ranchers—the Klostermeyers at Little Springs, the Grangers near Cedar Ranch and the Holmes at Red Horse. From there they would proceed to the homestead of Clancy Jennings on the canyon rim. They also had a winter route which took them around the eastern flank of the 'Friscos and through Deadman Wash between Sunset Crater and the Peaks."

Ryan, stopping Jeff before he could continue his monologue, fingered his handlebar mustache. "You mentioned Clancy Jennings.

That's the man I plan to see. My boss sent me out here for a story. I heard folks on the train talking about Jennings. What can you tell me about him?"

"Oh, I'll let you meet him and get your information first hand. I sense you are a reporter working on a story." Jeff seemed eager to resume his dissertation but Ryan wanted to confirm his suspicion.

"That's right. I am a chronicler employed by a large eastern newspaper. I can't tell you which one as I'm seeking an exclusive on Clancy Jennings." Ryan did not divulge his reputation as a newspaperman known in New York City to relentlessly hound his news sources.

Jeff Fox, enjoying the opportunity to spill his knowledge to a visiting stranger, continued. "Several Flagstaff businessmen and I joined with the Santa Fe Railway to establish this stage line. My partner Jay Watts and I own it. Our general manager is Matt Calendar and Sid Miller handles baggage, livery and our feed stables. Oh, and your driver today will be Roscoe Andrews."

When Ryan showed a genuine interest in his story, Jeff continued, "We opened for the season right on time, the third week of May. For that red Concord coach over there, we use either a team of four or six, depending on the passenger and freight load."

"What sort of schedule do you run, Mr. Fox?"

"Our stage leaves the depot at seven o'clock every Monday, Wednesday and Friday morning, and returns every other day. Our rigs are four-horse stagecoaches or a buckboard-style covered wagon with trailer pulled by a team of six horses. We can make the overland journey in ten hours with four relays of horses. We have established three stage stops or way-stations along the sixty-five-mile route and the terminus on the South Rim. That's where you'll meet Clancy Jennings and his rustic hotel, at present, the only accommodations on the rim."

Ryan withdrew a small notebook from his vest pocket and penciled a few notes on Clancy Jennings.

"If you'll excuse me now, I need to make sure the mailbag is ready. Besides passengers, it's the last thing to go onboard."

* * *

With tourists and luggage aboard, the stagecoach pulled away from the depot and wound its way, first through town streets, then through tall ponderosa stands, devoid of forest underbrush. The team took the wide curves in stride although Ryan felt they rolled along too fast. Passengers caught fleeting glimpses of the Peaks, their stark white summits gleaming in the early morning sun, as the four-in-hand raced across parks in a forest of stately ponderosa interspersed with white-bark aspen. Baggage and company freight for the way-stations bounced around in the boot at the coach's rear. The route at this early point in the journey skirted the base of the mountains, sweeping northwesterly past Leroux Spring, and across the park east of Kendrick Peak. Named after the mountain man Antoine Leroux, that spring held the title of being the most reliable in the area. Ol' Leroux scouted with Kit Carson, led the Mormon Battalion to California, guided the Army Corps of Topographic Engineers for a proposed railroad route along the thirty-fifth parallel, and even camped at the foot of the San Francisco Peaks where a town named Flagstaff would take hold.

The brief stop at the Little Springs Station at the northern edge of the mountains seemed only long enough to change horses and drop off supplies. Ryan saw a woman peering out of the barn loft opening, but never gave it a second thought. With the first sixteen miles behind them, first-timers, including Ryan, grew more anxious to see what lay beyond the northern slopes of the Peaks.

The stage also carried two middle-aged couples who expressed second thoughts about the reckless stage ride. They worried even more about their pending canyon descent on the so-called Whiskey Trail.

Ryan engaged in conversation with his fellow passengers. "Sorry folks, I meant to introduce myself back there. I'm Ryan Perkins. You plan to make the canyon descent too? I'm also reluctant about this whole adventure but my boss wants a story on Clancy Jennings and his canyon trails."

One gentleman revealed that he had run into Clancy many times in town. In fact, Clancy urged him to make the trip. Ryan, curious about Jennings, tried to coax information from the fellow.

"So, tell me what you know about this canyon character; I'd like to learn more about him before meeting in person," said Ryan.

"So would we," interjected the other couple, unable to avoid listening to the conversation in their cramped quarters.

"Well, I guess we have time to delve into Clancy Jennings for a spell," replied the man who seemed to know Clancy. He drew in a deep breath of high-country air and started. "Some say he was a private in the Civil War. Others say he was with Buffalo Bill during the Pike's Peak Gold Rush. We know he's dabbled in mining and trail-building, and his rustic hotel on the South Rim is the terminus for this overland stage line. But above all, Clancy is a storyteller. He often scrounges through memories of his gold rush days for nuggets of humor, but his dry sense of humor is low-grade like the ore in his mines." He paused for a minute to gaze out his window while Ryan scrambled for his notebook. Such an elegant double metaphor should not go to waste.

Ryan admired the gentleman's use of the English language. "Sir, you speak with compassion. Perhaps you should be a writer. I believe the prolific novelist Mark Twain said compassion is language the deaf can hear and the blind can see. Please continue."

"Well, as I was saying, Clancy Jennings considers himself a self-appointed guardian of the Grand Canyon. He entertains his captive audiences—campers and trail parties—with outrageous tales of his personal escapades. He relishes teasing tinhorns and toying with his listeners. Ol' Clancy Jennings is proud of his past, as mysterious as it is, but he stretches the truth so much that he himself no longer can differentiate between fact and fiction. As Mark Twain also once said, he never lets the truth stand in the way of a good story." The gentleman looked out his window again, trying to assess their progress.

"He must be a very lonely man living way out here," surmised Ryan, "missing the company of a fellow human being."

"Perhaps, but he's content with his superlative surroundings," added the gentleman. "As we'll see, the Canyon stirs the soul, or so I'm told."

From Little Springs, the stage continued north and even the casual observer noticed the ponderosa dwindling in size, and pinyon pine taking their place. Anxious eyes attempted to probe the vast plateau beyond the Peaks hoping to find a new wonder to occupy the mind—anything to escape, however vicariously, the constant jolting of the coach and the gusty snorting of overworked horses. Before long the pinyon gave way to stunted cedar and shaggy juniper as the stage made a turn to the west at Missouri Flats.

At Cedar Ranch, the stage line maintained a half-way house offering noonday meals as part of the twenty-dollar round-trip fare. Ryan, having befriended both couples, found the stagecoach ride a new experience for all. Cedar Ranch offered overnight lodging but, after a restful break, everyone continued the journey. With another eighteen miles completed and a fresh relief team pulling for the rim, the stage, with its lightened load of freight, lurched across the flatlands.

North of Cedar Ranch, the riders had a mesmerizing view of the Painted Desert outstretching to the east, as the Peaks shrank behind them. With the dull rumble of the coach on the hard-packed road, the passengers felt an ominous anticipation of a giant chasm lying ahead, yet no sign presented itself on the flats. The coach yawed like a galleon in a tempest. The passengers noticed smoother terrain as the stage passed volcanic cones of red and black cinders and bounded through a shallow draw that cattlemen called Jackrabbit Canyon. As the team lunged forward, cattle and sheep scattered at the last possible moment, then drifted back to browse in the dusty wake.

Twenty miles north of Cedar, at the junction with the old Moencopi road, they came to Red Horse Station. Amid the cedar and pinyon there stood stables, outbuildings and a single log cabin for the resident stationmaster. This point on the stage route is where ancient crossroads meet a turn-of-the century roadway. Here the stage crossed the old Moqui Trail between Cataract Canyon and the Hopi villages of Moencopi and Oraibi. The trail paralleled the South Rim and, in places, approached the edge of the Canyon. Mojave, Havasupai and Hopi used the trail in their east-west trade.

The passengers had just enough time to stretch their legs. As Ryan watched the unloading of supplies and the final change of horses, an elderly fellow leading two pack mules arrived at Red Horse.

"Would you happen to be Clancy Jennings?" Ryan asked.

"That old coot? He just sits around telling wild stories to his regulars—both of them! No, I'm not Jennings. My name is Levi Jackson. And you are?"

"Ryan Perkins, sir, new to the area and on my way for my first look at the Canyon."

"Well, mister, unless you want to walk the rest of the way," stressed Levi, "you are about to miss your ride."

Just then the stationmaster bellowed, "Hey stranger, if you are going with the stage, best get aboard now."

Ryan climbed back aboard and waved to Levi. "Intriguing fellow, that Levi," whispering to his fellow passengers, "I wish I had more time to talk with him."

With a crack of his whip, Roscoe had his fresh team running the final eleven-mile stretch. The coach felt like a torture chamber on wheels—lurching, pitching, yawing. The monotonous rhythm of hooves and wheels returned. Before long, the stage twisted and turned through tall stately evergreens.

"I've run into him a few times in town," stated the other gentleman.

"Who, that Levi fellow?" asked Ryan.

"Yes, he comes into Flagstaff a couple times a year for supplies. I understand he served as a Mormon scout, then a rough-and-tumble prospector, and now a trader with the Navajo. I've tried to get him to talk about the mystery of lost gold in the eastern reaches of the Canyon, but he always shrugs it off as a wild rumor." Ryan made a note about lost gold.

For first-timers, the real mystery loomed just beyond the forest. Inured to the lesser jolts, shocks and knocks delivered by the coach's drunken maneuvers—even somewhat mesmerized by the dull rumble of steel-rimmed wheels on rocky sections of the wagon road and the endless march of ponderosas—Ryan pondered what lay ahead.

Overwhelming desolation—augmented by mind-numbing vastness and breath-taking grandeur—invaded the passengers' psyches. Anticipation seemed tempered by the dizzy sensation of an ominous vacuum surrounding this enormous gash in the planet's crust, a vacuum created in a time beyond time when the land collapsed inward upon itself, a vacuum that drew one ever closer to the imagined border between life and surrender to the unknowable depths of eternity. Giddy stuff concocted by the excitable nineteenth-century mind. Repeat visitors reported harboring these same sensations of spinning or swaying. Sometimes they felt their surroundings moving instead of them. The Grand Canyon announced itself to man in mysterious ways, whether or not they approached as friend or stranger.

The road degenerated into muddy ruts as a late season snow melted in the afternoon sun. On the final run to the rim, the coach wallowed like a rudderless ship in a gale, slewing and sliding from side to side, while the team of horses cast gobs of mud towards the driver's seat. But lengthening shadows signaled an end to the ordeal.

Suddenly, the coach tilted on a slick turn, then rolled onto its right side! The team of squealing horses separated from the coach as Roscoe, having no chance to grab a leather tug strap, found himself jettisoned into a muddy hole. Slime oozed through the windows as the five terrified passengers tumbled over each other. The women screamed. The coach coasted to a stop, at least fifty yards off the road, with its luggage and remaining freight scattered along its path.

"Ryan Perkins, can you move? You're on top of my wife! Is anyone hurt?" The two gentlemen heard slight whimpering from the two ladies as they shifted position and strained to open the left side door.

"I can get out and help the rest of you," said Ryan as the three men pushed the door open and Ryan crawled out.

"Do you see our driver?" cried one lady, now free to crawl out of the coach with both men pushing from the inside. Ryan helped the woman to her feet as the second woman emerged, jumping from the overturned coach, then crawling through mud on all fours.

Ryan then spotted Roscoe. "I see our driver. He landed in the clear."

They saw their mud-slathered driver staggering back onto the road. Seeing that all the passengers escaped unhurt, Roscoe volunteered to go for help. "You folks stay here. I can walk the remaining miles to Clancy's place."

He no sooner started up the road when a wagon with a single driver rode towards the wrecked stagecoach. "Whoa," Monte pulled on his reins and brought his wagon to a sudden stop. "Roscoe, what happened? Is everyone okay? How many of you are there? Looks like you slid off the road and turned over!" Monte stepped down to assess the situation.

"I am sure happy you came along. My five passengers and I may have a few bumps and bruises, and a generous dose of mud, but we'll survive. The horses too. Do you think we can use all our horses to pull the stage upright before dark?" asked Roscoe, adding "Folks, this is Monte Bridgestone, canyon copper miner extraordinaire."

"Let's try it," replied Monte.

Using all six horses and considerable rope, they turned the stage back onto its wheels and pulled it back to the road. Monte helped Roscoe stow the luggage. With the four-in-hand reunited with the coach, the passengers reseated and with the crack of his muddy whip, Roscoe started the stage on a slow climb up the slushy road. Monte re-hitched his two horses, turned his wagon around, and followed the stage to its South Rim terminal. In the fading light, they arrived at Clancy Jennings' tourist camp—a village of tents, pending construction of more permanent facilities. A ranch-hand sallied forth—a young pistol-packing Hispanic woman wearing the buckskin mantle more typical of Daniel Boone or David Crockett—and serving as a porter, helped the passengers to their feet.

Teresa Cordova, dark and attractive, was also the relief driver scheduled to run the return trip the next morning. She descended from a long line of Butterfield Overland Stagecoach drivers in the southern part of Arizona Territory. "You're late, Roscoe. Looks like you took a spill. Hello Monte. Folks, I'll tend to your luggage." Teresa watched the party draw to the rim. "Folks, it's too dark now, you won't see the Canyon till morning sunrise," and with that she tended to her chores.

"Ahem, ladies and gentlemen, I am Captain Clancy Jennings, proprietor of this fine camp establishment and your trusty guide for tomorrow's trek below the rim." The visitors turned to see a haggard man in buckskins with a floppy hat and a leathered face that had seen a lifetime spent in the wild outdoors. He swung a lighted lantern. "Teresa tells me you've had a rough trip. From the looks of your stagecoach, it appears you spent part of it sliding sideways."

Clancy promised comfortable accommodations and a restful night's sleep but cautioned not to venture to the rim in the dark. "One of the great highlights of my Grand Canyon is seeing it for the first time at first light, when night shadows give way to dawn's oranges and reds. Tomorrow we'll venture deep into the Canyon and you'll see why I live here. I look forward to sharing my world amid the most spectacular backdrop on the planet."

As the two couples wandered over to their rudimentary accommodations, Ryan introduced himself. "So you are the Clancy Jennings I've been hearing about. I'm news-reporter Ryan Perkins and I hope to—"

Clancy cut him off, "Say, you don't look dressed for a canyon outing. I hope you have something more appropriate to wear on the trail."

Ryan explained that he wanted to travel light. He planned to wear his mud-splattered outfit. Clancy, who is rarely at a loss for words, strutted towards his cabin, mumbling something to himself. He then looked back at Roscoe and Monte deep in conversation.

"Monte, you can bunk with Roscoe tonight. And you are certainly welcome to join us for breakfast before you get started in the morning."

"Thanks Clancy, much obliged," said Monte as he and Roscoe tended to their horses.

* * *

The early risers hurried up a gentle slope in time for the magic hour when the sun's first yellowing rays played on Angel's Gate, then set vermilion walls of castles and towers aflame while the inner gorge lingered in dark shadows.

Ryan stood in awe, soaking in the silence and immensity of this gaping wonder, unaware that, far below, men rubbed their eyes as they woke to another long day of prospecting.

Yesterday's wild stage ride had delivered its human cargo to Jennings' rustic camp. Ryan Perkins and the two couples had skipped breakfast and climbed to the brink of Grand Canyon. Swallowed up in the sheer vastness of the abyss, the group did not notice Clancy, with his bandy-legged gait, approaching from behind.

Ryan had elbowed his way to the rim, crashing into the others with such force that he knocked one gentleman forward. The fellow teetered, precariously balanced on the edge, above the giant void. He swayed for a moment, then regained his balance and took several backward steps toward safety.

"Why don't you watch where you are going?" he demanded. "You nearly knocked me over the edge."

"Why don't you stay out of my way?" the belligerent reporter shot back. Clancy needed to calm his visitors, testy and grouchy after their long arduous stage ride and muddy spill.

"Now folks, settle down. You'll have plenty of time to gaze at my Canyon." Clancy started to describe the day's plan.

"Where's the trail, Captain Jennings?" Ryan interrupted their host. "We don't see it."

Clancy decided to put a little scare into his visitors, for their own good as they would need to be very careful in the day's descent. "You can see parts of my trail through them junipers." With that, he started his spiel, "For the first two miles, my Whiskey Trail is a sort of Jacob's Ladder, zigzagging at an unrelenting pitch down a steep decline caused by a sliding geological fault."

"Well, that's quite a description, sir," remarked Ryan, "Will we reach the river?"

"Sure enough, if you can handle the climb down," returned Clancy. "The trail is safe and practical for pack animals and for most pedestrians; ladies on rare occasion have made the descent and the return scramble. In places, I do not recommend going by horseback; in other places it is impossible," added Clancy. The passengers seemed aghast at his descriptions. He continued, "But at the end of two miles, a gentle slope is reached, and for nearly four miles, you can ride on horse or mule."

By now, the visitors hung on every word of their trail guide. In twangy cadences, he explained, "I have a rock cabin where we can dine and rest under the shade of cottonwoods that thrive alongside my spring."

"Sounds too good to be true; what comes next?" Ryan asked, the news-reporter in him showing skepticism.

"Well further on, the trail continues down a widening gorge and we will reach a clear rivulet, fed by my spring. We'll follow its windings to the end, but then you must abandon your animals," explained Clancy, taking care not to soften his description of the upcoming escapade.

Clancy then explained that the way narrows to a mere notch, challenging his group of greenhorns to the limit. "Then comes the hard part," he said. "I hope you are good climbers. The last drop is a forty-foot clamber down the side of a ribbon-like cascade."

"You expect us to climb down a waterfall? Are there ropes?" asked one of the lady travelers.

"Of course, there are ropes," snarled Clancy. "If you don't want to go, then you can wait with the horses at the top of the falls while the others go to the river."

Clancy continued, "If the adventurous visitor survives the last clamber down, he'll find himself, or herself, standing upon a sandy rift confronted by nearly vertical walls at whose base a brown muddy torrent pitches in a giddying onward slide. It is at that point, staring into the rapids, that a person has the sensation of slipping into the river."

"You sure put a scare into these folks," said Ryan, as the others walked over to Clancy's corral where Teresa Cordova waited to introduce them to their mounts.

"Wal, I do that to soften 'em up."

* * *

When the adventurous travelers reached the notorious Colorado River, they found it strangled by sheer walls, tortured by mid-stream boulders, and burdened with silt and driftwood. Well past noon, they marveled at Sockdolager Rapids and pondered Powell's river-running accomplishment. In Granite Gorge, one takes full measure of the river slicing through canyon rock walls and the continuum of time.

"Powell named these rapids Sockdolager. You can see standing waves fighting each other, forming themselves into clenched fists, and delivering crashing blows to the next standing wave."

Just when Clancy seemed ready to insist that they start their climb back up the falls before dark, one of the inquisitive ladies asked, "Cap'n, are there any beavers around here?"

Regardless of having to start back, Clancy could not pass up an opportunity to launch a story about one of his alleged desperate situations.

"Why sure." Clancy had his cue. "There is lots of beaver along the river and one time I caught one to keep me from starvin' to death."

The tourists were about to have the best of two worlds—reality and fantasy, the reality of this spectacular setting and the fantasy of a wild tale from the legendary Captain Jennings.

Suddenly there were two rifle shots in rapid succession followed by an explosion. The men, fearing for their wives' safety, left Clancy to his storytelling and climbed to higher ground to investigate. From a rocky ridge, they spotted two prospectors in a ravine, arguing about who set off the explosion. They eavesdropped on the conversation.

"Dagnabbit Chester, we'd not be having this debate if you remembered to bring the detonation cord."

"Well, at least my shot set off the dynamite," said the other prospector.

"That was my shot, not yours."

"No matter, Clyde, let's check for ore. Who knows, we may discover gold."

The tourists slinked back out of sight and scrambled back down to catch the end of Clancy's story. Ryan seemed to have had his fill of this story. "Now Cap'n Jennings, we may not know much about critters in this river, but we're not stupid. Surely, we're not supposed to believe using a stick for bait on a fishing line, you can haul a beaver in like a fish!"

Clancy, indignant but exuberant, responded, "I lived off that beaver until the river level dropped so's I could get out of the Canyon or I wouldn't be here tellin' you good folks this story today."

Clancy glanced over to the returning gentlemen. "What was that explosion?"

"Ah, seems two old fellows were prospecting with rifles and dynamite."

That made little sense to Clancy as he announced, "Time to go." They started back as Ryan and the women mentally reviewed Clancy's wild story. "I'm sure you agree, ladies," said Ryan. "We have just been bamboozled."

As they started their climb back up the falls to where they had staked their animals, Ryan asked, "Captain Jennings, how long will it take to get to tonight's campsite?"

"Why, are you in a hurry, Mr. Perkins?" Clancy glared at the reporter.

"Just wondering. I'm anxious to make my notes on today's adventure," said Ryan.

"For you folks, I'd say five hours. You'll find climbing up the falls is half the fun. The other two-thirds will be quite challenging and the remaining three-fourths will be downright drudgery."

"Sorry I asked," mumbled Ryan.

It only took Clancy's greenhorn tourists two hours to climb the falls and find a campsite for the night. They skipped supper and flopped onto their bedrolls. The next morning, they retraced their way to the Tonto Plateau and then ascended the trail to the rim. Compared to their venture below the rim, the journey back to Flagstaff seemed uneventful. Ryan wired his account of the party's canyon travels, minus the preposterous beaver story, to his editor in New York City.

* * *

The Whiskey Trail underwent improvements and rerouting to allow visitors to make the entire descent to the river on horseback or mule back. Also, another trail under construction at Summit Point, several miles west of Jennings' place, gave promise of a similar canyon experience on horseback.

Jennings himself had conducted impromptu excursions to this over-look. From this vantage point, a major portion of the Canyon lay open to his visitors' stunned eyes. The fabled Colorado River glistened as a tiny metallic ribbon upstream of Jackson Canyon—over ten miles away. To the southeast lay the vast evergreen forest of the Coconino Basin. As far as the eye could see, the landscape altered its appearance with the shadow of each passing cloud.

Chapter Nine

CANYON ANGEL

Take life one moment at a time, not one day at a time, and hold onto that pace.

Clancy Jennings sat in his rocker, smoking his pipe and enjoying the early evening summer breeze, when he noticed a lone rider approaching his cabin. Clancy called out, "Welcome stranger, I was not expecting any visitors this evening."

The lean, weathered fellow dismounted and hitched his white mule to a fence post, then spoke in low tones with a very distinct accent, "Bonsoir Monsieur, je suis Francois LaRue."

"Ah, a Frenchman, all the way from France?" asked Clancy. "I understand your country gave our country a huge copper Liberty Statue a few years back—a gift of friendship, I believe, but also a symbol of freedom."

"No sir, I'm not from France, I'm a French Canadian from Quebec," volunteered LaRue, adding, "I'm interested in finding work here at the Grand Canyon."

"Sit yourself down here and let's talk," offered Clancy, "and tell me how you found your way to this outpost of mine." He extended a handshake. "Captain Clancy Jennings at your service." LaRue explained that folks in town suggested if he followed the stage road, it would eventually lead to Jennings' tourist camp. He had read about the Canyon but this happened to be his first visit. With the sun sinking below the horizon, he would not get his first look until morning.

LaRue had a question, but hesitated asking. Finally, he said, "Mr. Jennings, I have a bedroll. Can I sleep on your veranda tonight? I apologize for any imposition and if you wish, I'll move along."

"As it so happens, I have no visitors scheduled this evening, or tomorrow for that matter. You're welcome to take the first tent in that row," Clancy said, pointing to a row of camping tents, "but it's still early, tell me more about yourself."

Clancy knew very well the long tradition in the West to accept a stranger at face value, so he clarified his inquiry. "I don't mean to pry, Francois LaRue. Certain things in a man's personal life should remain private but I'd be interested in knowing if you have any skills I can use here in my thriving tourist enterprise."

LaRue also knew that it would be bad manners to be too inquisitive or to undergo any cross-examination by a stranger; however, he seemed willing to share some information about himself.

"Nothing special but I'm a quick study. In Quebec I worked as a carpenter and a wheelwright, and in the Dakotas I did some prospecting during the Black Hills Gold Rush. I'm interested in learning all I can about the Grand Canyon, perhaps in sufficient detail that I might someday serve as a tour guide," explained LaRue.

"Well, you have come to the right place. I'm not trying to sound boastful but I consider myself somewhat of an expert on the Canyon," said Clancy, then in a half-hearted way he announced that he had appointed himself as guardian of the Grand Canyon.

"How's that mule of yours on steep trails?" Francois explained that he and Calamity Jane had no trouble rounding the Friscos.

"Calamity Jane? You named your mule after Calamity?"

"Yes sir, but she does not know that. I knew her when we were both drifting about in Deadwood. What a wild woman, yet she held a soft spot for 'ol Bill Hickok."

"Ah, now there we have a connection! I used to work for Wild Bill's brother. I named him Tame Bill," exclaimed Clancy.

"I knew them all, the Hickok brothers, Jack McCall and Martha Canary too," said Francois. "I left town after McCall shot Wild Bill in the back. That was about fifteen years ago. That mining town just got too wild for me so I moved on."

"I've spent some time in wild towns myself. Martha Canary, that's Calamity, right?" asked Clancy. "Seems you've been around the West and probably have had some wild experiences of your own. Now, back to my question. Have you done any riding on steep trails?"

"No, nothing like that; I presume you are referring to trails here at the Canyon," answered LaRue, hoping that such a blatant deficiency would not end their conversation.

"Okay, Monsieur LaRue, unsaddle ol' Calamity Jane over there and put her in the corral. And then I'll tell you what we'll do tomorrow. I'm going to give you some Grand Canyon training on a rim-to-river, round-trip excursion." As LaRue tended to his mule, Clancy kept talking.

"I'll indoctrinate you on the way down and test you on the way up. If you pass my test, you're my new trail guide. I can't pay much, only fifty cents per tourist, plus free room and board. It's seasonal work as there are times when the tourists stop coming."

"That sounds good to me but what if there are days like today when you have no visitors?"

"Then I'll employ you to perform carpentry, corral and fence repairs, firewood cutting, trail improvement, and maybe even some hunting. And the pay will be decided on a case-by-case basis."

Without reservation, LaRue accepted Jennings terms. "I promise, I won't let you down."

"Well, Francois LaRue, let's call it a night. Prepare to be regaled with canyon facts in the morning. The stage may bring some visitors I don't know about but no matter. The driver, either Andrews or Cordova, can show them around. I don't think anyone has signed up for going down my trails tomorrow."

LaRue felt Jennings may be running a rather loose operation but he let out a Sioux warrior whoop, grateful for the employment opportunity and excited about seeing this mystical canyon under the guidance of a self-proclaimed expert.

* * *

Clancy and Francois rose at sunrise, ate a quick breakfast of boiled pinto beans, bacon, biscuits and coffee brewed from toasted potato skins. Clancy ran out of coffee beans three weeks earlier. They saddled up Calamity and Clancy's mule, Dusty, and rode over to the trailhead.

"I'm going to tell you about the rock layers as we descend, wildlife, trees and plants, and watering holes so that you can answer questions from our greenhorn tourists. If you don't know the answer, make something up; I always do."

"For starters, what we're standing on is limestone caprock, some folks call it by the Paiute name, Kaibab limestone. It's the top layer and sometimes is rather craggy and crumbly, and in some spots, you'll see embedded fossils and sea-shells. It is usually white although further down it's an anemic light gray. Limestones and some sandstones are hard erosion-resistant rocks. That's why we have cliffs here at the Canyon. And now it is time to start down my Whiskey Trail."

"Why call it that?"

"Near the trailhead, partially hidden among the cliffrose, that shrub with tiny cream-colored blooms, I found an empty Twin Oaks whiskey bottle. And it just happens that Twin Oaks is my favorite brand, and my favorite brand of oxygen is the fresh canyon air that we are presently breathing. Now, the trees along this upper trail are pinyon, a very hardy southwest pine, cedar and scrub oak, and they'll peter out when we get to the Coconino sandstone. In some shady nooks just below the rim, fir trees survive but then any greenery further down dissolves into desert scrub. See that dirty white band out yonder on the North Rim? If you were over there, you'd see it on this side too. I call it the bathtub ring and right now we're standing on the rim of that giant tub. It's an impressive wall, looks to be fifty feet thick but actually it's more like three hundred feet thick. Fortunately, there are breaks where it permits a descent. In some places it is light yellow like beach sand. By the way, the North Rim appears level with the South Rim, but surveyors contend it is one thousand feet higher."

"You mentioned scrub oak. I'm familiar with oak trees." LaRue decided he would enlighten his instructor with some solid-oak facts. "Back in Canada, we regard oaks as symbols of strength and survival. We have an old superstition that says if you stand under an oak you'll be visited by a beautiful angel. We love oaks and believe their acorns are signs of good things to come, and it's always good to have a guardian angel with you." Clancy did not respond. Perhaps his mind still dwelled on Twin Oaks whiskey.

LaRue took note of the buff-colored cliffs perched on the red slopes while Clancy continued his canyon indoctrination. "One interesting thing about this magnificent corner of the world—the eye can train through the gorge where the river must be, but neither sight nor sound reveal its whereabouts. Another interesting thing is the way sunlight and cloud shadows play on the rose-tinged landscape. Towers and buttes seem to change shape and color in the shifting light."

"I see some big black birds gliding with ease overhead," said LaRue, craning his neck upward. "Ravens, right?"

"Yeah, they soar on currents rising from this huge abyss and they sure can be noisy when they start arguing. We also have hawks and if you look over there you can see a red-headed turkey vulture in that dead tree, overseeing his canyon realm from his lofty perch."

The two riders made their way through a steep break in the Coconino. Calamity, following Dusty's lead, managed this new adventure very well.

"Did you fill your canteen before we left, Francois?" By now, Clancy and Francois found themselves on a first name basis. "There won't be any water until we get below the Redwall. By the way, that red formation to your right, tilted by massive vaulting, is called Sinking Battleship."

"I have a full canteen, Clancy. By red, I presume you mean the sheer red layer that is so prominent; looks to be hundreds of feet thick."

"Yes, but right now we're coming down to two layers of crumbly shale. One is an angry rust red and slopes down rather abruptly. The other is a darker shade and has a gentler slope. These shale formations—often called talus slopes—are the reason the Redwall is red."

"I don't see how we can descend this Redwall of yours—it's a sheer wall of rock!"

"Well, fortunately there are a few breaks where it permits our intrusion. Without the breaks, there would be no way down. You might think it is red inside. Not so. The Redwall is pure limestone, a mottled light bluish color inside, stained red on the outside by iron oxides from the red shales above. Because of its true interior color, we call it blue lime."

"Any snakes down here? I hate snakes."

"Pink ones, rattlesnakes, so beware."

"Any spiders or scorpions?"

"Big ones, don't get bit. Another danger, at least when yer on foot, is the yucca in these parts. If your boots don't go high enough on your legs, you might get skewered; those stiff arrow-straight spines can be very painful. I call them Spanish bayonets." Clancy assumed the Frenchman was getting the drift of his descriptions.

It took some time to get through the Redwall but the riders finally reached a section of the trail that started to level out, an area with a layer of shale exhibiting a tinge of royal purple. Except for cactus blooms blazing red and yellow, the talus slopes appeared burnt and barren.

"Those flowers are real eye-catchers," remarked Francois.

"And prickly too. Okay, Francois, this is important. There's a layer of shale at the base of the Redwall. Shale is nearly impervious to water so this is where springs and seeps are found. Coming up is my Whiskey Springs camp where I have a rock cabin and some shade trees. We'll rest here, water our mules and refill our canteens."

"So, this is an important stop for your tourists, a good place for a lunch break."

"Now you're catching on."

LaRue could not help noticing the fleur-de-lis design on the iron door of Clancy's camp stove. "Those fleur-de-lis designs on your stove represent a legendary flower heralding French royalty. They represent the spirit of man's journey through life." Clancy seemed to ignore the comment.

"When we leave, we will be out in the open, on what we call the Tonto Plateau. No shade, no water except where springs trickle through an eroded gulley and form a rivulet. That only happens in a few places. But beware, there are monsters down here." Clancy waited for that revelation to sink in.

"Monsters? Are you joshing?" asked Francois, wondering if he heard Clancy correctly.

"Yes, monsters—gila monsters or what we call heely monsters— big fat poisonous lizards, some as big as your arm, pink and black blotches like the walls of the inner gorge. They have a fearsome look and a bad temperament, and are most active in the morning after a good night's sleep. On foot in rocky areas, that's when you might stumble upon one of these carnivores. Their bite is excruciatingly painful, but not usually fatal; you'll just be sick for a week or two. They tend to clamp down and not let go, so again, beware of these tenacious canyon monsters. I got a little careless with one about two years ago and lost the end of my right index finger." Clancy went on to say the largest animals one might encounter below the rim are bighorn sheep which usually turn tail and run.

"I've stayed overnight in my cabin here many times, which reminds me, there's another critter I need to tell you about. He's cute, but very sneaky. At night, the ring-tailed cats come out. These scavengers tiptoe around in the dark, silently going about their business looking for food. You'll recognize them right off—large eyes and ears and a long tail with alternating black and white rings. And most interesting of all, when they surround your campfire, like in my camp here, their eyes glow in the dark."

"Are they dangerous? Like mountain cats, I mean lions?"

"No. Not at all," Clancy paused for a few minutes, then resumed his spiel. "The Tonto sits on greenish-gray shale; oh, throw in some tan for good measure. Also, there's some sandy-colored limestone in places. Right below that layer is a dark brown sandstone or what I call mudstone because it's really petrified mud. In some places you'll see ancient critter tracks in the rock. That combination of shale and mud-stone lies on top of the oldest rocks in the Canyon—hard black granite with specks of mica and the whole formation is turned slantwise. Geologists say these black walls of the inner gorge show signs of a very troubled past. Bear in mind that all the stacked layers have been horizontal sedimentary rock, but the granite has been turned nearly vertical by forces far beyond our comprehension. Yep, this here Granite Gorge is where all geologic hell broke loose."

The riders crossed the Tonto, with its braided burro paths, following a main route through sagebrush, and edged up to the brink of the ever-deepening Granite Gorge.

"This has been quite a lesson in geology, Clancy, and now I finally see the river," observed Francois.

"Just imagine that roaring river cut through all those rock layers we just passed through and now is working on the hardest rocks of all," said Clancy. "Follow me and I'll show you how my trail makes it to river level. There are a few small creeks, including my Whiskey Creek, that follow breaks in the granite and there at the bottom you will almost always find a set of ferocious rapids, formed of course by boulders being pushed down the side canyons during flash floods and into the swirling Colorado River. I meant to point out another prominent landmark on the north side of the river," added Clancy, pointing to the northwest. "We call that formation Angel's Gate. Use it as a guidepost if you lose your bearings in these side canyons."

"Why the name Angel's Gate?"

Clancy thought for a minute, then conjured up an explanation. "Notice the gate is open. Lightning bolts have a habit of striking Angel's Gate, it being high and isolated. Unlike your Canadian superstition about oak trees and visiting angels, that towering rock is very dangerous. I'd say any angels hereabouts fled so quickly during a lightning storm, they left the gate open, and then flew through a hole in the wall on the North Rim. We call that Angel's Window."

"I see how you are Clancy, toying with a newcomer's mind. But I'll remember this when I'm guiding your paying customers into the Canyon. If one asks about Angel's Gate, I've got the story straight from the Canyon's self-proclaimed guardian." Heading off a retort, Francois quickly changed the subject.

"Several times you have said we, meaning there are other canyon pioneers besides yourself, right?"

"Yes, but I was here first, built the first trails, established the first lodging facilities, and guided the first tourists. Now mind you, I'm not bragging, I'm just stating the facts. And I do respect tinhorns. My philosophy is to never look down on anyone unless you are on a higher switchback on the trail." Clancy paused. "Oh, you asked about others. Yes, you may encounter some prospectors down here. Let's see, there is Clint McCarty, Monte Bridgestone, Stuart Casey, Cole Campbell—to name a few. Oh, and then there's the burros. If you haven't seen one, vous regardez—see, I know a word or two of French—look over there at those three buff-colored fellows with black markings on their shoulders—always snorting as they browse among the Tonto sagebrush. And if their snorting is not enough, their nauseating heehaws shatter our blessed canyon silence. We prospectors and miners have managed to wrangle a few and use them as pack animals."

The men approached a stand of trees and a cool stream in a shaded gulch, then dismounted and hitched their mules with enough slack to reach the precious water source.

"This is as far as we can go by mule until I get a chance to improve the trail. Unless Calamity knows how to rappel down rock cliffs on ropes, we need to proceed on foot," explained Clancy, "it will be rough going for a while."

An hour later, Francois remarked, "Those rapids are getting louder as we draw closer."

"Powell, the Colorado River explorer, named them Sockdolager Rapids, a weird name. A few years back, I ran into a scruffy fellow in his mid-forties by the name of Hawkins down here." Clancy pointed. "He was just sitting on that rock, watching the rooster-tail waves in the river. He said he was on Powell's river expedition in sixty-nine and wanted to revisit the spot where they first entered this Granite Gorge. He remembered the Major saying he was going to name these rapids Sockdolager. When Hawkins asked why Sockdolager, Powell said it meant a heavy knockdown blow."

"Did you believe him?"

"Not at first, but he seemed to know all about Powell and the men who manned those tiny rowboats. Hawkins said he was a young scrappy Union soldier in the Missouri Cavalry during the Civil War and like many young men looking for new adventures, traveled west after the war. He signed on as cook and journeyed from Green River City way up north through the Canyon. Powell ended his historic river journey at Grand Wash Cliffs but Hawkins and another feller continued all the way down the Colorado to Yuma. He said he settled down in the territory, somewhere south, maybe Tucson or Phoenix. I never saw him after that."

"Anyway, LaRue, I digress, but I should mention instead of Sockdolager Rapids, I would have called them Jennings Rapids but that name has already been taken as I am improving another trail about two miles upriver that ends in the same violent manner. I mentioned a prospector named Monte Bridgestone. He did some work on that trail but has since abandoned it, so I've taken over. In many places, this river turns into a snarling torrent. I have never understood how Powell made it through." Clancy added, "If you pass my Grand Canyon test, you might be able to lend a hand on my Redrock Canyon Trail." Clancy neglected to mention that Monte had blazed that trail initially and all he planned to do is make some minor improvements.

On this day, the river flowed as a gush of somber brown water, laden with silt and debris. It roared in anger at the dark rock walls that imprisoned it, pressing inward from both sides. On the north side of the river, walls with fluted pockets of polished granite glistened in the sun. Clancy often dreamed about these as cubbyholes for gold nuggets. He pointed out that in these ancient rocks, time is encapsulated in a geologic record, in fact, to scientists the fossils in canyon rocks reveal the beginnings of life on the planet.

Clancy eyed Francois and stated, "Here's a question you are sure to be asked: 'Are there any fish in the river?' I'm asked that on every trip."

"I don't know about fish but I'm sure you are going to tell me", answered Francois, immediately regretting that he probably came across as rather flippant.

"The answer is yes; you can say there are squawfish, known to grow six feet long. They are rather boney and not very good eatin' but they sure put up a fight when you and this denizen of the muddy deep are at opposite ends of a fishing line."

Clancy and Francois refilled their canteens at a point just ahead of where the clear water of Whiskey Creek mingled with the dirty Colorado, and then started the long climb back up to where their mules were waiting.

"If a tourist asks you how deep the river is, what would you say?" Both men were finding that trudging up the rocky draw in the heat of the day to be bone-wrenching, in fact, quite challenging.

"I have no idea; you have not said anything about that," countered Francois.

"Actually, no one really knows. I would say a couple feet where the river is wide and maybe twenty or thirty feet where it is narrow;

sink holes could be even deeper. And the river probably averages three to four hundred feet across and is a vertical mile below the South Rim."

The men reached the steep walls where ropes were needed.

"What color is the Redwall?" snapped Clancy.

Francois answered quickly, "bluish white on the inside, red on the outside."

"Correct. Name three poisonous critters, most lethal first."

"Rattlesnakes, heely monsters and I'm guessing scorpions, although you did not say much about them."

"Close enough. Name three canyon prospectors."

Francois could only remember two. "Monte Bridgestone, Stuart Casey, and, let's see, Clancy Jennings."

"Yes, I keep my hand in prospectin' so I'll let you get away with that one. We're coming up on our last rock climb and then we can rejoin our mules. What's the name of this trail we're followin'?"

"That's easy, Whiskey Trail."

Calamity's braying indicated the men had reached a rest stop and another opportunity to fill their canteens. They sat in the shade of spindly alders, ash and swaying willows while Clancy continued to reel off a series of questions for the Frenchman.

"What rock layer caps the black granite? Name three species of trees on the rim? What do I call the thick white band of sandstone? And what is the name prospectors use to describe the black rocks?"

Francois tried to remember each question. "Mudstone, ponderosa, oak, cedar, bathtub ring and I have no idea on your last question. With all due respect, Monsieur, you failed to mention that."

"I'm just trying to trip you up. You are doing very well on your test, but we're not done. We refer to the black granite as black diamonds because it is peppered with glitter. I see it as the bedrock of the planet. You probably could find some in Quebec if you dig deep enough. Let's mount up and head for my cabin. It's late so we'll hole up there for the night."

After another hour, the men closed in on Clancy's camp at Whiskey Spring. Both mules brayed and to the men's surprise, a horse neighed back.

"Clancy, I thought you said you were not expecting any visitors on your trails today," asked Francois as the two entered camp. A solitary camper with a slouch hat and a holstered six-gun crouched beside a cooking fire.

"Ahem, mister, who do you think you are, making use of my camp and helping yourself to my firewood?" Clancy, not that displeased about the intrusion, feigned anger for effect. The stranger stood up. A long braid swung around to her back.

"You're a woman!" exclaimed Clancy. "A rare sight indeed in these parts."

"Yes, I'm a woman and it never ceases to amaze me how surprised men are when you discover me down here," said the woman.

"So, you are in the habit of surprising us old codgers, are you?" asked Clancy.

"No, I heard you two coming for the last twenty minutes. I usually scamper off and remain hidden but this time I already had my supper cooking so I decided to stay and face the situation, hoping you would be friendly. Can you forgive a stranger for taking over your camp?"

"Certainly, but who are you and what are you doing way down here?" questioned Clancy, looking over to Francois with a friendly smirk.

"My name is Sabrina Jaffa and I'm on a prospecting trip. This is my horse, Serendipity. It's her first trip down here but she also knew you were closing in long before you showed."

"This here is Monsieur Francois LaRue who is here on a training mission. And I am Clancy Jennings. Perhaps you have heard of me. I have a cabin on the rim and . . ." Sabrina cut him off.

"Heard of you? Of course, everyone has. We all look up to you as the single authority on all things Grand Canyon!" Sabrina placated the amiable pioneer and saw right through Clancy's glory-mongering. Still, she put on an air of barely being able to contain her excitement. Clancy looked over to Francois, "Listen up, Francois, she knows what she's talkin' about."

"I've been avoiding you and everyone else roaming around down here; just minding my own business, staying out of folks' way, while I poke around these canyon rocks. In my former life, I was treated like a piece of property rather than a person. The independent streak in me said I need to start looking out for myself, so here I am, looking out for myself—in your camp."

Clancy mumbled to himself, "More like helping yourself to my camp." She may have been hiding something or perhaps playing some clever game, but he put those thoughts aside. "Welcome to Whiskey Camp, Sabrina Jaffa; we'll all be spending the night together. You've probably noticed my rock cabin over there and my fine spring. Now, I have just one question for you Miss Jaffa. What's for supper? We're right hungry."

Sabrina dipped into her supply of canned meat, green beans and corn, cut up some more potatoes, and converted her simple fixings into a fine stew. She had real coffee beans for brewing and opened a paper-wrapped package containing thick slabs of bread. Although they seemed to be off to a rocky and stilted beginning, Sabrina felt she could set things right. She seemed confident that she would be well accepted after a hearty chuckwagon-style meal and fresh-brewed coffee.

"Supper is almost ready. You have two choices—take it or leave it."

"Smells good, I'll take it," answered Clancy. "Moi aussi, mon ami," repeated Francois. Following the lead of his instructor, the Frenchman answered "I'll also take it."

As they sipped their coffee, both men could not help gawking at the attractive woman. She caught them peering over the rim of their coffee cups but muffled her girlish giggle.

"Francois, I remember what you said about standing under oaks and being visited by a beautiful angel," said Clancy, tilting his head toward Sabrina. Francois, despite his shyness when first meeting a woman, just had to comment. "Miss Jaffa, these are very fine vittles. Don't you agree, Clancy?"

Clancy nodded in the affirmative, but obviously had a question. "Sabrina, what meat did you put in this stew?"

She toyed with the idea of keeping it a secret, perhaps claiming a recipe handed down from a distant grandmother. She decided to tease the fellows. "I call it mystery meat."

Clancy was not satisfied. "That does not answer my question. Where's that can? Maybe the label will tell me what yer hiding from us."

"Never mind, I'll tell ya. It's a delicacy—potted ox tongue!"

Clancy's expression revealed his skepticism, but Francois seemed well pleased. "Madamoiselle Sabrina, I found your stew to be very tasty and thank you for the fine meal."

"Thank you, Monsieur LaRue. In the morning, I'll fix flapjacks and coffee for you fellas before we go our separate ways. I assume you're headed for the rim. I'm headed east across the Tonto for some more prospecting." Sabrina felt she had made amends for borrowing Clancy's camp and decided she had opened up enough about herself.

She became decidedly quiet after supper and bedded down under the stars near Serendipity. Clancy and Francois slept in the rock cabin.

* * *

The men woke to the smell of fresh coffee and a pile of flapjacks on a flat rock next to the campfire. Sabrina and Serendipity had already slipped out of camp.

"Strange woman, that Sabrina; she never said goodbye. She reminds me of the assistant working in the Recorder's Office. Francois, I think we have just witnessed the first female prospector in the Grand Canyon. That's assuming she is really down here for that purpose. Yes sir, she's a strange one."

Francois added, "Strange yes, but not as wild and free-wheeling as Calamity Jane of the Dakotas. I'm sure we'll cross paths again sometime."

After breakfast, the men saddled their mules, broke camp and headed up the trail. Clancy decided that Francois had met his requirements for a trail guide. "Francois, I'm not going to ask you to answer any more questions. Congratulations, you passed my test. You are the new guide on the Whiskey Trail. My work philosophy is quite simple; take life a moment at a time, not a day at a time, and hold onto that pace; if you like what you do, you won't have to work a day in your life."

Francois smiled, quite pleased about how he played along with Clancy's game of questions and answers. And he thoroughly enjoyed his first venture into the canyon depths. He would make this exquisite wonder his new home.

Chapter Ten

STEPPING STONES

Secrecy can lead to the wildest imaginings.

At sundown, the creaking supply wagon rolled into camp at Deadman Flat. Since leaving Flagstaff mid-morning, Monte Bridgestone, Clint McCarty and Ben Saxton made good time following the road that skirted the eastern slopes of the Friscos. From Deadman Flat they rumbled northwest, passing red and black cinder cones on both sides of the wagon road, and rejoining the stage road ten miles north of Cedar Ranch. They camped for the night at Red Horse.

At eleven o'clock the next morning, they arrived at Jennings' camp, unloaded the wagon, and sent Saxton and the team back to town. While the *Frontier Times* reported the men planned to search for a lost gold mine, Monte and Clint intended to work on their Shooting Star Mine.

After dinner they stowed their outfit—twenty-five pounds of giant powder, a box of blasting caps, pickaxes, shovels, six-shooters, hunting carbines, cartridges, blankets, heavy rope, skillet, coffee pot, tin tableware, oaken bucket, lanterns and provisions for two weeks, including sealed boxes of flour, bacon, coffee and beans—against the north wall of Jennings' vacant cabin. Then each man packed a load on his back and proceeded down the trail to the rock house at Whiskey Spring. There they camped overnight with Francois LaRue and three strangers.

"Bonjour, Messieurs McCarty and Bridgestone; I spotted you in town once but we have not met. I am Francois LaRue and I'm guiding these gentlemen on Jennings' trail. I arrived a few months ago and have been prospecting for myself and also working part-time as Clancy Jennings' new trail guide. Pardon my strong accent; I'm French-Canadian from Quebec." LaRue had a friendly disposition, sparkling eyes, and a complexion bronzed by exposure.

"Yes, we've seen you in town too," said Monte. He had to ask, "How in blazes did you find your way from Quebec to Grand Canyon?"

The bewhiskered guide answered, "Others have asked that same question." Monte assumed the hope of finding valuable ores, coupled with living in an awesome corner of the world, must have been strong inducements for the grizzled old-timer to adopt Grand Canyon as his new home. He waited for LaRue to get around to how he found his way to canyon country.

LaRue explained. "Years ago, I had been working as a joiner and a wheelwright in Bellevue, a city in southern Quebec, surrounded by mountains, rivers and lakes—far different from this place. I grew tired of handcrafting door frames, bookcases and wagon tongues in a closed workshop full of wood shavings and sawdust. I longed for the great outdoors. So, I traded carpentry for the life of a vagabond and journeyed into the American West. I was in no hurry, and chose a roundabout path that crisscrossed the Great Plains and the Desert Southwest, and that's how I ended up here."

"LaRue, I'm surprised we have not crossed paths down here before now," stated Monte, still intrigued by the man from Canada.

"Well, it's a big canyon, Monsieur Bridgestone, and I spend considerable time at my canyon enterprises, west of the Pioneer Trail. Perhaps you know Slim Broadway. We have several mining claims there."

"We know Slim. He helped us build that trail, but he never mentioned you. I have to admit, I have never been to your part of the Canyon." With that, campfire talk ceased. The only sounds were the crackling fire and the snoring of LaRue's novice explorers, exhausted from their day's journey.

* * *

At daybreak, the prospectors borrowed a bay mare from LaRue and shuttled their outfit over to the first side canyon leading up to the mine.

"Monte", said Clint, "after you fell asleep last night, I talked more with that French feller. He's a colorful character. I would not normally press a man for details of his private life, but this time I couldn't help myself."

"I assumed he had wandered into the Canyon the same way we did," Monte responded, "maybe in search of the same thing. Secrecy can lead to the wildest imaginings, Clint. Reckon you should not have been prying into his life. He could be a fugitive on the run from a dark and secret past."

After ten minutes of silence, Monte blurted out, "Okay, now I'm curious. What did LaRue tell ya?"

As the men worked their way around to the east side of Windsong Mesa, Clint shared LaRue's story. "Apparently our French-Canadian friend met Calamity Jane in a Deadwood saloon while passing through Dakota Territory. And although employed by Clancy, LaRue has his own place twenty miles to the west of us. He lives alone at Cliffhouse Springs, a hidden recess in a sandstone wall. He says he staked several promising claims at the mouth of Spotted Tail Canyon, wherever that is, including one named Crazy Horse—Chief Spotted Tail's nephew— and two on the South Rim, one named Wild Lady of the West, perhaps after Calamity Jane. If she had known he named one of his mules Ca- lamity, she would not be amused."

Clint continued as they rounded Windsong Mesa. "LaRue tells me he took care not to appear in any decennial census reports, perhaps to perpetuate the mystique about himself."

Monte chewed on these revelations for a while. He heard Calamity Jane spent considerable time in Sioux Country. Had LaRue really met her? Or had he borrowed names from dime novels? One could speculate that the mystique surrounding LaRue and the old-timer's reluctance to waste words are traits gained by close association with those proud warriors of the doomed buffalo culture.

LaRue shared information gained from Clancy and his abiding love of the Grand Canyon with early tourists. He seemed sensitive and reticent, but not aloof or ornery. LaRue's new frontier worked its own brand of magic and transformed the French-Canadian into an American westerner.

Francois LaRue's trail through life, with teasing twists and shadowy switchbacks, is as difficult to follow as the trails he cut along canyon walls. At times, this quiet fellow seemed somewhat of a recluse; at other times he associated with other prospectors, trail-builders and canyon pioneers. "A mysterious fellow that Francois LaRue," thought Monte.

Monte and Clint settled into the rigorous task of packing supplies and equipment down the trail to the mine and around Windsong Mesa to Cottonwood Camp. The pack horse borrowed from LaRue helped.

Clint remembered something else from his late-night discussion with LaRue. "Monte, I forgot one other piece of news that LaRue shared with me. When Clancy and Francois came up from the river, they found a female intruder at their Whiskey Spring campsite!"

Monte shielded his eyes from the sun and asked, "So who, or are you going to leave me guessing all day? Wait, let me guess. Not Calamity Jane, likely Sabrina Jaffa."

"Yes, that woman prospector we encountered some time back!"

"Oh yeah, how could anyone forget a good-looking prospector?" said Monte. "Sabrina seems to have unlimited stamina as she has been exploring down here for years, never hesitating to venture into the Canyon alone. Last time we saw her, she didn't seem to know much about prospecting. Some of us have been calling her the mystery lady."

Clint added, "LaRue mentioned he usually becomes tongue-tied around ladies, but not around the sassy Sabrina Jaffa."

Clint, still young and single, seemed eager to question LaRue more about meeting Sabrina. He assumed the Frenchman camped at Whiskey Spring would need his mare soon. What a great opportunity to learn more about the female prospector. Meantime, Monte started for the mine with a canteen of water, shovel and carbine. He then trudged back to where they had left their packs.

Clint, finding no one at Whiskey Spring, arrived thirty minutes later with another load. Early summer heat proved to be gruesome for traveling on the shadeless Tonto. They straggled into camp with bedding and coffee pot. The next day, they awoke sore and stiff. Too exhausted to go to the copper property, they chose to stay in camp.

Cottonwood served as a permanent mining camp. It offered fluttering shade and a trickling spring among a stand of water-guzzling cottonwoods. Here, the miners built a wooden platform over which they pitched their canvas canopies to serve as rain shelters.

Although still tired from their trail-packing ordeal, Monte and Clint climbed up to Windsong Mesa and worked most of the day on an early prospect hole. The next day they awoke to heavy rain. With no relief in sight, the men suspended a hole-ridden wagon sheet on the windward side of their camp floor and huddled in bedrolls to keep dry. Clancy Jennings, with a pack horse and burro, visited the two bedraggled miners in camp. He offered fresh venison for dinner. The three miners spent the balance of the day next to the campfire, drying bedding and clothing and reviewing each other's mining claims.

Monte took this opportunity to tell Clancy what he thought of his so-called trail. "That's not a trail, Clancy, it's a primitive pathway."

"Dagnabbit, it's a right good trail, built it ma' self," snapped Clancy.

"Well, I have a better plan, an alternative route that will put your tortuous pathway to shame," said Monte. "With the terminus near Summit Point, I plan to build a trail with a direct connection to our mines here on the mesa." Annoyed by Monte's plan, and feeling he may lose some tourist traffic to a competing trail, Clancy departed for his cabin on the rim, grumbling to his four-footed companions, "Dang newcomers, gonna get crowded down here."

"Blamed if you didn't put a damper on things, Monte. You gave Clancy good reasons to go and no reason to stay. I had planned to ask him what he knew about our mystery lady." Too exhausted to argue, no further conversation took place that evening.

The next morning, Monte and Clint went to work at the mine. Late in the day, despite a menacing storm, the men climbed down the east wall of Windsong Mesa and retrieved the rest of their water-soaked packs, discarded four days earlier. With all of their gear and grub in one place, and with camp well established at Cottonwood, the men set about developing the Shooting Star Mine.

* * *

Clint described the frustration of finding nothing and the thrill of striking good mineral.

"Monte, we have worked on this claim all day and found it looking none the better." Indeed, the men prospected the entire next day and again found nothing of value. They returned to camp at sundown, not feeling the best.

On the third day, they prospected all morning and again found nothing. But then early that afternoon, Clint hit the bonanza!

"Monte, take a look!"

"Finally! Keep digging, Clint, this is what we need to make the claim worthwhile."

The men worked hard on the new copper strike and by late afternoon had taken out fine mineral. They first thought, as many a poor man had before them, they are rich beyond their wildest dreams, but after two more hours of digging, the fine mineral gave out. Clint and Monte realized they are still poor as ever, but returned to camp feeling much better, with hopes to strike it rich the next day.

Monte's diary captured the highs and lows of prospecting below the rim: "Clint struck the glory hole. Within two hours, we dug it all out. By four o'clock we were ranting, ragged millionaires; by six, no millionaires but ranting and ragged all the same."

They continued prospecting the next day and made another strike in the limestone. Monte noted that, from all appearances, it must be blue lime. Clint offered, "I've heard there is no regulation to blue lime formations."

With nothing else to say, Monte shrugged. The time had come for a break. The men spent the day resting in camp, washing clothes, sunning bedding, cooking beans, and shooting lizards.

After another week working with pick and shovel in the mine, these canyon miners needed supplies and planned to meet Ben and Slim on the rim at Jennings' cabin. After a brief reunion, and a report on discovering some high-grade copper ore, the four men packed provisions down to Cottonwood. Each journey on the Whiskey Trail built a stronger case for a more direct, more forgiving rim-to-mesa trail. With the next week came another sign of trouble with one partner.

Slim, Clint and Monte worked on the mine. Ben watched them work for a while, and then returned to camp. The next day, it being Sunday, everyone stayed in camp and all took a bath in Cottonwood Creek, even Ben. The following day Ben and Clint put a shot in a boulder, then Ben announced he felt queasy, and returned to camp. As the week went on, the men worked on the mine and built a blacksmith's forge. Ben started for the rim for grub, but at the foot of the Whiskey Trail he met a man coming to cook at the mine. He figured the newcomer could not look at the mining operations without an escort so he came back. Monte muttered to himself, "Lollygagging again. Another day frittered away, just like Black Ben."

Everyone saw Ben Saxton as an illiterate man, laconic in speech, with a bumpkin demeanor, a perpetual frown and shifty, downcast eyes. The sallow-faced forty-year-old always seemed to grumble about something. He looked for easy ways to get out of work and gave sidelong glances to his partners, all of whom he thought conspired against him.

While Ben had contributed to the planning and construction of the Pioneer Trail, the partners could no longer depend on him. For the past two years, he nursed his bitter resentment at the obvious injustice when the men barred him from ownership of the trail. While a winter storm delayed his return with supplies for his stranded partners, he took the blame. Why he remained a partner for so long is a mystery. Perhaps Ben saw the loss of his share as insignificant compared to the wealth he expected to gain from the Shooting Star Mine. Regardless, he continued to annoy Monte and Clint, seeming to shirk his share of the work.

While Slim cut juniper wood for making charcoal, Monte and Clint worked on the mine. Ben trudged back to the rim and did not return with grub until the next day. Monte bristled, noting that it took Ben two days to make what should have been a one-day round-trip. After another week's work on the mesa, the men had set up a forge and had retrieved a bellows and some tools from one of their downriver camps.

The mine now penetrated over one hundred feet into Windsong Mesa and the men began the grueling task of stockpiling high-grade copper ore near their rock corral, intending to pack it out by burro later. As usual, Ben complained about a gut ache and stayed in camp for the next three days. By Friday afternoon, he had recovered. The partners returned to the rim and met Cole Campbell and his wife at Jennings' place. That evening, they enjoyed another reunion. When Monte and Ben started back to Flagstaff, the others returned to the mine where Amanda Campbell toured the underground workings. Monte wished Marcy would show a similar interest in their mine or at least make a trip to the Canyon. That would be a first for Monte's uncompromising wife.

Matters came to a head late that summer. Ben needed to go with Monte to Flagstaff for supplies. The plan called for Ben to return to the Canyon with a wagonload of equipment and provisions. He and Monte drafted a bill of goods at Bergner's general store, but then Ben balked, starting a long series of excuses about not being ready to go back. The men at the mine depended on the wagon's prompt return. Meanwhile, the newsman Perkins, now living in Flagstaff and working for the *Frontier Times*, and unaware of Ben's sulking or Monte's frustration, posted an uplifting story about the rich copper ore of the Shooting Star Mine.

Otto Bergner read the glowing story aloud as Monte listened with pleasure, a bright spot in his harrowed day. "That the Grand Canyon has mineral of every kind is beyond dispute. That it has the richest copper deposits in the world is also beyond dispute. This week, Monte Bridgestone and Ben Saxton brought in some of the richest copper ore ever taken from that mining district. Together with Clint McCarty, the men located this property last year, and a few weeks ago they resumed work on the claim, and have taken out about fifty tons of ore, including native copper. They have burrowed into a geologic formation called Windsong Mesa to a wye about one hundred and thirty feet from the entrance, at which point two tunnels branch off in different directions, each penetrating another seventy-five feet into the blue lime rock. The men plan to use a pack train to haul ore to the rim, then haul it to town by wagon. Whenever there is enough ore to fill a railcar, a freight train will deliver shipments, hopefully on a regular basis, to a smelter."

"How's that for progress, Otto? We'll soon be able to repay you for grubstaking us," said Monte as Otto folded up the newspaper.

"I'm impressed, Monte. You fellas have a great start with the Shooting Star. But there's still the matter of hauling the high-grade ore out of the Canyon and shipping it to smelters," cautioned Otto, while still taking care not to discourage Monte and his men.

Delays and excuses of the bull-headed Saxton continued for another week, but he finally started back to the Canyon. Monte, who faced intense problems of his own at home—enough to put him into a deeper foul mood—caught up to Ben at Cedar Ranch where they drew water from a reservoir.

While the men packed supplies and water to the mine, Ben became most difficult. Recriminations flew back and forth. Ben contended that they had a conspiracy against him. He threatened to take his share and throw the mine into litigation. All work stopped. The men returned to Flagstaff to settle the matter once and for all.

After their first winter of prospecting, the partners had acquired Jesse Parks' one-fifth interest in the mine with the understanding they would settle the account at Bergner's store. As for a one hundred-and-eighty-eight-dollar balance, Ben had yet to post a single dollar to that account. As the men rolled into town, the squabbling turned to accusations that Ben had not done his share of the work. Monte added, "Ben, I'm going to say this flat-out, if you have ever done a day's work on any of our claims, I don't know of it and don't think you do either."

Ben, seething with anger, snapped back, "Not true and you know it. I've done more work than any of you!"

Unaware of the bickering among the partners, the paper carried more news of the Shooting Star Mine: "McCarty, Bridgestone, Broadway and Saxton have returned from their mine in the Grand Canyon. They brought in some fine specimens of copper ore, now on display at the *Frontier Times* office."

While the work in the mine brought out the best in copper ore, the disagreement brought out the worst in the miners. Monte set his mind to banishing Ben from their partnership. Having no tolerance for a free-loader, he had papers drawn up to transfer Ben's share. Frustrated by petty arguments and delays, the partners chafed to get back to the Canyon. They made final arrangements for a two-month stay at the South Rim to build a rim-to-mesa trail from Summit Point to the mine, more direct and more forgiving than the one in use. Monte, Clint and Slim urged Ben to sign legal documents so they could get back to work. When Ben appeared ready to sign his interest over to Clint McCarty, arguments ensued about who would pay the two-dollar recording fee for transferring his interests.

Ben stonewalled for hours, refusing to complete the agreement. "Monte, I'm not signing any papers until I am paid for all my work on the Pioneer Trail, my long trips back and forth between the Canyon and town, and all my back pay for my work at the mine."

"Back pay? What back pay? Dang it, Ben, we've turned that page in the ledger. It showed no back pay for you," yelled Monte.

Ben continued his balking. "And I'm not paying any of the recording fees, or assessment fees, or any other fees," howled Ben. Dejection loomed on the horizon.

The men, disgusted with his delaying tactics and belly-aching, left Saxton behind in Flagstaff, and returned to the Canyon. Later they filed a notice of forfeiture, claiming they filed documents certifying completion of assessment work on the Shooting Star Mine for the past two years. They notified Saxton that if he did not pay his full proportion of expenses within ninety days his interest as co-owner would cease. In time, they banished him from the partnership and Clint McCarty assumed his share of the mine.

Did McCarty stir up the others against Saxton to create a path to increased ownership? What about Bridgestone? A mild-mannered and fair-minded man, his diary entries about Saxton seemed out of character. Perhaps McCarty influenced the others and turned them against Saxton. McCarty is the one who had the most to gain from Saxton's ouster.

Regardless of who appeared to be at fault, or who conspired against who, getting back to the Canyon and continuing to stockpile high-grade copper ore mattered most to Monte.

* * *

In early August, an overloaded, squeaking wagon, with Monte Bridgestone, Clint McCarty and Kirby O'Brien aboard, rolled across the Coconino. Beneath the canvas wagon cover jostled drill steel, iron rods, wheelbarrow, canned goods, sacks of flour and potatoes, red flannel shirts, and corduroy trousers. And from San Francisco, a box of new copper-riveted overalls made by a German immigrant named Levi Strauss, lay crammed under the driver's seat.

The men camped overnight at Red Horse. The following day, they travelled another five miles before stopping. Sensing the increasing importance of the Grand Canyon Stage Line, Monte located the Moqui Mining Claim and Clint staked the Wagon Wheel Mining Claim within fifty feet of the stage road, in effect exploiting the Mining Law loopholes. They camped that night at Jennings' cabin and filled their water barrels. No one seemed more eager to begin work on the massive Summit Trail project than Monte. He had hired Kirby O'Brien, known to be a dependable worker, to replace Ben Saxton.

From its start to its completion, the trail would be Monte's consuming obsession. The men knew a direct well-built trail would save time and labor in the long run, and that would translate to respectable profits. Even given the superior grade of the ore waiting in the mine, the time and labor required to transport it to the smelter could still negate any chance of profit. All agreed—they needed a practical alternative to Clancy Jennings' rugged trail.

Monte seemed further motivated by a spirit of rivalry. He considered himself a master trail-builder compared to the grizzled old tale-spinner. Taciturn and direct, Monte's nature often clashed with that crinkled old man. Clancy, like Levi Jackson, followed fading Havasupai and Hopi pathways into the canyon depths. Nothing original about that, Monte thought. He recalled the impossible turn on Clancy's route where he lost one of his pack horses. He would blaze new territory—strike a trail straight down the banded rock walls. He would not make the same mistake on his zigzags. He would engineer his trail, hone it from ancestral rock, bridge stubborn barriers, and build a durable pathway that would last a century or more.

Monte tired of Clancy's constant bragging and repeated claims of having single-handedly cut the first entryways into the Grand Canyon. He muttered to himself: "All Clancy ever did is smooth away brush and rubble and dangle rope ladders over difficult climbs." His Summit Trail would outshine Clancy's primitive track, perhaps even make it obsolete.

The men cut juniper logs on the rim and dragged them to where they built bridges, cribbing and retaining walls on the Summit Trail's switchbacks. They devoted weekdays and Saturdays to trail work and set aside Sundays for sharpening tools, cutting pole pines for another cabin, digging water retention basins on the rim, and hauling water. On Sundays, they also entertained themselves by teasing greenhorn stage arrivals at Clancy's place.

According to Monte's ledger, he, Clint and Kirby each worked twelve full days on switchbacks. They valued their labor at four dollars per day, three times the rate for lumbermen, cowboys and soldiers. The most difficult sections of trail construction lay along the cliff faces. These represented a challenge which the trail-builders met with daring, skill and hard work. They blasted out some sections of the limestone and sandstone walls—others involved installation of an intricate trail bed suspended on steel-pinned logs and hung on the sheer canyon wall.

The route selected for this new trail began east and south of Summit Point, the highest point on the South Rim of the Grand Canyon and traced a no-nonsense course to Windsong Mesa. The trail clutched vertical ramparts and spiraled down terraced slopes, and unlike the Pioneer Trail tucked into giant ravines, this trail exposed itself on north-facing cliffs.

From their precarious work stations, the men could see great expanses of canyon country, filled with stranded buttes and jagged side canyons. Majestic in any of its moods, the Canyon manifested itself as a panorama of unknowable and immeasurable antiquity, done by a force far more patient and powerful than all the men and giant powder in existence. Below the Navajo Palisades, which separated the Grand Canyon from Painted Desert, they could see the work of the Colorado River, cutting and excavating each band of rock that provides this stunning vista—from the milky-white rimrock that vibrated their pickaxe handles to the even harder black diamond-studded walls of Granite Gorge.

By late August, the trail-builders had started work on the first bridge. And who happened to be on the scene, observing the construction, but reporter Ryan Perkins. "What do you mean? You're building a bridge on the trail?" as he adjusted his wire-rimmed glasses.

Monte drew a deep breath and described the construction. "We're building a bridge-like structure by anchoring rough-hewn juniper logs with steel pins to form cribbing," he explained. "This involves drilling holes in the wall and jamming a long steel rod into each hole. The rods have square heads for pounding or eyelets for fastening steel cables. Long cedar timbers form the outer edge of the crib." Monte observed Ryan scribbling notes, trying to keep up with the trail-builder's narrative. "We backfill the space between the logs and the canyon wall with rock and rubble. Then we cut slabs of sandstone and fit them edgewise into the bed. Our plan is to complete this first mosaic bridge of interlocking stepping stones in four days."

"Ah," Ryan sighed, "then you build a second bridge, and then a third. Now I understand what you mean by trail bridges."

Ryan seemed engrossed in trail construction. Monte chuckled when he realized Clancy may read his report in the *Frontier Times* and learn something about real trail-building. Perhaps Ryan will headline the story "Bridgestone Builds Stone Bridges".

Monte continued to supply Ryan with details. "Sometimes we drill a series of holes with a sledge or jack, and insert loose-fitting rods and wedge-shaped lengths of steel—we call them feathers—on either side of the rods. By alternately tapping the feathers and listening to the tone or timbre of the responding pings, a skilled rock-splitter can control the fracture and separation of large blocks of stone." Monte allowed Ryan to catch up on his note taking.

"The alternative approach to removing large sections of rock is rather crude: the men drill holes in the face of the rock wall, then with a miner's spoon ladle blasting powder, and finally string fuses into each hole. Then comes my favorite part; we light the fuses. What follows is a sharp rap of man-made thunder echoing across the Canyon, reverberating off the Redwall and muffling itself in various side canyons."

As Ryan closed his notebook and prepared to leave, he had an unrelated question for Monte.

"Say, Monte, there are rumors floating about town about a mysterious lady prospector roaming about the Canyon. Just wondering if you have seen her?"

"Oh, you mean the Mystery Lady," exclaimed Monte. "As far as I know, no one has seen her in months. She's quite the loner and by now may have given up looking for a place to stake a claim. I guess I don't have any news for your readers. Oh, except she goes by the name Sabrina Jaffa. Sorry, that's all I know."

"Thanks Monte. If I get a chance to interview her, it could be an interesting story."

In town, the *Frontier Times* carried the following news: McCarty, Bridgestone and O'Brien are building a trail from their Grand Canyon mine to the rim. When finished the trail will make the trip to the river and back much easier. Ryan's report described the details of constructing the Summit Trail and the hard labor to wrest valuable minerals from canyon walls. It concluded by stating that if a man needed an obsession, the search for canyon gold may be a good choice.

Work on the trail and cabin near Summit Point continued through the fall. Two more hired hands, Jeremy and Dexter Livingston, joined Kirby. The three men earned miner's wages for their work on the trail. At one steep switchback in the cross-bedded yellow sandstone, they constructed a ramp to bridge two walls. Again, they hammered steel rods into the slope to support the base of cobblestone walkways—stepping stones inserted edgewise into the trail-bed—and to prevent the entire assembly from unraveling block by block. The men reached a saddle in the sandstone, a notch perched atop the red beds—a milestone in the construction of the Summit Trail. With most of the difficult work completed, the men earned a break. By the second week of November, they arrived back in Flagstaff.

* * *

Late one Saturday night in a back alley a few blocks from the railroad depot, Ben Saxton, skulking about, stumbled toward another saloon. The moonless night darkened his mood. He startled a drunken cowboy, known around town as Simon Nelson, humped over an empty beer barrel. Nelson drew his empty six-shooter, pointed it at the dark intruder and pulled the trigger.

Saxton, just as soused as Nelson, pulled the trigger of his short-barreled, forty-four caliber Winchester carbine but it jammed because he loaded pistol cartridges in his carbine. He then emptied his Colt pistol but his shots went wild. This seemed anything but a quick-draw gunfight. Saxton, left with no usable shooting iron, drew a sharp double-edged knife.

Nelson suddenly appeared three feet away, jaw clenched, fists clenched, eyes blazing with fire, knife in hand, about to thrust it into Saxton's chest.

Saxton seized his wrist and held it while lunging for Nelson's belly. But Nelson caught Saxton's arm and the two men became locked in a deadly battle. Nelson roared, "I'll teach you for taking shots at me, you drunk!" No townsfolk noticed the scuffle going on in the alley. Nor did anyone respond to the gunshots, a common occurrence on wild Saturday nights in Flagstaff. "You tried to shoot me but you're so drunk you had no bullets," countered Saxton.

The two no sooner struggled to their feet than Saxton tripped Nelson who again went down, pulling Saxton down with him, then rolling over him, breaking loose his wrist. Strong like Saxton, he held him tight, his knee on Saxton's throat, his left-hand holding Saxton's right wrist, his dreadful knife poised.

Saxton, sneering at his grizzled foe, jerked free, his head turning aside as Nelson's blade went through his bandana and plunged into the alley dirt. Saxton then bit Nelson's ear.

Nelson howled with pain and released his grip on Saxton's right wrist while trying to seize his knife with his left hand. But Saxton reached the knife first. "I'll teach you not to tangle with me," said Saxton as he stabbed Simon Nelson multiple times, thrusting the long blade between Nelson's ribs, and killing him. He let out a brittle snicker and struggled to his feet.

Two days passed before anyone discovered the lifeless body. Silas Taylor identified him as the accidental killer, the man who shot John Bridgestone years earlier. With no witnesses, Nelson's murder remained a mystery. Only Ben Saxton knew what happened that dreadful night, and even his recollection seemed foggy.

Chapter Eleven

MYSTERIOUS EXPLOSION

A man could bury revenge deep inside but only until it becomes the lighted fuse of retaliation.

A week after the bloody, back-alley knife fight, Flagstaff citizens buzzed when the flamboyant Colonel William "Buffalo Bill" Cody, the Wild West hero and showman, arrived in town. Like Clancy Jennings, Cody's life boasted a mix of legend and fabrication. Both spent time on the Kansas plains, worked for wagon-freight outfits, and tried their luck as "Fifty-Niners" by dabbling in the Pikes Peak Gold Rush.

Unlike Jennings, Buffalo Bill rose to fame as a national folk hero in dime novels and shared the printed page with the frontiersman Kit Carson, the raucous Calamity Jane, and the notorious outlaw Billy the Kid. He staged his first Wild West show in North Platte, Nebraska. His famous shows dramatized historical events and frontier life in the American West, including a hunt with wild buffalo, a Sioux attack featuring Sitting Bull and his band, a Pony Express ride, and even Custer's Last Stand in which several Lakota, who fought in the battle, played a part. Buffalo Bill's Wild West exhibition opened in London with a command performance at Queen Victoria's Golden Jubilee.

For three decades, the shows proved to be enormous successes. In between these outdoor extravaganzas, Cody escorted Easterners and Europeans on hunting expeditions in the West.

Cody arrived in Flagstaff in the company of a large contingent of Englishmen interested in establishing hunting lodges on the Kaibab. The party, which included the Queen's personal guard, stepped off the train and onto wagons supplied by several Kanab businessmen. Under the gray skies of a brisk November day, the visitors continued their journey north for their first look at the Grand Canyon. They planned to stay one night at Clancy's rustic hotel.

"Well, I'll be damned," squealed Clancy, "it's Bill Cody himself." He jumped up from his rocking chair and stepped down from his cabin porch. Cody beat him to a handshake. "Howdy, Clancy, I haven't seen you since we were panning for gold in Colorado."

"Bill, I had no idea you were coming."

The skies cleared as the two walked over to the rim where Cody soaked in canyon views, rinsed by blond sunlight.

"What a magnificent sight; it certainly puts the Grand Canyon of the Yellowstone to shame—Clancy, we made a last-minute decision to visit the South Rim before going over to the North Rim. I hope you can accommodate my entourage." That night Cody penned his name and his impression of the Canyon in Clancy's visitor's book.

When most of Clancy's guests had retired to their assigned sleeping quarters, he and Cody took advantage of the quiet evening, and the radiant heat from Clancy's fireplace, to review each other's exploits.

"So, Bill, what have you been doing since our pitiful gold-panning adventures in the Rockies?"

"Hunting buffalo and supplying meat to transcontinental railroad workers in Kansas. I also scouted for the U.S. Cavalry. That's about the same time my partner, Texas Jack Omohundro, and I guided General Philip Sheridan, General George Custer, Lakota Chief Spotted Tail and the Russian Grand Duke Alexis on a buffalo hunt near North Platte. What about you?"

"Well, let's see." Clancy welcomed the opportunity to talk about himself. "For a spell I worked as a mule-skinner for Lorenzo Butler Hickok, brother of the notorious Wild Bill Hickok," explained Clancy.

Cody perked up, "Oh, Tame Bill! He and Wild Bill and I are long-time friends! So, you helped Lorenzo supply army forts with buffalo meat, probably from buffalo I shot on the plains." Cody grinned; he could not help gloating about his buffalo kills.

Clancy continued, "I reckon so." Clancy had mixed feelings about the near extermination of the American Bison. He only killed animals for the meat he himself needed. He despised the hide hunters but stopped short of thinking of Cody as one of those killers. "After the Civil War, I was a dispatch rider out of Fort Leavenworth, Kansas. As you know, the Army built that outpost to protect traders and settlers on the Santa Fe Trail."

"I know it well," interjected Cody, "from my own Army days."

"Yeah, like you, I also dealt with the Army," Clancy added, "including the Navajo's forced march from Fort Sumner, New Mexico to Fort Defiance, Arizona; leading settlers down the Santa Fe Trail from Fort Union, New Mexico and west to Fort Whipple, Arizona; and moving wounded Apache braves, women, and youngins from Camp Verde to the San Carlos Agency."

"Clancy, it appears you've had as many dealings with the Army and Indian affairs as I have," Cody remarked. He placed two logs on the fire. Looking up at Clancy's fireplace mantle, he noticed a picture frame next to a stack of dog-eared issues of *Harpers Weekly* magazine. "I share your philosophy on life: 'Old wood to burn, Old wine to drink, Old books to read, Old friends to trust'. I believe that is a quotation about age by Sir Francis Bacon; after what we've both been through, it's time to slow down." He waited for Clancy's next escapade as he enjoyed tales of his wild adventures, but Clancy digressed.

"Well, I don't know about that Bacon feller but I like the part about old books to read," Clancy said. "My favorite books are those written by Mark Twain. He stretched the truth a mite and I do the same in my stunning stories. Ol' Twain often told downright lies and, well, I have been known to do the same." Twain's writings had a big influence on Clancy and his wild tales. Both storytellers served up ample helpings of absurdity, sentimental feelings, questionable relevance and uplifting humor.

"Cody, I think I lost my train of thought," added Clancy, "whatever you do, don't get old like me; you'll live to regret it."

"Clancy, I believe the alternative is worse."

"Oh, I remember. I ran a stagecoach between Canyon Diablo and Flagstaff, punched cows and broke horses on the Coconino, eventually leading me to early encounters with this magnificent place." Clancy peered out his window at a full moon flickering through ponderosa branches. "You could say I hitched my wagon to the Grand Canyon," added Clancy.

"I've had a similar series of experiences," volunteered Cody. "For the past twelve years, I've been on stage more than I've been on the frontier. It's probably best." Cody paused in deep thought. "Clancy, the frontier is about gone and so ends the era of the Wild West. I've been trying to hang on to the old days by forming a theatre troupe that included Wild Bill Hickok, Calamity Jane and Texas Jack."

Cody again paused in deep thought. "Clancy, there's a plan developing to stage a World's Fair in Chicago City. I'm trying to get the organizers to agree on having my Wild West show as part of the Fair but I'm running into a lot of opposition. They keep telling me the event is to celebrate the discovery of America by Columbus and to showcase all the great inventions and progress America has made since then. They see the Wild West as a thing of the past and tell me it's time to move on. Our frontier days are past history now."

Cody drew a long breath and let out a deep yawn. "And with that, I reckon I need to turn in. Big day tomorrow."

The party split the next morning, with Clancy escorting several members back to Flagstaff to catch an eastbound train while Cody and his hunting party traveled overland to the Kaibab Plateau by Lee's Ferry and House Rock Valley. Fortunately, at that time of the year, the river ran low and slow, allowing a safe crossing.

* * *

Flagstaff townsfolk continued their chatter about Buffalo Bill, but also about the proprietor of the Ponderosa Tavern and his wanton wife. Rumors flew from parlor to saloon. With impressions colored by youthful romanticism, many a young buck remembered Marcy Bridgestone as an attractive woman. Townsfolk sympathized with her complaints about being abandoned while her husband ventured into "that cursed canyon".

Monte had traded the civilized life of a family man and popular saloonkeeper for the more rugged life of a canyon prospector. He knew a man foolish enough to leave a beautiful wife alone in a rough town spelled trouble. A woman claimed few rights, and life on the frontier—even in a frontier town—proved as hard on the spirit as on the body. Marcy expected the support and companionship of her man. Women in the West, coveted by men not blessed with their company, remained the one serious deficiency in the male-dominated territory. Even lonely prospectors imagined inserting their necks in the noose of marriage. And in Washington Territory, lonely lumbermen looked forward to their mail-order brides, shipped overland like freight.

Monte won Marcy by the sympathy and care he provided in her bereavement. His quiet dignity and sensitivity put her at ease. But now, through the town's gossiping tongues, he caught fleeting rumors about Marcy's roving eye, and her inability to stay faithful to her man. Vague stories about Marcy and a traveling salesman—others said a gambler, still others identified the man as Ben Saxton—circulated widely. Explosive rumors flew about town—perhaps originated by Marcy herself—that her husband, too, operated as a philanderer, worse that he ran with the famed Jackson Trail horse thieves.

Monte, stubborn yet optimistic about expected improvements in their situation, staked their marriage on unproven mining claims. But Marcy saw nothing but lonely days and nights, abandonment by a husband more interested in mining than raising a family. His brief homecoming did not result in a joyful occasion for either himself or his wife, or their four year old son Ben. His suspicions about mistreatment of young Ben during his absence remained unabated. Monte needed to get back to the Canyon.

* * *

Monte and his men resumed construction of the Summit Trail, picking up where they left off at the Coconino saddle. He needed to supervise the Livingston brothers and Kirby O'Brien. He estimated another four weeks to extend the trail to the Shooting Star Mine. The team looked forward to pulling high-grade copper ore out of Windsong Mesa's tunnels.

Ben Saxton, his hands still bloodied from killing Simon Nelson who shot Monte's brother, quietly slipped out of town, circled around the east side of the 'Friscos and journeyed north to the Canyon. Unseen, he descended Clancy's Whiskey Trail, worked his way over to Windsong Mesa, and climbed the Redwall to the mine, avoiding the work party on the Summit Trail.

With all work focused on the last segment of the new trail, the mine lay dormant. Saxton paused at the tunnel entrance to light a kerosene lantern, then hunching, entered the down-sloping tunnel. Heavy timbers lined the sides. Saxton wheezed as he labored to breathe the stale air. He leaned against a heavy timber during a brief dizzy spell in the stifling tunnel. At a fork he lost his sense of direction, but then remembered to veer left. In the feeble lantern light, he shuffled along the tunnel until he reached a dead-end—and a discarded keg of black powder right where he left it months ago.

Saxton backtracked to the fork where he planned to set the charges, rolling the powder keg over the rubble on the tunnel floor. Having planned his escape, he pulled a coiled fuse from his coat pocket, cut off a short piece and inserted one end into the keg. After using the lantern flame to light the fuse, he turned to run. In his haste, the blithering scoundrel ran down the other dead-end tunnel, then turned back to the fork. Only a few feet of fuse remained. Now confused, he stumbled on a chunk of limestone, and smashed his lantern against the tunnel wall, extinguishing the light. He scrambled to his feet, broke into a run in the dark, only to crash into the wall again.

The explosion swept Saxton off his feet as a strong out-rush of stale air and dust roared past him. Timbers creaked, and one cracked overhead like thunder. He groped his way up the tunnel as the ceiling and walls collapsed around him. With only lime dust to breathe, he felt stinging in his lungs. He gasped for air while stumbling over shattered rock but dragged himself out of the debris field, coughing and trembling. He knew he had to scamper down the east wall, retrace his footsteps to the Whiskey Trail, and escape from the Canyon.

Kirby O'Brien and the Livingston brothers, working on the trail below the saddle, heard the distant rumble.

"What in tarnation? Did you hear that?" sputtered Kirby.

"Sounded like an explosion!" returned Dexter. Kirby sprang to his feet. "The mine!"

Monte, finishing up a set of cribbing on the upper trail, also heard the blast. He ran down to where his crew stood gawking at the mine. "Hey, Monte, we think we heard an explosion at the mine," shouted Jeremy.

"Yeah, I heard it too. Let's go!"

When the men arrived at the mine, they saw dust spilling out of the entrance. With no one working in the mine for the past month, each man offered a different idea on what caused the mysterious explosion—lightning? volcanic eruption? static electricity? Monte suspected sabotage but the identity of the culprits boggled his mind, certainly none of his fellow miners working on other canyon claims, a fraternity of mining men—kindred spirits in the mining profession. While they did not always agree on issues, they respected each other's talents and good intentions.

As the dust cleared, Monte shouted, "The entrance is still intact! We can get in." Looking at Kirby, he added, "If one wanted to shut down a mining operation, you would think closing off the entrance would be the goal. Instead, the culprit set off the explosion deep within the mine. Run up to the cookhouse and grab a couple lanterns." Kirby returned twenty minutes later.

The men entered the mine and stepped over broken timbers and rubble. Kirby still panting from his jaunt to the top of the mesa and back, trailed behind as they approached the location of the wye. The pungent smell of gunpowder hung in the air. Monte thought to himself, "Whoever did this had no idea what he was doing. If he had used giant powder instead of black powder, the mine would surely have been destroyed." The explosion transformed the wye into a chamber with fissured walls and rocks piled several feet high on the floor.

Monte broke the dusty silence. "Men, whoever did this, did us a big favor." Pointing, he added, "Look up there."

Jeremy shouted, "Ooh-eeh, that's copper!"

The blast exposed a large section of bright shiny metal, mixed with blue green carbonates—a rich vein of pure copper.

* * *

Marcy Bridgestone sat in her rocker, enjoying the radiant warmth from her fireplace and thinking about her lot in life and the long days and nights while her wayward husband worked copper claims deep in the Canyon. Young Benjamin was staying overnight with a friend. She heard the backdoor creak but assumed the bitter November wind, putting a chill in the air that night, made the sound. Then it creaked louder. Startled, Marcy jumped from her chair as a big man came up behind her. Trembling, she turned quickly. "Oh—you frightened me. Why didn't you knock on the front door?"

"I am sorry for that Mrs. Bridgestone," then pausing, "you are very beautiful in the firelight." With venomous animosity for Monte and the chance to even the score, Ben Saxton looked her over and commented, "Certainly is a pretty skirt and blouse yer wearin'—they suits ya well," as he forced a smile.

"Thank you kindly but I did not know you were stopping by," as she made sure the backdoor was closed.

"Well Marcy, you didn't seem to be so skittish when Monte used the backdoor," remarked Ben as he grasped her hand. She figured he must have spent hours watching the house, perhaps peering into windows while lurking in the shadows, all to study Monte's routine and habits at home.

"Mr. Saxton, you have no right to speak to me like that. If you will be so kind as to leave me alone; I'm expecting Monte any time now." Marcy knew that not to be true as she had little knowledge of her husband's comings and goings. She again pleaded that Ben leave, trying to conceal her fluster.

"Come now Marcy—or must I say Mrs. Bridgestone—cannot a man express his admiration? For sure you will not be haughty towards a friend."

"I recognize you as the freeloader dismissed by my husband and that does not make us friends so please go out the way you came in." Marcy opened the door and motioned him out.

Ben hesitated a moment at the doorway and putting his hands around her slender waist he said, "Now then, let's talk awhile and become friends." An alarming gleam in his steely gray eyes unnerved her.

"Sir, I do not welcome your attentions, please unhand me," and stepping back she shook off his grasp.

Ben laughed, "Now here I thought that ladies liked fancy compliments. I seem to recall that you accepted Monte when he gushed forth with his pretty sayings, although I do not recall seeing you that close of late."

Marcy's eyes narrowed at Ben's words. She felt uneasy as he continued speaking.

"For certain you welcome the attentions of Monte in a gentler fashion. Sometimes I've observed that you have greeted him—shall we say—rather intimately!"

Ben's rudeness shocked her. She realized that when she and Monte thought themselves alone, a stalker lurked nearby. Marcy had an urge to slap Ben for his impertinence but now she feared him. She looked at him squarely in his bewhiskered face and seeing the smirk of amusement he displayed at her discomfort, she seethed with anger. Drawing herself up, she tossed her head in defiance, her hair flying past him, and replied, "Mr. Saxton, your boldness astounds me. Will you please get out!"

"Well Miss, I have not entered your home to be dismissed so lightly. Let us talk awhile for I can be as charming as the next man," cajoled Ben, and taking her arm, he added, "You need to be more friendly."

"Monte will not be friendly towards you when he hears of your forward manners."

"Well, he isn't around to hear anything, is he? I know he's at the Canyon. Now why don't you be nice and let's sit for a spell."

"No, please leave." Marcy panicked and started for the front door.

Ben seized her by the waist and drew her close, saying, "Not so fast, lady," and pressed his lips to hers. Struggling against his body she pounded his chest with her fists and wrenched free and darted back to the door. With quick strides Ben reached for her and pulled her against his chest saying, "Ah my sweet girl, be nice now."

"Let me go—let me go please!" Marcy pleaded, now frightened more than ever as she saw Ben's lustful expression.

"Aha! I imagined you'd be a fiery one," Ben whispered. He grasped her hands and folded her arms behind her back. His tall body towered over her and holding her helpless, he covered her mouth with his in a long, suffocating kiss. Marcy struggled and working her arms free she pushed him off but Ben grabbed the neckline of her blouse that then broke open and he pulled her back, forcing her onto the floor. Screaming and kicking she tried to get away but he overpowered her. Fumbling for her breasts, he unlaced her bodice while muttering, "My little beauty, you are a well-endowed lassie and I will have my way with you."

Marcy let out a piercing cry, "Stop!" and with all her strength, she lurched back and swung one arm free despite his weight upon her. With her freed hand she clawed at Ben's face, raking the skin under his left eye. Surprised by Marcy's action he released her and raised his fingers to his torn, bleeding cheek as she rolled out from under him.

Just then, a shadow fell over them and a man's fist clutched Ben's shirt. Marcy screamed and crawled away, then turning her head she saw Monte standing over the intruder. She struggled to her knees as Monte exploded and yanked Ben to his feet.

"You swine! How dare you molest my wife," Monte shouted, then he swung at Ben and landed a fierce blow that sent the scoundrel staggering backwards. Ben held his cracked jaw and muttered, "Where in hell did you come from?" and then he fell back as Monte struck him again and again with quick jabbing blows. Ben tried to defend himself with both fists but he proved no match for the outraged husband. Monte's explosive anger continued to land painful punches. Soon Ben begged for mercy. "Enough Monte—enough—I am sorry." But Monte continued his relentless pounding.

Marcy slumped into her rocker—holding her pale Irish face in her hands. Her throat constricted as she struggled to breathe. She blinked, trying not to cry. But then a warm tear escaped. She felt it trickle down her cheek and salt her upper lip. She looked up at the fighting in time to see Monte knock Ben out cold—sockdolager as Powell would have described it. He lay sprawled on the floor—dead still. Marcy, though, numb with fear, gradually realized that Monte, with his timely arrival, spared her from ultimate violation.

"You all right, Marcy?" she heard Monte ask. She rose to her feet and feeling dazed she tried to regain her wits. Mortified and trembling she grasped her bodice, trying to close the unlaced portions as Monte added, "That rat will never bother you again, that's for sure." He then wrapped a towel around his bleeding hand.

Marcy looked around the room. Ben lay still on the floor—bleeding profusely from the long deep scratch she had inflicted. A trickle of blood seeped from his mouth from Monte's final blow. Shocked by Ben's inert form, she cried out, "Oh Monte, you have killed him, he does not move!"

"He will recover. I knocked him out good. He deserves much worse for I am appalled that he would dare assault you." Monte felt a scoundrel like Ben Saxton could bury revenge deep inside but only until it becomes the lighted fuse of retaliation.

"Monte, I-I-I, I believe—I mean—I think that you arrived just in time—before—uh before—" and Marcy burst into tears again. Monte supported her as she slumped against him. "You have had a terrifying time. Where's our son?"

"Staying—staying overnight at McCarty's."

Marcy glanced again at Ben Saxton's prone body with confused emotion. She felt ashamed and attempted to smooth her skirt and gave a futile pass through her tangled hair. Marcy could not believe that Monte's former partner tried to attack her; she felt both angry and shocked by the incident and felt remorse for Ben's bloody condition yet she remained furious at his uncontrolled action. Then her mood changed and she directed her anger and embarrassment at Monte.

"If you had been here with me, where you are supposed to be, this would never have happened. It's as much your fault as Ben Saxton's. This is the last straw." With that, Marcy left Monte standing over her intruder and ran into the street, leaving the front door wide open.

Ben stirred and Monte pulled out his six-gun. "You going to shoot me now, Monte?"

Monte strained to see where Marcy went while keeping his gun trained on Ben. When he peered out the door, Ben tried to grab his foot. Then a single gunshot pierced the night calm.

A few days after the awful incident, a deputy sheriff arrested Monte for shooting Ben Saxton in the inside part of his upper thigh. He claimed the shot was accidental, "I fired a warning shot when Saxton regained consciousness. He stepped in front of the bullet." The judge agreed and dismissed the case, but rumors circulated, obscuring what may have transpired. Despite no further scrutiny, the damage to their marriage signaled the end. Monte long suspected Marcy of infidelity and possible abuse of their son. And in the back of his mind, he wondered if Black Ben, who reeked of guilt, caused the mine explosion.

One late December Sunday, Monte and his son secretly boarded the eastbound Overland Express. He placed his son in the care of the Sisters of Charity boarding school, in the obscure village of San Miguel, on the Santa Fe Railway in northern New Mexico. Marcy filed for divorce on the grounds that Monte did not provide the necessities and comforts of life. She demanded custody of their son and dissolution of their marriage. When the court granted their divorce, it ordered custody of their son held in abeyance, pending further order. After the divorce, neither Marcy nor Ben Saxton appeared in town again. Rumors circulated that Marcy returned to New Mexico.

* * *

With winter coming on, Monte and his Summit trail-builders started back to the Canyon. They camped overnight at Leroux Spring in the Friscos and by firelight read the newspaper. The lead stories featured talk of statehood, Grover Cleveland's election, mining and drought. Stockmen hoped for heavy snowfall as the winter ranges lacked water. Several cattlemen already lost most of their herd.

The trail-builders, eager to finish their construction project, wanted to get back to mining copper, including the rich vein exposed by the explosion. Monte sold his Ponderosa Tavern to Silas Taylor, his trusty bartender, and now that Marcy left town and Benjamin accepted life in a distant school, he planned to spend most of his time at the Canyon.

Upon arrival at the rim, the men cut enough roof poles to complete the Summit cabin and claimed the surrounding five acres as the Shooting Star mill-site. The cabin served as Monte's new residence and a base camp while he and his partners developed the Shooting Star Mine. What began as a log house on the rim, Monte hoped would grow into a grand tourist complex.

The mill-site, filed in the names of Monte Bridgestone and Clint McCarty, sat two miles west of the Whiskey Trail, a half-mile east of the Summit Trail, three and a half miles southeast of the Shooting Star Mine, and a half-mile above the mine. While never used as a mill-site, Monte regarded it as a valuable piece of South Rim real estate, serving first as the original trailhead of the Summit and perhaps later as a popular tourist destination.

Progress continued on the mill-site as Monte and Kirby worked on the tank, erected a stock fence, and hurried to complete the cabin as heavy gray clouds moved into the Canyon. The men, flirting with an early winter storm as the dark gray sky began spitting ice pellets, worked to put a roof on the cabin. It snowed hard in the afternoon and all the next day.

The men spent the next few weeks mud-chinking the cabin walls and working on the tank. They borrowed a plow and scooped out broken caprock and half-frozen earth from a swale leading to the rim. Early in January, the tank, twin man-made rim-side depressions, stood ready to collect snowmelt. The partners looked forwarded to the day when they no longer depended on others for water.

The last stretch of the Summit Trail hugged a ridge and sliced through gentle slopes of red shale to the top of the Redwall and Windsong Mesa. With only a few more weeks of work, it connected to the

Shooting Star Mine, ready for travel by horseback; but more importantly, ready for packing stockpiled copper ore from mine to rim on burros and mules.

The Summit Trail basked in the stunning vistas and blissful solitude of the Canyon. It served as an enduring monument to a remarkable group of mining men—and it was nearly finished.

Chapter Twelve

TRAILS AND RAILS

If it were not for mining men having bad luck, they'd be having no luck at all.

The Shooting Star Mine's vast deposits of high-percentage copper ore overshadowed all other mining claims, considered the greatest mineral discovery at the Grand Canyon, enough to supply the world! Monte Bridgestone often said, "She's the queen of canyon mines."

Such rampant optimism in northern Arizona towns along the transcontinental tracks led to renewed discussions of building a railroad to a point on the South Rim—a spur line from Flagstaff, Williams or Ash Fork. Buckey O'Neill predicted, "A canyon railroad will provide transportation of ore from canyon mines and deliver tourists to this spectacular wonder of nature."

* * *

To promote a canyon railroad, the Territorial Legislature enacted tax exemptions, giving any company building a railroad in Arizona, including a spur line from the Santa Fe tracks in Flagstaff to the Canyon, freedom from property taxes for six years. A town meeting promised help in securing rights of way and in providing support services for any company willing to accept the challenge, but financial backing seemed to be just out of reach. Major proponents of the rail line included prominent Flagstaff residents—lawyers, merchants and sawmill managers. These men did not lack foresight, but they lacked the financial means, and eastern capitalists with the means lacked the willingness to take the risk. With Flagstaff as the new county seat, these men set their minds on making their city the gateway to the Grand Canyon.

But Williams also wanted the railroad spur. Forty miles north of Williams, Buckey O'Neill found limestone outcroppings riddled with copper along Shaski Wash and near Tusayan Well. When asked about this discovery, he replied, perhaps to play down the location, "It don't amount to a damn; it's just a surface showing."

While northern Arizona suffered devastating drought, stockmen hoped for heavy snowfall to rejuvenate their tinder-dry grasslands, but the ranges received little relief from winter snows and spring showers. On prairie lands, overrun with hideous cracks, the grass withered to a sandy brown. Dry southwest winds and blazing sun scorched all but the hardiest vegetation. A nationwide financial panic caused a drought in the marketplace as well.

Jesse Parks, a respected banker, explained the situation. "I attribute this devastating depression to the Sherman Silver Purchase Act that required the U.S. Treasury to buy millions of ounces of silver, driving up the price, and pleasing only western silver miners. This dilemma undermined confidence in the gold standard and resulted in a run on the nation's gold supply. New mines, so vital to fledgling communities in the West, flooded the market with silver, causing its value to plummet."

Monte, a former silver miner, expressed a different reason for the depression. "I blame the railroads. In all the newspaper accounts I've read, it appears the railroads overbuilt their lines and incurred expenses that outstripped revenues. British investors, who speculated in American railroads, lost confidence in the U.S. economic system and unloaded American securities. So, as railroads failed, the fortunes of their allied industries and banks took a downturn."

With mounting concern for the state of the economy, people rushed to withdraw their money from banks. Gold reserves sunk to low levels. At the peak of this economic panic, the New York stock market crashed. Over fifteen thousand businesses failed, six hundred banks closed, fifty railroads became insolvent, and unemployment soared. The Atlantic & Pacific Railroad, already in receivership, sold out to the Santa Fe Railway. Losing jobs and life savings meant people could not meet their financial obligations.

Western silver mines closed, and many never re-opened. A number of mountain narrow-gauge railroads, built to serve the mines, also went out of business. With the President nearing the end of his term of office, he sought re-election despite national labor strikes and economic depression in the agrarian South and West.

Canyon miners, encouraged by the exceptional high-grade copper ore of the Shooting Star Mine, determined to buck the economic trends and ship copper ore from their canyon mines.

* * *

Monte returned to Summit Point with his most dependable hired hand, Kirby O'Brien, somewhat of an itinerant drifter and a venerable wind-bag, yet a very hard worker. "Kirby, I'm hiring you because I can depend on you to get things done, but I have a low tolerance for your long bone-dry recitations, picked clean by buzzards. Keep that in mind. Now, we need to concentrate on completing this trail. It's only three or four feet wide so it should not be too difficult."

Kirby could not let it go at that. "Yeah, but it is five miles long!"

At the end of a three-week period of steady work, Monte and Kirby completed the remaining trail work and set about building a three-wheeled cart for a special mission. With the help of the ever-obliging

Slim Broadway, the men eased their modified cart down the new trail. The operation took an entire day, and when the contraption finally rumbled onto Windsong Mesa, it needed repairs.

They loaded the cart with a two-hundred-pound block of copper carbonate that dropped from the roof of the mine during the explosion, and so began the laborious trek to the rim. In bad weather, the cart with its precious copper cargo sat abandoned on the trail. Occasionally, the men devoted a day to hitching a mule to the heavy cart and dragging it closer to the rim. It screeched in continuous protest. On several switchbacks, they needed block-and-tackle rigging to nudge the stubborn rock around tight turns.

The wheeled monolith became the brunt of colorful banter and profanity and called into question devoting so much labor for an exhibition seventeen hundred miles away with so much work to do at the Canyon.

"Monte, why are we wasting our time with this chunk of limestone?" groused Kirby.

Before answering the question, Monte jammed a rock under one of the wheels. He feared the cart might teeter over the crumbling edge of the trail, sending man and beast to a dreadful end.

"Kirby, this is not just any chunk of limestone. It has a special purpose and a special destination," Monte explained, knowing his hired hand needed a better answer. Just then, Monte recognized the ominous sound of a rattlesnake. A quick scan of the trail located a four-foot pink, diamond-checkered body uncoiling from around a low bush and heading for Kirby's foot.

"Jump back, Kirby, now!" yelled Monte, with his inner thoughts thanking the rattler for at least giving them fair warning. Its fangs primed to strike, Kirby withdrew his six-gun, fired two shots, and missed both times. The rattler's sensitive tongue darted in and out of his cocked mouth to challenge Kirby's poor shooting.

"Leave him alone, Kirby, let's go."

Despite the nationwide depression, it was an active year for miners and prospectors at the Canyon. Monte Bridgestone and his team extracted blue-green ore from the Shooting Star Mine in record quantities. Its superior grade kindled a small copper boom.

* * *

One cool January day, two strapping young drifters, Morton and Sykes, journeyed by horseback to the South Rim, trailing a braying mule with their canvas boat strapped to its back. Using the Pioneer Trail, these roustabouts carried their makeshift craft to the river's edge.

"Morton, I ain't going first," proclaimed Sykes, a mysterious hawk-nosed fellow with a pointy hat and a fixed stare.

"I'll go," volunteered Morton. "But I'll need you to play out the rope as I paddle across."

"What are you fellers talking about?" Surprised to find someone else on the trail, Morton turned around to find a middle-aged man sitting on a rock ledge, watching the river and whiling away the day. Morton responded, "Oh, we're hauling our boat down the trail for a river crossing. Who are you?"

"I'm Slim Broadway. I helped build this trail. Just thought I'd take a day off and admire our handiwork."

"I'm Morton and this scallywag is Sykes. We built something too—this one-man canvas boat. We thought we'd test it out on the river. Let's go Sykes, the day is getting away from us."

"This I've got to see. Good luck; yer gonna need it." Slim had a good vantage point to watch the emerging fiasco.

The novices stood gawking at the wild swirling current, known to intimidate man and discourage trespass. While Morton watched the river squeeze between sinister black canyon walls, Sykes unstrapped the canvas boat and let it fall to the ground.

"You idiot; you have probably broken some of the ribs, maybe even the keel," cried Morton, "I should make you go first now."

After checking for damage, the men launched their tiny craft and, with some trepidation, Morton stepped aboard. "Sykes, don't let go of that rope, just let it play out as I paddle across. He edged out onto the brown flood as the boat slewed sideways. Slim watched Morton paddle across, both amused and amazed that he reached the north shore.

Morton and Sykes suspected each other of being former outlaws, perhaps still on the run, each thinking the other escaped the law by hiding in the Canyon. These scoundrels obviously left trouble behind, but also seemed to be looking for trouble ahead. The squint-eyed Sykes, a bundle of nervous energy, looked the part and the happy-go-lucky Morton bragged about a train robbery near Canyon Diablo.

When Morton reached the opposite shore, Sykes pulled the empty boat back for his own waterborne excursion. He coiled the rope on the bottom of the canvas hull and jumped in, just short of bouncing overboard. Slim let out a cheer when he saw Sykes reach the other side. They stowed the boat in a patch of willows and in the brooding twilight trudged over the boulder-strewn creek-bed and disappeared.

* * *

Inspired by the Shooting Star Mine—and driven by the need to make more claims before the Federal government attempted to exercise control at the Canyon—prospectors in the district staked a record number of lode claims. They knew about talks in Washington City during the Harrison administration to set the Grand Canyon aside as a national reserve.

Not knowing the timing or impact of federal legislation on mining activities, the prospectors initiated a massive search for new claims. During a brief period spanning two Sundays in February of eighteen ninety-three, a blizzard of claim-staking activity swept both sides of the river. Grubstaked by Ernst and Otto Bergner and other townsmen, the prospectors scurried to stake more and more claims.

In the meantime, Kirby and Slim measured the Summit Trail from rim to river to prepare for filing a toll road. "Kirby, last month near the foot of the Pioneer Trail, I watched two unsavory characters paddle across the river in a canvas boat. It was rather comical to see these adventurers, one introduced himself as Morton, the other Sykes, arguing with each other over every detail of the crossing," said Slim.

"And they made it across? The river has been running high and swift for weeks. What were they saying?"

Slim answered, "I could not hear much of the conversation but I watched them disappear up Skeleton Creek. For all I know, they could still be there."

"You should let Monte know about these strangers. They could be claim-jumpers, or worse, wanted outlaws." With that, Kirby and Slim resumed measuring the trail.

Clint McCarty, on behalf of the men who built the trail, recorded the Summit Toll Road with the county. The trail extended from the rim near Summit Point to Windsong Mesa, down the west wall of the mesa to Cottonwood Camp, and then followed Cottonwood Creek to the river.

A week later, as if someone had signaled the prospectors with a rifle shot, sharp and urgent, they put down their picks and shovels and journeyed to Cottonwood and assembled in camp. Buckey O'Neill and Francois LaRue rode in from the area west of the Pioneer Trail. Monte Bridgestone, Clint McCarty, Kirby O'Brien and Slim Broadway sauntered in from Six-Gun Creek. Stuart Casey, Cole Campbell and Clancy Jennings came up from the river. Sam Thornton, a recluse whose diggings occupied a bluff overlooking the Pioneer Trail, failed to show. Kirby acted on behalf of the old-timer Levi Jackson who by then lost interest in prospecting and mining.

The mining men gathered for a historic meeting among the cottonwoods. They planned to formalize the organization of the Grand Canyon Mining District by hammering out district boundaries and rules for locating, filing and working lode claims.

Casey started the meeting, "Ahem, gentlemen, I call this meeting to order. When gold was discovered in California there were no statutes that authorized appropriation of minerals from the public domain. Miners of the California Gold Rush assumed their right to prospect, to claim, and to mine. It is different now. We are operating under the Mining Act which confirms our right of free entry on public land, our right to prospect for minerals on that land, and our right to claim valuable deposits and occupy the land containing these deposits."

He cleared his throat and continued, "As you know, the Mining Act specifies the need for discovery of a valuable deposit before location of a claim and establishes a set of standards and minimum requirements for maintaining a claimant's rights against rivals. In effect, the County Recorder recognizes a miner's claim as property. He could exclude others, even the United States government, from entering for non-mining purposes."

The men listened. "After the California Gold Rush, thousands of prospectors journeyed here and to Colorado looking for new gold placers. They panned streams, hoping to carry away a fortune in nuggets and gold dust. As placers played out, prospectors searched for gold, silver and copper lodes. To protect themselves from outside parties, and to exercise the rights and privileges provided under the Mining Act, miners organized mining districts. Each district had its own set of rules and regulations for claim size and monuments, the form of public claim notice, and requirements for maintaining ownership. Throughout the American West, this mining district concept traveled from one region to another as men discovered mineral deposits."

Casey's long spiel seemed like a lecture. He continued. "After the Civil War, men established mining districts in the Colorado Rockies, where Monte had been engaged in prospecting and mining in the Quartz Creek Mining District, and where Clancy tried his luck when gold was discovered in Colorado's Boulder Canyon. And I should mention Dakota Territory where Francois caught "gold fever" in Deadwood Gulch during the Black Hills Gold Rush. I came to Arizona Territory from the gold fields of California's Sacramento Valley and now I am helping to form mining districts in northern Arizona."

Buckey O'Neill, always one for pressing his own luck, asked Casey about his experience in panning for gold in California.

"Well, like you say, we were panning for placer gold. That's not what we're doing here in the Canyon, but I'll tell you how it was."

Kirby tossed two more logs on their campfire, and Casey began his tale about a lucky strike, although not his own.

"There we were, Harley Shaw and I, bending over in ice-cold water, dipping our pans and sieves into an unnamed tributary of the Bear River, he on one side, me on the other." Casey scanned the group to make sure he had everyone's attention. "Neither of us were having any success. We shifted position often, turning over a rock to check the sand and gravel that collected at its base. I was cold, miserable, and hungry, and a voice inside kept telling me to give up the hunt. I had spent four weeks in the gold fields, and with sorry results, in fact, no results." The men let out a collective groan.

"Harley continued non-stop, driven by a compulsion to succeed, scooping up sand from the stream bottom, swishing it around in his pan, then dumping the worthless contents. Foolish and stubborn, we both hated to admit failure."

"I would have given up two weeks earlier," interjected Kirby. "Me too," added Slim.

Casey continued, "Well, dejected and exhausted, I just sat on the bank and watched Harley. Then suddenly Harley shouted 'Gold!' My heart pumped wildly—there were seven bean-sized, yellow-colored stones in his sieve! 'Stay back!' he warned, 'This is my side of the stream.' I watched him carefully note his location relative to trees and rocks along the river bank, then clamber ashore to stow nuggets in his gold poke and tighten the rawhide strings. In the short span of four weeks, he had several pokes, earning as much as he could have made in a year on his valley farm. I had earned nothing but misery and regret."

Monte had to ask, "So did you pull up stakes and move on?"

"We both thought now is not the time to quit," Casey answered. "I watched Harley return to the same spot in the stream and make a bigger discovery, a walnut-size nugget, accompanied by gold flecks in his pan. I waded back into the icy stream but gold never flashed in my pan. After a few more days Harley had accumulated enough gold dust to equal the weight of his nuggets."

"Harley, with a slight mean streak, kept making matters worse, yelling 'Casey, if it were not for you having bad luck, you'd be having no luck at all.' I left Harley to his gold strike, tried two other spots downstream, then gave up, disgusted, disappointed and kicking myself for thinking I could get rich quick. I was so embarrassed about my gold panning days, I gathered up my belongings and, without looking back, Sarah and I left California with empty pockets."

"Well Casey, as you know, it's different here in the Canyon," argued Monte, "where we're staking lode claims and finding good copper showings. It's hard rock mining and involves investment of more equipment than placering and an organized pool of laborers. No gold fever here but we're doing the right thing in formalizing our district."

Buckey interjected, "Fellas, before we get down to the business of forming a mining district, we should listen to a Fifty-Niner."

Kirby blurted out, "We've heard of Forty-Niners like ol' Casey here, but Fifty-Niners?"

Buckey looked straight at Clancy Jennings, "Well, we have one right here. Clancy, tell us about your experience in Colorado."

Clancy looked around and it seemed everyone wanted to hear his story. He emptied his smoldering pipe in the fire and started in. "Some fool prospector discovered gold in a creek bed in them foothills of the Rockies, just west of the frontier town of Denver City. It started a wild stampede. Disgruntled panhandlers, destitute after the California gold fields played out, scurried over them Rocky Mountains, like fire-ants pouring outta an anthill, in a rush to beat the winter snows. And from the East came hordes of gold-seekers ridin' in wagons emblazoned with the words 'Pike's Peak or Bust', all converging on the Rockies." Clancy had the men's undivided attention.

"I was just a young whippersnapper, a flatlander mind you, from Missouri," continued Clancy, "and knew nothin' about pannin' for gold but I went along with the wagon trains. By the time I arrived in the hills west of Denver City, the place was crawlin' with panhandlers. I borrowed a pan and tried my luck. The fella I borrowed from, standin' just fifteen feet away, collected a whole passel of yeller flecks while I collected plain bits of gravel and sand. After two or three days of wading in a cold stream—probably as frigid as your California stream, Casey—I returned the pan and said my goodbyes. I've always wondered if there was a better way to catch gold in some contraption but I figured the pick n' shovel method we're doing here is best."

Buckey jumped back into the discussion. "Thanks Clancy for that tale of woe and misery. Francois, you've been rather quiet. Anything to add to our discussion?"

"Sorry fellas, I tried panning for gold in the Black Hills but, like my friend Clancy here, had no luck at all. And I'm still learning about hard rock mining here in the Canyon," confessed Francois. Buckey jumped back into the conversation.

"So, men, even though Casey had no luck in California, Clancy had no luck in Colorado, and Francois had no luck in the Dakotas, there's always a chance we might discover gold here at the Canyon. We simply don't yet know how much wealth can be extracted from canyon rocks." There followed a series of grumblings, nothing intelligible. Clancy rummaged through his pack for two small bottles of whiskey.

At Cottonwood Camp that momentous day, the men elected veteran Stuart Casey as chairman and railroaded Monte Bridgestone into taking notes. The men felt it quite proper that Casey and Monte be the ones to guide the members of the district. As recording secretary, Monte later transformed his notes into official rules and regulations adopted by the Grand Canyon Mining District and filed the papers with the County Recorder.

That night, gathered around the campfire, its smoke curling through the cottonwoods, the miners hunkered down on crude benches fashioned by spanning logs from one sandstone boulder to the next. They passed bottles of Twin Oaks whiskey to celebrate the official organization of their mining district and to counter the night chill. Firelight flickered and danced against a canopy of leafy tree branches as the men pondered what they just accomplished.

The canyon miners had hammered out an agreement in which they partitioned off two hundred square miles of the Grand Canyon and set down on paper stringent operating rules for the Grand Canyon Mining District. The area spanned the rims and stretched from Whiskey Rapids to Bighorn Rapids.

On the same day—in Washington City—President Benjamin Harrison, with only two weeks remaining in office, issued a proclamation creating the Grand Canyon Forest Reserve. Inspired by photographs of Grand Canyon, Harrison long advocated setting the Canyon aside for all to experience and enjoy. As a U.S. Senator from Indiana, Harrison had introduced proposals to set up Grand Canyon National Park. But with the national park idea still new, his proposals failed.

With the passage of the Creative Act, which authorized national forest reserves by presidential proclamation, Harrison took the first step toward creating Grand Canyon National Park. To prevent undue degradation of America's scenic wildlands, the act passed. Harrison seized the opportunity to establish a forest reserve encompassing the Grand Canyon. Forest reserves closed all operations permitted by public land laws, including the Mining Laws. Closing national forest reserves to prospecting and mining—an oversight, perhaps also an overstep, by the Government and an unintentional restriction of the miner's right of entry—ignited a long conflict at the Grand Canyon.

The Grand Canyon Forest Reserve included the most scenic areas of the Canyon and large tracts of forest on both rims—a region of twenty-nine hundred square miles. At first, Harrison's presidential proclamation had little impact on closing the area to entry; several years passed before Congress authorized funds for government supervision of Federal Forest Reserves. But, in time, the government and the miners on the reserve became entangled in the interpretation of the law.

For years, Federal agents challenged the rights of mining men. The men doubted the fairness of the government and arguments by all parties pushed patience to the limit. In organizing the Grand Canyon Mining District, the canyon pioneers found their mining operations in direct conflict with the Grand Canyon Forest Reserve. Of the two entities born on that midwinter day, only one would survive.

Chapter Thirteen

PRIZE ROCK

Hard times build strength, patience and character; financial commitment, skilled labor and teamwork build railroads.

The day after the historic meeting at Cottonwood Camp, Monte Bridgestone, Kirby O'Brien, and four other men resumed the work of hauling the two-wheeled cart with its heavy chunk of copper ore along the steepest section of the Summit Trail. Their groans and strains ended in triumphant cheers when they gave the dreaded cart a final push onto the rim, then loaded it onto a wagon. While Slim took three men to work at the mine, Monte and Kirby started for town with the block of copper ore destined to be the centerpiece in Arizona's mineral exhibit at the Chicago World's Fair.

For a few hours, Monte and Kirby remained quiet, enjoying the ride, a chance to relax after hauling their prize rock. Then Kirby broke the silence. "Monte, what's this fair up in Chicago City all about?"

"You don't know? Well, as I understand it, it's a year late. Its proper name is something like the World Columbian Exposition to celebrate the 400th anniversary of Christopher Columbus' landing in the Americas." Monte kept his wagon team moving across the Coconino, ready to continue his explanation when Kirby interrupted.

"Who is this fella Columbus?"

Monte looked at him in awe. "Kirby, didn't you go to school?"

"Yeah, for a few years, but I don't remember studying Columbus." Monte sighed and dropped the subject.

Another bone-jarring hour passed on the rocky stage road. Then the wagon hit a large stone protruding from the roadbed. The jolt catapulted both riders out of their seats but the block of copper ore barely moved. "Whoa. Kirby, check that left rear wheel."

He jumped out and reported the wheel appeared undamaged but he noticed something else.

"Monte, there's several wagon parts hereabouts."

"Of course, Kirby; where there is a bump in the road, there are always wagon parts. Do you see anything we might need?"

Kirby climbed back aboard, "No sir, nothing."

Monte happened to glance behind them as he snapped the reins. He thought he saw a lone rider dart into a grove of junipers. "Whoa," roared Monte.

"What's the matter now, Monte?"

"I think I saw a woman astride a dark chestnut horse but now I don't see her." He snapped the reins to get their two mules started again.

Five minutes passed, then for a second time, Monte saw the mystery rider on a gallop along a devious path through cedars and junipers, skirting the wagon road to get past, perhaps unseen.

"Well fancy that. There she goes," pointing to the rider, holding her hat down and thrashing her reins from side to side.

"Looks like she's trying to avoid us; who is she, Monte?" The horsewoman disappeared into the trees.

"Don't rightly know," drawled Monte, although in the back of his mind he thought it might be Sabrina Jaffa.

* * *

The great Chicago Fair, despite the nation's troubling economic times, proved successful. When he was President, Harrison signed the legislation designating Chicago City as the site of the six-month exposition. After several years of construction delays, the organizers finally completed the fairgrounds.

President Cleveland conducted the honors for the grand opening. Despite the economic panic, the prestige and glory of the World Columbian Exposition gave the nation a heady outlook on the future, albeit somewhat temporary. Many of the products displayed at the exposition became everyday features of American life. The nineties marked an era when the tandem bicycle surged in popularity, the newfangled telephone and the electric light took their place in history as absolute revelations, and dime novels created western heroes overnight.

The exposition took place near the shores of Lake Michigan. As the first world's fair with a separate amusement park on the adjacent mile-long Midway, it featured carnival rides. A huge wheel with riding chairs, invented by a civil engineer named George Ferris, became the signature attraction of the World Columbian Exposition. Over two hundred temporary buildings occupied the fairgrounds. Visitors flocking to the fair saw a temporary escape from the growing economic problems of the country, which deepened into a four-year depression that summer. The fair hosted twenty-seven million visitors—one quarter of the country's population.

Although the organizers denied Buffalo Bill's Wild West show a spot at the Midway amusement Park, Cody arrived in Chicago to set up his popular season-long exhibition just outside the park. He cleared seven hundred and fifty thousand dollars—profit he did not have to share. The spurning of Buffalo Bill by fair organizers proved to be a poor financial decision.

The World Columbian Exposition featured America's mineral wealth. It displayed coal and iron from the Alleghenies, phosphates from Florida, silver and lead from the Rocky Mountains, copper from Arizona, and gold from California. The Arizona Territory Pavilion comprised mineral specimens—a dazzling showcase of the territory's rich mineral resources—carbonates, oxides and native copper. Geologists hailed Arizona's collection of copper ores as the most exhaustive and complete copper exhibit ever assembled for a public showing.

Buckey O'Neill, as president of the board for Arizona Territory's contribution, made sure that Arizona's mineral display included copper ore from the Grand Canyon. In fact, the two-hundred-pound block of azurite that Bridgestone and his crew hauled up from the Shooting Star Mine emerged as the star attraction. At the base of the block lay a display of malachite, contrasting with the deep blue and rich green carbonates. The block which fell from the mine tunnel roof during the mysterious explosion contained 80% copper and won first prize.

The exposition closed at the end of October, in fact, on the same day that the U.S. Senate repealed the Sherman Silver Purchase Act. Repeal of the act demonetized silver, causing many silver boom towns like Tombstone to go bust overnight.

Chet Kennedy, of the Flagstaff lumber industry, and now a prominent Chicago businessman serving on the board of trustees of Chicago's Field Columbian Museum, made sure that the Canyon's copper legacy would live on. After the exposition, through donations and purchases, the new museum gained thousands of objects exhibited at the fair. The award-winning block of canyon copper ore sold for one dollar per pound. Chet became the first president of the museum's board of trustees. When the Field Columbian Museum opened, visitors once again experienced many of the exhibits featured at the Chicago World's Fair.

* * *

With the Summit Trail and formal establishment of the Grand Canyon Mining District finished, efforts turned to copper ore production. Monte returned to Summit Point with ten more burros and four hundred heavy canvas ore sacks. He planned to increase ore production by shift work in the mine and to pack ore to the rim by burro for stockpiling. Until development of a railhead nearer the Canyon, wagons hauled ore to Flagstaff for shipping by rail.

One mid-March rainy day, County Sheriff Clint McCarty escorted railroad advocate Brayton Holmes down the Summit Trail to Cottonwood. Jeb Johnson and Art Thompson also made the trip. Jeb served as deputy sheriff under McCarty. Art worked for the North Rim Cattle Company, a sprawling outfit on the Kaibab Plateau, where William Cody's party visited. Monte and Slim declared a miner's holiday and accompanied the men to the river. Despite the weather, they stayed several nights in Cottonwood Camp where miners and townsmen discussed the advantages of a railroad line to the South Rim.

Cottonwood Camp, at the point of convergence of the two forks of the creek, seemed to be ill-placed. While settling down in camp at night, with the roll of thunder, the flashes of lightning, and the splatter of spoon-sized raindrops, the men worried about a flash flood. The swish of wind gusts through upstream cottonwoods imitated the sound of rushing water. Like a ghost, heavy cold air came sliding into camp, spilling around rocks and trees, then moving on downstream where it sank into the depths of the inner gorge. Every rustle of leaves, every change in the creek's gurgle, every flutter of some flying creature in the dark begged for an explanation that did not come. The men endured a restless night. Sleep came in brief snatches as they braced for the flood that never came. Monte and his partners vowed to build a safer camp on Windsong Mesa, but postponed the work, as it represented another distraction from the important task of extracting copper ore from the Shooting Star Mine.

By sunrise, the gusty winds had subsided, clear skies returned, and after a hearty breakfast, Holmes, Johnson and Thompson asked for a tour of the Shooting Star Mine. With the damage from the explosion cleared up, Clint obliged.

Monte winced at Clint's politicking and boyish charm. While he too favored getting rails to the rim, Clint's cunning antics seemed frivolous, if not downright counter-productive. Slim too did not feel good about squandering three good workdays. In Slim, Monte saw a kindred spirit, most helpful in getting that dreaded block of copper ore on its way to Chicago. He mirrored Monte—retiring and reticent, eschewing the limelight of public attention for the quiet life of a dead-serious, hard-working man with little tolerance for nonsense.

With their kerosene lanterns held at arm's length, the visitors followed Clint through the tunnel. Everyone used care in stepping around open shafts and ducking under overhead timbers as they moved deeper underground. Juniper logs from the rim served as uprights and cross-members to prevent cave-ins. Near the end of the tunnel, temporary supports creaked and groaned as fine lime dust streamed from cracks in the ceiling. There the danger seemed most in evidence and caution most in demand.

The visitors did not linger long in one place as the shoring needed completion and the caustic chalky dust from drills, picks and shovels made breathing difficult. Despite the deafening clatter, Clint explained the mining operation. Those in the back of the line could not hear him at all, so they watched Clint collect a few ore samples in a burlap sack. Miners stepped aside as the party passed, then resumed their underground drudgery. Shaking his head as he examined the timbers, Holmes finally had to ask, "Since the mysterious explosion, have you had any cave-ins?"

Before Clint could answer, Jeb interrupted, "Seems a ventilation duct with a gasoline-powered blower is in order."

Clint explained, "Yes, the blower is on order from Denver City and we have stockpiled the ductwork on the rim. We want to get the tunnels shored up before installing our ventilation system. And no, Mr. Holmes, no cave-ins."

The men breathed fresh air and a sigh of relief when they emerged from the mine. Blinded for a few moments by dazzling sunlight, they brushed the chalky dust from their clothes.

"I have a new appreciation for the men who work twelve hours a day in a mine," commented Holmes.

"Me too," said Thompson, "And no wonder they drink and play hard when they get to spend time in Flagstaff saloons."

Johnson chimed in, "I can just hear the short-tempered miners complaining of low wages, high risks, long hours, and poor working conditions."

"A miserable job indeed," added Holmes.

Clint emptied his sack of ore samples onto a wooden bench. The visitors could now see the quality of ore that the Shooting Star produced. Half of the rocks showed blue-green carbonates but the other half showed native copper—bare shiny metal!

"Now that looks high-grade!" exclaimed Holmes, seeing the bronze glint of copper, but not knowing the first thing about metals.

"Yep," nodded Clint, "the explosion opened rich veins of pure copper bound in the sedimentary rock we see here on the mesa. Were it not for the explosion, we might have missed this concentration of copper ore."

On his journey back up the Summit Trail, Brayton Holmes mulled over thoughts of a spur line to Summit Point and what it could mean to have an efficient means of shipping ore from the Shooting Star Mine direct to a smelter.

* * *

The men worked in the mines throughout the summer. Sometimes tourists from Clancy's rustic hotel visited, determined to test their skills on horseback by descending the Summit Trail.

One blistering hot day in July, a single woman accompanied a group of visitors. She registered at Clancy's as Sharlot Hall. That day she experienced her first look at the spectacular opening which divided vast sections of northern Arizona. At age twelve, Sharlot came to Arizona with her pioneer family and settled ten miles southeast of Prescott. Later, as the Arizona historian, she became the first woman to hold territorial office. Now as a skilled writer, she determined to popularize the strip of land wedged between the North Rim and the Utah line.

Sharlot's writings captured the awe and magnetism that this grand chasm evokes, its great power to intimidate, its menacing river that roils and eddies, tortured by channel rocks, squeezed for eternity between stupendous granite walls. She envisioned no other place in the American West with such a congregation of what she described as petrified russet ramparts and sun-scorched sage-green esplanades.

On this first canyon visit, Sharlot journeyed east by wagon from Clancy's place. With her guide, Seth Westbrook, she traversed the Coconino Basin, hoping to visit Levi Jackson at Jackson Crossing. She found Levi sitting in a rocker and Molly working in her garden.

"Mr. Jackson, I am Sharlot Hall, Arizona Territorial Historian. I'm on my way to Lee's Ferry. I understand you know the region well. I'd like to ask a few questions," she explained, trying not to appear intrusive.

"Historian? Didn't know the territory needed such a person," said Levi, growling like a bear. "What do ya want to know?" Levi looked haggard, leather-faced and older than his years. To Sharlot, he seemed surly and gruff, perhaps unwilling to answer questions from an uppity historian.

"Well, I heard you were visited by a party surveying the river while working in your mine. Can you tell me about that?" Sharlot prodded.

Levi hesitated a few moments, then opened. "I was doin' some prospecting when them river men happened along," stated Levi in a deep raspy voice. "They seemed real interested in whether I was finding any mineral of value. I felt they were prying, so I didn't tell them much. Then my dad-blamed partner showed the trip leader a hunk of copper ore and his men went wild. He had to call them back, and they shoved off. Truth is, that was one of the few pieces of good ore we found."

"Still, you found it important to set up a mining district." Sharlot kept prodding. "I think you called it the Little Colorado Mining District."

"You know about that? So, you've been snooping around in county offices." Levi paused, sizing her up, thinking this woman to be more knowledgeable than she let on. He then explained why he quit prospecting in the Canyon. "I had good luck during the California Gold Rush and hoped that my luck would follow me here. But back then we were panning for placer gold; here it's different. It's hard-rock mining with pick and shovel. After several disappointing prospect holes, I quit mining all together."

"And it's a good thing," piped up Molly, glaring at Levi as she placed her garden harvest on a wood table. Then, she directed her remarks to Sharlot. "Pardon my outburst, Ms. Hall. Levi works hard as a horse, but he's stubborn as a mule. I need him around here to tend to our ranch, not roaming the Canyon in search of rocks."

Levi stopped her short. "They were not just rocks, Molly, they were intriguing pieces of copper ore, and if you had not complained so much about me being away, I might have found enough to haul out!"

She countered, "Levi Jackson, you know darn well you would not make any money with copper rocks; you even said that one time when you came home empty-handed."

Sharlot, realizing she had touched a nerve, bid her goodbyes. Despite the Jackson arguments, she planned to return to canyon country as an ardent supporter of Arizona's mineral resources and the burgeoning mining industry.

* * *

The stage drew up before a log cabin surrounded by a dozen or more tents. In front of the cabin on a wood bench sat a sturdy man of about fifty, his tawny hair and beard sprinkled with gray. He wore a dark brown coat and a scruffy broad brimmed hat. He rose and came forward, smiling and doffing his hat; and stage driver Roscoe Andrews said, with a great flourish of his coiled whip: "Ladies and gentlemen, allow me to present to you Captain Clancy Jennings, who knows more about the Grand Canyon than any man living."

Later, Roscoe took the visitors aside. "I doubt Clancy has any right to the title of Captain, but it pleases him to no end. So, I'd just let it pass, no harm done; after all, when a man reaches a level of popular esteem, he should be so honored."

Clancy papered his cabin walls with pictures and lithographs of Mark Twain and Buffalo Bill in every pose they ever struck. "Bill

Cody!" Clancy used to say, "Shucks! I knew him long before he took to play-actin'."

Folks in Flagstaff warned tourists before they journeyed north: "Clancy Jennings will tell you some awful stiff yarns but be sure to get him to tell you about the time he and Smokey tumbled over the edge of the Canyon."

There is an old Winchester carbine resting on a ledge near Clancy's tourist camp, weathering storms, surviving a falling rock or two, and rusting away. Clancy often lamented about losing Smokey—his favorite gun—over the edge while hunting deer. He checked on ol' Smokey from time to time and stored away stories about the mishap to have a ready tale should the need arise.

One that he concocted and repeated became famous throughout the Southwest. No doubt, Clancy believed it himself. To spur him on, all one had to do is ask, "Captain, what has been the greatest danger so far in your life here at the Canyon?"

Clancy would reflect for a few moments and then say, with the utmost composure: "I reckon about as near as I ever come to going to heaven was when I tripped and went over the edge."

After a minute of agonizing silence, someone always commented, "And we see the fall didn't kill you."

"Naw," drawled Clancy, "I reckon I hain't got sense enough to git killed. It was just a little east of here, not more'n a half-mile. I'd been hunting and came across a big buck. Suddenly he charged me, and the hunter became the hunted. He chased me toward the rim where I tripped over a log. Now mind you, I still had my gun but there was no time to turn around and take a shot. And the buck was still racing toward me. It was plain to see I couldn't stop, an' I sez to myself, 'Clancy Jennings, I reckon your time's finally come!' But all the same, I was a-figgerin' how I could avoid broken bones, or worse, serve myself up for a vulture feast. Wal, I jest reached out for a twisted cedar root that hung over the caprock and grabbed it with one hand. I was desperate for a better hold but I didn't want to part with my trusty gun. Live branches above me swayed in taunting gestures and the root made cracking noises. There I was—dangling like a giant spider on a single strand of its web, root in one hand, gun in the other. I was on the verge of losing my grip." He paused to scan the faces of his spellbound crowd, then resumed his tale.

"Wal, it was time to drop my gun. I let her go and grabbed the root with both hands. As I pulled myself to safety I shouted, 'Smokey, try to land as softly as you can and I'll come back later with a rope.' Smokey landed on a narrow ledge, about two hundred feet down. And it fired a shot, I think at me. I moved further back from the rim, none the worse for wear."

"What happened to the buck?" someone asked.

"By the time I regained my composure, he was nowhere in sight."

Someone else asked, "How did you feel when you saw your gun hit the ledge?"

"Oh, 'twas sad," replied Clancy, "it was in several pieces but I didn't blame it for taking a shot at me. The two of us go way back and I let ol' Smokey down."

After a moment, the same visitor remarked: "Now, Captain, you cannot expect us to believe such a story as that."

Leaning forward, wagging a finger at his gullible listeners, Clancy replied, "Dagnabbit! I never tell stories I can't prove." Then rising, he motioned his audience closer to the edge. "Come over here, all of ya," he called. "Look right down thar in the Canyon; do you see a Winchester on that ledge?" Several visitors acknowledged that they could see parts of an old gun. "Wal," with a supercilious grin, a triumphant sweep of his right arm and his voice rising to a screechy crescendo, "that thar is the parts of poor Smokey a-rustin' away. No sir, Clancy Jennings may have very little sense, but he don't never tell no stories he can't prove."

The visitor with all the questions could not leave it at that; he had to have the last word. "Captain Jennings, you said the big buck chased you about a half a mile from here." Pointing, he continued, "So how did the pieces of your gun get piled up down there?"

Clancy, rarely caught flat-footed, clarified, "Ah, sorry, I remember now; he charged me right here; I meant to say I was comin' back from hunting on the rim a half-mile away. That's where I have a second cabin, right on the rim, built for the canyon views."

Eastern newspapers used to say "the best way to know what wonders lay hidden in the Canyon is not to go and search them out with patient daily toil, but to ask ol' Clancy Jennings. His tales match the Canyon and ought to be true if they are not."

A few years later, a visitor from New York City, having just completed a trek below the rim, stepped onto Clancy's cabin porch. "Where's your guest book, Captain Jennings? I'd like to make a note." Clancy pointed to a small table as the visitor fumbled for a pencil in his vest pocket. After a minute or two, he said, "There you go; all the best to you, sir."

When the visitor disappeared in tent city, Clancy picked up his guest book to see what the fellow wrote. "Glorious and certainly laborious. Happy to be back, thanks to the legendary Captain Clancy Jennings, a splendid trail guide, despite his habit of stretching the truth."

* * *

Two days before Christmas, Cole Campbell and a young prospector named Mark Warren packed provisions from Summit Point to the Shooting Star Mine. They camped that night on Windsong Mesa and left some provisions at the mine. The next morning, they departed for the river with six burros, following the lower part of the Summit Trail along Cottonwood Creek.

At the river they set about ferrying supplies by boat at Casey Crossing. They swam the burros across two at a time. Crossing in makeshift canvas boats required cutting the proper angle on the current and maintaining a respectable paddling speed to avoid being swept downstream into formidable rapids. The men then packed their load to the Apache Plume and Silver Feather asbestos mines in Willow Creek Canyon. That Christmas Eve, they joined six others for a yuletide celebration on a granite bluff more than a thousand feet above the river.

The men, their stomachs filled with sow belly and beans, sat around a crackling campfire, singing carols and passing a bottle of Twin Oaks whiskey.

Brought together by a kindred spirit, the prospectors listened to Clancy's tall tales. "Hey barkeep, give me a shot of whiskey," stammered Clancy, simulating a saloon conversation. "I'll bet you fellas don't know where the expression 'shot of whiskey' came from," queried the congenial old prospector, teasing his campfire companions.

"I'm sure yer gonna tell us straight away," smiled Casey as he whittled off a piece from a stick of dynamite.

"Wal, I invented that expression. You see, back in the old days, a forty-five-caliber slug for a six-gun cost ten cents and it just so happened that a mug of Bumblebee whiskey—the liquor with a real sting— also cost ten cents." He paused to make sure his spiel captured everyone's attention. "If I got low on cash, I just pulled out a bullet from my gun-belt and slapped it down on the bar as payment. Without hesitation, the barkeep accepted this, hence the expression—a shot of whiskey."

And with that, Casey nonchalantly threw a two-inch piece of dynamite into the fire. Mark cautioned, "That dynamite has highly sensitive nitroglycerin in it; fellas, speak softly when whittling that stuff." This good-sized piece of incendiary mischief burned with a fury, then simmered until Clancy completed another yarn, a short one about running out of reading material, resorting to his dictionary, and then complaining about frequent subject changes. Casey sprinkled nitro-laden dynamite shavings on their campfire, whipping the flames into a fiery frenzy.

"Wanna hear another?" Clancy did not wait for an answer. "I used to play poker with my dog, and I always won. Whenever his hand, I mean paw, had four-of-a-kind or a straight flush, he wagged his tail. If he had a royal flush, he'd pant!" And with that Casey tossed another two-inch piece of dynamite in the bonfire. Everyone jumped to their feet to avoid flash burns.

"I remember your dog, Clancy. He was always yelping and spoiling the hunt, said Mark. "What ever happened to that ol' critter?"

Clancy assumed a mournful tone, "Aw, he ran off. He always got agitated around burros."

Mark added, "He probably tired of losing at poker."

Just then, a tumultuous rumble in the next tributary side canyon downstream of their Christmas campsite interrupted the miner's reverie. "Sounds like a rockslide!" Mark charged. "Casey, you best stop throwing chunks of dynamite on our fire. You might trigger an earthquake."

"Aw, settle down," said Casey, railroad builders use dynamite all the time. It's quite safe, you know."

Mark shot back, "Well, maybe, but they don't throw it in fires; they use it to blast tunnels and railroad beds. And speaking of railroads, we need one to service our mines."

"You don't think I know that?" Casey countered, "I've been championing the cause for years. But these are hard times."

"Yes, and hard times build strength, patience and character."

Casey responded, "And financial commitment, skilled labor and teamwork build railroads."

* * *

On Christmas day, Mark Warren and Clancy Jennings saddled their pack animals and started back across the river to Cottonwood. While Mark headed back to Flagstaff, Clancy butchered one of six yearlings Casey had driven into Cottonwood Canyon so the prospectors would have fresh meat during their winter months below the rim. Not satisfied with just the beef for Christmas dinner, Clancy went fishing in the river and caught a three-foot suckerfish which he intended to add to their Yuletide feast. Again, he crossed the river, loaded his burros on the north shore and climbed the sheer cliffs to rejoin his friends. As for his river catch, the men reminded him that suckers are like squawfish; they are very boney and not good eating.

At their camp atop the north wall of Granite Gorge, the men continued to celebrate, pleased with their accomplishments over the past year, and happily optimistic about the future—a future they hoped would bring rails to the rim.

Chapter Fourteen

SERENDIPITY

Sleeping under the skies, searching under the guise.

One afternoon, outside one of Flagstaff's saloons near the railroad depot, Clancy Jennings took out his shooting iron and gave a young fellow a silver Liberty head quarter-dollar with instructions to toss it high
in the air as passengers stepped off the arriving train.

"Okay, now, let 'er go," instructed Clancy. Up it went about fifty
feet and he fired. "Got it! A direct hit!" exclaimed Clancy.

A well-dressed gentleman from the train, intrigued by the sideshow,
walked over to Clancy. "How do you know you hit it?"

"Wal, it's a case of mind over matter; if you don't mind, it don't
matter! Nah mister, I'm just joshin' ya. Even though I was squinting as
the sun was beginnin' ta' set above the buildings over there, that didn't
bother me none. I know I scored a direct hit 'cause the coin landed on
the spread-eagle side," explained Clancy to the stranger, "I killed it!"
And with that, he picked it up, holstered his gun, and went inside for a
drink. The stranger followed.

"Yes sir, mister, that quarter landed spread-eagle." Clancy slapped
the coin down on the bar, spread-eagle side down again. "I can prove
that I shot it." He flipped the coin over. "Look here; see that deep
scratch across the eagle, gouged out by my bullet?"

"Well, let me buy you a drink," said the stranger, and with that he
slapped a five-dollar gold piece down. The barkeep would not accept
either Clancy's damaged silver quarter-dollar or the stranger's five-dollar gold coin.

"What's wrong? Our money not good enough fer ya'?" complained Clancy, knowing he could not produce another coin.

The stranger added, "I've got several more five-dollar pieces," as he went for his vest pocket.

"Well, today, with these coins, I must tell you, your money is no good," answered the barkeep. "Let me explain. I was nearly snookered by a man on yesterday's train when he tried to pawn a gold-plated five-cent Liberty head as a five-dollar gold piece. I'm saying both of your coins are counterfeit and won't spend worth a darn."

Several nearby railroad workers raised their beer mugs in salute to the barkeep for standing his ground. Clancy railed against the group and the stranger vowed that they would not go thirsty that morning. He reached into his trousers and pulled six or seven five-cent pieces from his pocket. The barkeep inspected the coins, accepted several as cash payment and poured two beers.

"Let me introduce myself," said the beer buyer, "My name is Percival Lowell. I'm planning to build an astronomical observatory in your fair town."

"My name is Clancy Jennings, Grand Canyon expert, and . . . you're building an observatory? You mean for gazing at planets and stars?"

"Yes, especially Mars. For the past month I've had men surveying a site on that hill above the lumber mill, on the western edge of town, determining what it will take to build the observatory. Flagstaff may be on the verge of becoming a major center for astronomical research." Lowell took a gulp of beer and continued. "Grand Canyon expert, you say?" He felt Jennings looked more like a prospector but seemed willing to hear more about this self-proclaimed expert. "By the way, you can call me Percy."

Clancy plunged into his standard spiel about being the first to build a tourist enterprise and trails from the rim to the river and mines with good showings of valuable minerals. Lowell, intent on learning more, bought another round, and the two continued their conversation, with Clancy doing most of the talking.

In some respects, Percy Lowell saw some of his own traits in Clancy Jennings—a visionary with an engaging style, an intellectual in his own right, yet a rather curious character. And both served as self-interest promoters—Percy in the science of what lurks out in the universe and Clancy in the mystique that lurks within the Canyon.

* * *

The two four-in-hand stages of Jeff Fox's line left for the Canyon at seven o'clock in the morning in gallant style. The tough, wiry Arizona horses knew the road, and, in the hands of Teresa Cordova, Jeff's most skillful driver, and Roscoe Andrews, the chartered coaches made good time—an average of six miles per hour over the entire distance.

Onboard Roscoe's coach sat transcontinental railroad officials, intent on observing the lay of the land between Flagstaff and the Grand Canyon. The party included the General Manager of Los Angeles operations, the superintendent of Albuquerque operations, and a representative of the *Los Angeles Times* newspaper. Onboard the second coach—a new acquisition by Jeff Fox—a refined lady from Hartford hung on to a side strap while chaperoning her two younger sisters and a rambunctious daughter. The women had shown the good sense to dress for stage travel. The sisters took turns occupying the driver's box with Teresa and appeared to enjoy every mile of the drive.

The railroaders noted that the stage road from Flagstaff to the Grand Canyon crossed country much flatter than supposed. Except close to the San Francisco Peaks, inclines and declines appeared challenging but not difficult. They surmised that a railroad line through the forests and across the prairie land, though somewhat out of harmony with Nature in her grander moods, would offer the ideal means of reaching the Canyon in comfort and with good speed.

The officials considered such a railroad, with an iron horse instead of spirited broncos hitched to the passenger coaches, entirely workable. The distance from the main line in Flagstaff, about seventy-five miles, could be covered in two hours, instead of twelve by stagecoach, and the gradients would be less than those found on many sections of transcontinental routes.

The news reporter overheard the two railroad officials discussing a locomotive called the Shay steam engine which they considered well-suited to work on a line to the Canyon. Shay locomotives, geared for high traction needed for pushing or pulling heavy loads on steep grades where the ordinary railroad engine would buck and stall, seemed ideal for the proposed route. Already in use for hauling timber in northern Arizona, the Shays proved themselves on twists and turns in mountainous terrain. "If these wood-burning steamers could haul logs to lumber mills," one official stressed to the other, "they certainly could haul ore to copper mills."

The Shay locomotive could overcome most of the natural elevations on the route without resort to any expensive grading. The railroaders believed these engines could successfully scale the flanks of the San Francisco Mountains, and only a short section of the mountain line would need grading. They noted that building materials in untold quantities, stone and cinder for ballast and timber for ties, stood ready for the hand of the constructor, subject only to control in those regions where the road would pass through government lands.

If Congress refuses to authorize rails in the Grand Canyon Forest Reserve, as occurred in Yellowstone, construction would stop at a point within fifteen miles of the South Rim. From there, the rest of the journey could be a pleasant stage trip. There were plenty of tall pines for building rustic log depots, and along the whole line, only a few places require bridges or trestles, and none need labor-intensive earth fills. If water for the steam engine becomes a problem, a tanker car on the train puts such concerns to rest.

The officials believed following the laying of track, traffic to make such a line pay already existed. When it became known the grandest work of nature in the entire country is accessible by an all-rail route from either side of the continent, the trend in tourist travel would be toward the Grand Canyon.

The general manager thought to himself that the owner of this stage line would not like a rail line to the South Rim. The iron horse, with comfortable coaches, could render his horse-drawn coaches obsolete.

The two stagecoaches rolled down the last slope, and the parties finally arrived at Clancy's camp—tired, hungry and dusty. Stepping off the stages, bodies stiff with long sitting hobbled to the brink and gaped in awe at the canyon walls, tinted red and sublime. Souls steeped in profound reverence, teetering spellbound on the edge as any first-time visitor does when he confronts the Canyon, watched the impressive mingling of shapes and colors at day's end. Sprawled out before these railroaders and passengers lay the most stupendous gorge known to man—and in the minds of the railroad officials raced thoughts of a canyon rail connection.

* * *

Buckey O'Neill journeyed to New York City and Chicago City several times to interest high-minded business executives in canyon copper. Monte Bridgestone, representing the Black Diamond mine, suggested Buckey contact their mutual friend Chet Kennedy in Chicago about such an investment. The influential businessman, having worked with the canyon prospectors to make sure their prize copper ore went on permanent display at Chicago's Field Columbian Museum, always seemed willing to help his old friends in Flagstaff.

After more discussion, a group of developers formed the Black Diamond Development Company, named in appreciation for Monte's referral. Buckey pushed for a railroad from the Santa Fe's main line to the Canyon, with the idea copper would justify the investment, including construction of a tourist hotel on the rim. He continually emphasized the mining potential of the Canyon.

One day, Buckey met Thomas Applegate at the Flagstaff train depot and, having made arrangements for relay horses along the stage route, drove him by carriage to his cabin on the rim, built more like an office for entertaining prospective business partners. The view almost guaranteed putting a prospective investor into a receptive frame of mind. The men drove to the copper deposits south of Tusayan Well. Applegate, impressed, assumed that the mines would be profitable if a railroad spur from Williams, which had a good water supply for trains and smelters, could reach them. His company bought Buckey's copper claims for twenty thousand dollars.

While the Black Diamond Development Company managed its mining interests, it could not tap enough investors to finance a railroad. Applegate himself spent many months trying to raise enough money and even approached the Santa Fe which declined participation in the venture, although they viewed a spur line as a workable rail connection. Applegate seemed perplexed by their expressed reluctance.

Meantime, Buckey took the matter straight to the people most affected by a railroad spur. He stirred up competition for a line by using a tactic he learned in Tombstone—raise the ante and buck the tiger. First, he went to Flagstaff, and bursting into a town hall meeting, announced to officials engrossed in a budget discussion: "We're building a railroad to the Canyon!"

One townsman rose from his chair. "O'Neill, can't you see we're conducting official town business here? You are not on the agenda."

"I'm telling you, we will build a railroad to the Grand Canyon!" repeated Buckey.

Another townsman beamed with joy, "On the agenda or not, that is great news! It will ensure many years of growth and prosperity for Flagstaff."

Buckey took a chair and leaned back, propping his feet on the table. "Yes, I imagine that could be the case, but Williams is favored as the junction point."

That got their attention. The town fathers exclaimed, "Williams? Are you out of your mind? Flagstaff is the logical point, not Williams!"

"Too far," Buckey asserted, then added, "perhaps we could run a longer line from Flagstaff if the town offered additional financing."

The town leaders huddled, then the Mayor countered, "Certainly, the town will vote a subsidy!"

Buckey agreed, without change of expression. "Great, but you must bid higher than Williams."

The town fathers scoffed, looked at each other, then asked, "How much have those high-minders bid?"

"Well, I can't tell you," Buckey returned with all honesty, and with no hint he actually did not know. "Place your bet, I mean bid, and I'll let you know." As Buckey left the town hall, he sensed the Mayor might want to talk to him in confidence.

"Gentlemen, I declare a fifteen-minute break, then we'll get back to our remaining agenda items." With that, the Mayor pushed away from the table and hurried out the door, hoping to catch Buckey.

As Buckey turned the corner, he heard the Mayor calling. "Dagnabbit, Buckey wait, we need to talk." It was the response he hoped he would get. Mayor John Atkins, an overweight, backslapping politician, waddled rather than walked. Known to be gullible to a fault, he often bungled town business. He sought the limelight of public attention and saw landing a canyon rail line as a way to put on a good front in the eyes of Flagstaff citizens, not to mention enhancing his chances of re-election.

"What is it now, Mr. Mayor? I've told you all you need to know to assemble your bid." O'Neill had provided little information, but he oozed with enthusiastic sincerity and public spirit.

"I need—I mean we need more details on railroad construction standards, route preferences, material costs, schedules and—"

O'Neill cut him off. "Mr. Mayor, getting those details is up to you. It's part of the job of preparing a credible bid. Now, if you don't mind, I'm on my way to Williams."

"Hold up there a minute. When you get back, if you could give me some idea of how high Williams might bid, I could manage a private bonus for you in appreciation for helping to make Flagstaff a better place." Mayor Atkins, realizing his statement sounded like a bribe, figured he best not say anything more. Buckey, knowing the mayor's reputation as a tight wad, shrugged off the offer and went on his way.

Buckey repeated this scenario the next day in Williams. The town organized a group of stalwart investors and made a bid. Flagstaff canvassed its own investors and bid more. Williams raised, but Flagstaff went higher, even to the point of illegally emptying its town coffers. The bidding war went on for weeks. Williams' investors finally prevailed and Buckey reported to Black Diamond Development Company that the town planned to pay for their railroad. He had accomplished in just a few weeks what Applegate could not do in months.

The Santa Fe continued to appear uninterested in a canyon spur line. It had its own motives. While it could be risky letting another enterprise build the line, in the long run its strategy focused on waiting, letting that enterprise do the pioneering work and then, at just the right time, take over at a bargain.

* * *

For ten days, Sabrina Jaffa roamed the Tonto and side canyons between Cottonwood Creek and the Little Colorado River. She considered herself a free-spirited woman but nothing like the free-wheeling, pistol-packing hellion known as Calamity Jane. And yet Calamity's foray into the male world inspired her, even to the point of dressing like a male rancher.

Sabrina had come west with her husband and settled on a ranch near the railroad town of Winslow. After his accidental death, she remained in their wood-frame house, lonely but restless. She remarried on a whim but after a few months, that marriage dissolved into mistreatment and mistrust. Somehow during the divorce proceedings, her second husband, a ne'er-do-well freeloader, became sole owner of the ranch. Sabrina held a private conviction that men are bumblers—inferior beings all.

She moved to Flagstaff and took a position as assistant clerk in the County Recorder's office, even though society had not yet embraced women aspiring to careers or office positions.

While professional assayers had a moral obligation not to divulge information about a prospector's ore samples, county recorders—such as in the office where Sabrina worked—felt no such obligation, in fact, mining claim information became a matter of public record.

Only in her late twenties, Sabrina dared to be different. She had an insatiable thirst for adventure and the temerity to make her own way in life—to be in absolute control of her own destiny. She wanted more out of life than what her clerking job offered although she felt gratified that at least for a time she had trod into male territory. Even though she did her level best, she felt stifled in her office job and tired of looking like a frump. Self-confident and defiant, and without giving notice to her supervisor, she quit her job and started exploring the Canyon. Sabrina felt more at home in the wild than sitting at a desk in Flagstaff. Wisely, she regularly put part of her meager pay aside, enough to get by for a while, without dipping into an inheritance from her first husband. She longed for the pioneer way of life—an American institution—before it became history.

Below the rim, upon the rare occasion when she encountered fellow man, she projected herself as a woman prospector in search of shiny metals. To Sabrina, digging up minerals in the Canyon while burying one's past made good sense. She avoided other canyon prospectors and travelers. Down there, women seemed scarcer than gold.

A few years ago, Sabrina had traded her swayback mule for a spirited chestnut mare she named Serendipity. She trailed a young jenny, her pack mule, loaded with equipment and provisions. Serendipity brandished a long mane like her rider—for both—their most arresting feature.

Sabrina featured a striking figure, radiant green eyes and auburn hair. She wore a beige long-sleeve cotton shirt, light-weight trousers, a red bandana around her neck and a slouch hat. Binding her waist-long hair in a bun at the back of her head worked in her clerical job but not on the trail, not with her floppy hat, so she let it tumble down her back or hang braided off to the side.

After several forays into the canyon depths, Sabrina learned that a route that seemed impossible from the rim became plausible from a closer vantage point. The descending call of the canyon wren beckoned her to explore deeper into side canyons. She rode the newly built trails, the creaking of her stiff leather saddle and Serendipity's mild snorting being the only sounds of her patient descent. She carried a six-shooter and a Winchester rifle. With the latter, she considered herself a sharpshooter, almost as good as the legendary Annie Oakley of Buffalo Bill's Wild West show.

She found poking around rocky ravines far more enjoyable than clerking for the county. However, under cloudless turquoise skies, she found few scraps of shade—and even fewer traces of water. It did not take long for her to discover that cottonwoods in a deep gulch marked the course of water—cool clear water seeping from sandstone ledges and pooling in time-sculpted shale basins, then overflowing into rivulets. Sabrina often made camp in these shaded oases.

On one occasion she accidentally set up camp close to a group of prospectors. A whiff of woodsmoke and muffled voices gave her quite a start. With the setting sun's rays splashing the Canyon's buttes with yellows and oranges, she led Serendipity and Jenny out of the cottonwood stand and across a mesa to the head of the next side canyon. With fading light, and no desire to travel in the dark, she camped on the mesa. Nothing stirred her soul more than the majestic sunsets of the Grand Canyon, with modulating hues of yellow, then orange, and finally gold—colors that radiate a beauty born of ruggedness.

As Sabrina traipsed eastward across the Tonto, she savored sagescented breezes that whispered secrets every prospector wanted to know. Where were the sparkling minerals—the telltale signs of copper, silver and, ah yes, gold? With hope in her heart and a small pickaxe in her hand, she scratched stone walls and cracked open suspicious rocks. While sedimentary bands of limestone and sandstone measured passing eras, they did not reveal their hidden secrets. She stumbled upon pottery shards and walls with decrepit portals—laying in mute testimony of those who came before—but passed them off as useless clues.

On this trip, Sabrina had no planned route or timetable. As long as her supplies held out, she would keep scouring the carved stone corridors, hidden ravines and crevices, and rocky nooks. She hoped for a discovery that would set her up for life, before depleting her savings and inheritance. Serendipity served as her driving force and her faithful horse. The name stood for the curious phenomenon by which one stumbles upon something exquisite—that chance encounter, that stroke of luck—often while searching for something quite different. Could Sabrina Jaffa's excursions below the rim be secret searches for lost gold—searches conducted under the guise of prospecting for minerals worth mining?

Sabrina made her way along a narrow ledge, peppered with fist-sized chunks of shattered limestone. A sheer five-hundred-foot drop hovered on the outer edge of the trail. She dismounted and led Serendipity and Jenny in single file. One misstep would plunge them all to certain death on the rocks below.

Serendipity whinnied, signaling something amiss. Then Sabrina heard a faint rumbling sound just around the bend. The rumble grew louder until it became a sustained roar from above. "Rockslide!" shouted Sabrina, as if she needed to warn others.

Thundering down the boulder-laden talus slope, rocks hurled over the lip of an overhang. Sabrina immediately moved to protect herself and her girls from falling debris. She pressed against the canyon wall while steadying her livestock, hoping the ledge and overhang would hold firm. If either crumbled, it would be their last trail ride.

The rockslide stirred up massive clouds of dirt and dust, so much that her vision was obliterated. The world around Sabrina and the girls darkened and breathing became difficult. With a bandana pulled over her face, she pressed harder against the cliff. It seemed like an eternity but in a few minutes the roar subsided and finally faded away. She stood stone-still for another five minutes under the overhang, in case a teetering boulder set the whole affair in motion again. Serendipity shuffled her feet, anxious to move along.

The precious quiet of the Canyon returned, the air cleared, revealing a ghastly gap in the trail. Apparently, a heavy boulder knocked off a three-foot section of the ledge, leaving only a narrow strip hugging the wall as passable. Looking back where they came from, Sabrina discovered cracks in the rock shelf, some showing daylight, erasing any thoughts of turning back. She and her horse and mule found themselves trapped, stranded on a cracked ledge littered with fragmented rocks, and no one knew they were there. Other more seasoned prospectors probably avoided this dangerous route.

With so many shattered rocks on the ledge, her girls shuffled their feet, causing additional debris to plunge over the edge. Sabrina studied the remaining trail along the wall. She cut Jenny loose and paused for a spell, wondering if her livestock could be coaxed along the treacherous strip that remained. Convinced it was her only way out of this dilemma, she took a deep breath and inched sideways along the wall, with Serendipity's reins wrapped double around her right hand.

Sabrina made it across the gap and tugged on her horse to follow. Jenny hung back, waiting for her turn. Suddenly Serendipity decided to jump. She barely made it across but sent more rock breaking off the trail-bed and debris clattering into the canyon as she scrambled to gain a footing, her hind legs kicking more rubble over the side. The scramble knocked Sabrina off her feet. Parts of the ledge crumbled under Serendipity's eight hundred pounds. Sabrina tightened her grip on the reins as her legs dangled over the ledge. A growing sense of fear invaded her mind, causing her body to shudder and her legs to thrash violently. Serendipity kept a strain on the reins, allowing her rider to crawl back onto the cracked shelf, and saving her life. Just as she reached firm ground, a stray rock smashed against her right knee. Her scream caused Serendipity to rip the reins out of her hand and at the same time startled Jenny who decided to jump the gap.

Finally, all three moved away from the rockslide while a few more boulders tumbled into the abyss. Sabrina led her frantic girls along the trail another five hundred feet, limping all the way. They settled in a shady ravine where the trail veered away from the edge of the canyon. Sabrina removed Serendipity's saddle and Jenny's pack. After that scare, Sabrina called for a long break.

She found shelter and shade in an alcove. Her knee swelled but she doubted she broke any bones. Her mind swirled with regrets and thoughts of abandoning her dangerous forays into the Canyon. Her independent streak, her daring to be different, her determination to do things her way, her wild defiance and thirst for adventure—in a nearly inaccessible canyon of all places—almost cost their lives.

"Girls, I'm sorry I dragged you into this. What were we thinking? We almost died, and for what? Shiny metals? We need to quickly decide—whoa, what was that?"—the sharp sound of a rock splitting and earth shaking interrupted her attempt to quiet her team. "We need to decide if we should continue our exploration or find the shortest way out of this mess." Serendipity whinnied and Jenny brayed as another section of the ledge broke away and thundered into the gaping void. Sabrina hunkered down in her rocky nook, bracing for another rockslide. She located a tiny seep, enough of a trickle to keep a shallow depression filled with life-giving water.

Planning to camp for a few days, Sabrina stretched a rope between rocks for hitching her livestock and poured out some grain from a feed sack. This rest stop gave her time to evaluate her lot in life.

On her second day, while cooking breakfast, she heard slurred voices of men approaching from the east, griping about the trail being just a burro path, certainly not the work of man. No wonder wayward prospectors and horse thieves warned against trying it.

Sabrina hunkered down but still felt rather exposed. Jenny gave away their position; discovery of their open trail camp came easy, even without the braying of a mule. As two scruffy riders, obviously half-drunk, closed in, Sabrina reached for her Winchester.

"Morton, I'm telling you, burros made this path. It's not a trail and I'm not letting you talk me into another scamper into this canyon."

"Sykes, don't be using my name. There could be others snooping around here—oh, what have we here—a woman and her horse and pack mule right in our path!"

"Stop right there! My guns are loaded and I'm a very good shot." Sabrina suspected these two whiskey-soaked ruffians might be outlaws on the run. The blurry-eyed, weather-beaten one called Sykes appeared menacing, his hand shaking over his six-gun. The rotund one called Morton teetered in his saddle while trying to focus on Sabrina.

Morton had to ask, "What in tarnation are you doing down here? See what I mean Sykes? Someone else really is snooping around down here."

"I'm prospecting. Now move along!" Sabrina wrestled whether she should force these drunks to turn back or warn them about the damaged trail ahead. "Go back where you came from."

"We ain't goin' back, little lady, we're headed west," growled Sykes.

"You may regret it," cautioned Sabrina. "There's been several rock-slides."

Sykes dismounted and confronted Sabrina. "Whatever your name is, you can't tell us what to do or where to go. And we're not worried about rockslides. We're experienced trail-riders. Morton here was born in the saddle."

Morton jumped back into the fray. "Sykes here is stubborn as a mule and dumb as an ox. But if he says we're headed west, then that's where we're going."

"Your choice, now git!" Sabrina fired a shot in the air. Sykes, undeterred, moved closer and yanked Sabrina's long braid.

"Yer not very friendly. Let's take some time to get to know each other."

Sabrina jabbed her rifle barrel into Sykes' gut. He bent over in pain.

"She's going to shoot you Sykes. Let her go."

"Your sidekick is right. Now let go of me and move out—now!" shouted Sabrina.

"Dang it, I'm just trying to be neighborly," whined Sykes as he released her braid and stepped back.

"Come on, Sykes, she's not bluffing."

Sabrina watched them head toward the rockslide, then set about breaking camp, wanting to put as much distance as possible between herself and those drunken drifters. She felt guilty about not being more adamant in discouraging westward travel on the terrifying route but at the same time she felt relief about their departure. She looked forward to intercepting the Jackson Trail, but ever cautious, she stopped several times to be sure they were not followed.

* * *

Morton and Sykes dismounted and studied the hideous gap in the trail where a rockslide obliterated all but a narrow ledge along the wall, no longer wide enough for a horse or mule to get by. Sykes wanted to jump across. "Go ahead, I'll watch you plunge to your death, you fool! Then I'll turn back."

The two roustabouts argued for at least an hour. "Sykes, we're at a dead-end! The trail is gone! What's left is not wide enough for a coyote. I'm for backtracking."

"Morton, we've already been there. I want to continue west. That's been our plan all along. If you don't agree, maybe this is where you and I part ways."

"You are forgetting who is back there, Sykes. We can trail that good-looking woman prospector and find out what she is really up to, maybe compare canyon ventures, and get to know her better. That's what you wanted to do when we stumbled upon her camp."

"Alright, Mort, I'd like to spend some time with her. Let's go."

About the Author

Dick Brown has always been fascinated by western history— mountain men, wagon trains, gold rushes, cattle drives, notorious outlaws, ghost towns, and transcontinental railroads; however, he has concentrated much of his recent writing on one region of the American West in particular—the Grand Canyon. He has spent decades researching the early pioneers and the Canyon's bumpy road from unbridled backcountry to a national park. It is the venerable pioneers of the late nineteenth century, with their struggles to survive and thrive on the ragged edge of this tremendous abyss, that inspired Dick to write this historical novel.

During his writing career, Dick has authored and co-authored six award-winning books and has been published in numerous periodicals. He is a retired systems engineer and past president of the Grand Canyon Historical Society. As a former Navy submariner, he is a regular contributor to the journal *The Submarine Review* for which he has won three literary awards. He is also past editor of the magazine *Ballooning*. Dick lives in the forested mountains of central New Mexico, enjoying retirement with his wife and two feral cats.

Upcoming New Release!

DICK BROWN'S

HEART OF GOLD
UNDER THE CANYON SKY
BOOK TWO

Heart of Gold, is a historical novel, Book Two in *Under the Canyon Sky*: about the early Grand Canyon pioneers. It is the story of gold discovery, copper mines, rockslides, outlaws, beer-drinking burros, a railway on the brink, conflicting federal regulations, and badgering by a flourishing commercial tourist industry that fiercely opposes independents...

The Grand Canyon's long journey from unexplored wilderness to a great American national park involves tangled bureaucracy, greedy schemes, fraudulent mining claims, and competition between favored commercial operators and private entrepreneurs. The government's rough start in managing this natural wonder and the pioneers conducting their own tourism enterprises create bitter conflicts that last for decades.

For more information
visit: www.SpeakingVolumes.us

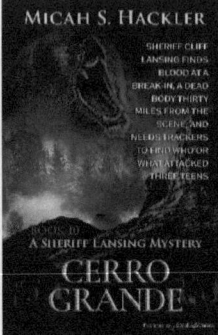

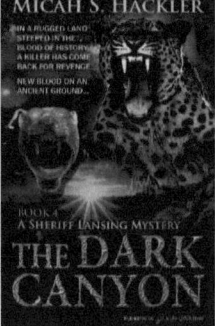
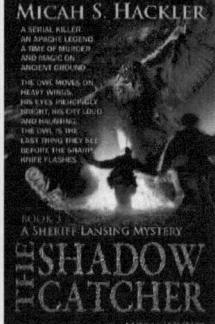

Now Available!

AWARD-WINNING AUTHOR
MARK WARREN

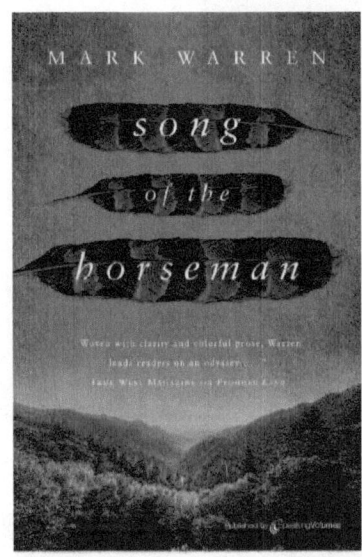

For more information
visit: www.SpeakingVolumes.us

Now Available!

SPUR AWARD-WINNING AUTHOR
PATRICK DEAREN

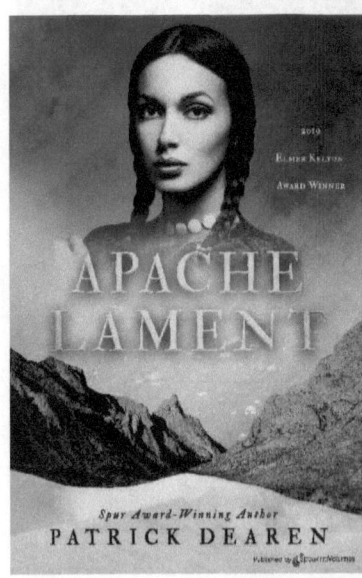

For more information
visit: www.SpeakingVolumes.us